THE FACTS IN THE C... A. POE

ANDREW SINCLAIR was b... ...ucated at Eton
and Trinity Colle... ...\merican History from Ca... ...reer in the
United States an... ...ile he was still
at Cambridge, we ...aking of Bumbo (based
on his own experie... ...uards, and later adapted for
a 1970 film written a... ...inclair) and *My Friend Judas*. Other
early novels included *T*... ...*ct* (1960), *The Hallelujah Bum* (1963), and *The Raker* (1964). The latter, also available from Valancourt, is a clever mix of Gothic fantasy and macabre comedy and was dedicated to Derek Lindsay, the pseudonymous author of the acclaimed novel *The Rack* (1958), who inspired the title character. Sinclair's best-known novel, *Gog* (1967), a highly imaginative, picaresque account of the adventures of a seven-foot-tall man who washes ashore on the Scottish coast, naked and suffering from amnesia, has been named one of the top 100 modern fantasy novels. As the first in the 'Albion Triptych', it was followed by *Magog* (1972) and *King Ludd* (1988).

Sinclair's varied and prolific career has also included work in film and a large output of nonfiction. As a director, Sinclair is best known for *Under Milk Wood* (1972), adapted from a Dylan Thomas play and starring Richard Burton and Elizabeth Taylor. His nonfiction includes works on American history (including *The Better Half: The Emancipation of the American Woman*, winner of the 1967 Somerset Maugham Award), books on Dylan Thomas, Jack London, Che Guevara, and Francis Bacon, and, more recently, works on the Knights Templar and the Freemasons.

Sinclair was elected a Fellow of the Royal Society of Literature in 1972. He lives in London.

By Andrew Sinclair

FICTION
My Friend Judas (1959)
The Breaking of Bumbo (1959)
The Project (1960)
The Hallelujah Bum (1963)
The Raker (1964)*
Gog (1967)
Magog (1972)
The Surrey Cat (1976)
A Patriot for Hire (1978)
The Facts in the Case of E. A. Poe (1979)*
Beau Bumbo (1985)
King Ludd (1988)
The Far Corners of the Earth (1991)
The Strength of the Hills (1992)
Blood & Kin: An Empire Saga (2001)

SELECTED NONFICTION
Prohibition: The Era of Excess (1962)
The Better Half: The Emancipation of the American Woman (1965)
Guevara (1970)
Dylan Thomas: Poet of His People (1975)
Jack: A Biography of Jack London (1977)
John Ford: A Biography (1979)
Sir Walter Raleigh and the Age of Discovery (1984)
The Sword and the Grail (1992)
Francis Bacon: His Life and Violent Times (1993)
The Discovery of the Grail (1998)
Death by Fame: A Life of Elisabeth, Empress of Austria (1999)
The Secret Scroll (2001)
An Anatomy of Terror: A History of Terrorism (2004)
Rosslyn (2005)

SCREENPLAYS
Before Winter Comes (1969)
The Breaking of Bumbo (1970)
Under Milk Wood (1972)
Blue Blood (1974)

* Published by Valancourt Books

THE FACTS IN THE CASE OF E. A. POE

EDITED AND WITH A NEW INTRODUCTION BY
ANDREW SINCLAIR

VALANCOURT BOOKS
Richmond, Virginia
2014

The Facts in the Case of E. A. Poe by Andrew Sinclair
First published London: Weidenfeld and Nicolson, 1979
First Valancourt Books edition, January 2014

Copyright © 1979 by Andrew Sinclair
Introduction © 2014 by Andrew Sinclair

The right of Andrew Sinclair to be identified as Author of this work has been asserted by him in accordance with the Copyright, Designs and Patents Act 1988.

Published by Valancourt Books, Richmond, Virginia
Publisher & Editor: James D. Jenkins
20th Century Series Editor: Simon Stern, University of Toronto
http://www.valancourtbooks.com

All rights reserved. The use of any part of this publication reproduced, transmitted in any form or by any means, electronic, mechanical, photocopying, recording, or otherwise, or stored in a retrieval system, without prior written consent of the publisher, constitutes an infringement of the copyright law.

ISBN 978-1-939140-72-2
Also available as an electronic book

All Valancourt Books publications are printed on acid free paper that meets all ANSI standards for archival quality paper.

Cover by M. S. Corley
Set in Dante MT 11/13.2

INTRODUCTION

Poe believed he had a split personality and often wrote about himself as such, particularly in 'William Wilson' and 'The Purloined Letter'. He liked to divide his rational and irrational personality and hold a conversation between the two of them, as in the opening dialogue between I/Poe and Dupin in 'The Murders in the Rue Morgue'. He also invented the inductive detective Dupin, which led on to Sherlock Holmes and the rest of the sleuths to come.

So Poe himself suggested the method of writing his own biography, since every biography is an autobiography in one sense, and every analysis a self-analysis. In this book, the narrator Pons in 1979 was 'I' – a modern man (not myself!) who was obsessed by Poe and believed himself to be possessed by him. 'I' chose an analyst because he was called Dupin – a mere chance. The analyst became his friend over the years and slipped into the role of the fictional Dupin, because it seemed to apply to the patient. *The Facts in the Case of E. A. Poe* begins with 'I' in a bad state of obsession, and his psychiatrist suggesting that the only way to rid himself of his obsession is to work out who the actual Poe really might have been.

After that, the method of the book is much that of *The Quest for Corvo* or *The Mask of Dimitrios*. A century later, 'I' visits all the places where the historical Poe used to live – Richmond, Stoke Newington, Charlottesville, Baltimore, Philadelphia, New York. He slowly reconstructs the life of Poe and the interpretations of him – Freudian, Parisian, hallucinatory, horrific and logical. A translation by Baudelaire or a Roger Corman film – these are the methods of cutting back from 1979 to 1837, and so creating a mosaic or a mesh. Finally, 'I' reaches the end of the acts and the legends of E. A. Poe, and his mentor Dupin tells him that his cure lies in writing an analysis of the historical figure. This 'I' does – and when it is complete, he has a strong sensation that the real Poe is sitting in the other chair in his room. 'I' is no longer possessed. Poe has left him at last. But through his greed and chicanery, the analyst Dupin engineers a gothic and macabre ending for his client, worthy of the mystery and tragedy in Baltimore that killed Poe himself.

The nature of the American poet and tale-teller was contradictory. He was a master of ambivalence. He had the manners of the Southern and English gentleman, which he was not born to be, although he was educated in those ways in Virginia and London society. As Melville wrote of him, he was *The Confidence-Man* of many parts. 'Nothing could exceed his look of picturesque Italian ruin and dethronement', while as a 'shatterbrain, he made a bow, which for courtesy, would not have misbecome a viscount'. Equally, he was seen as 'a cunning vagabond, who picks up a vagabond living by adroitly playing the madman'.

Both caricatures were true enough. Poe could be a conformist, but also a charlatan. He swung between the pit of despair and the pendulum of evading dire circumstances by flight. Anywhere might be better than where he was now. For he always felt himself an outcast, capable of any ruse to survive, but also a victim of the greedy money-changers of New York. If he flipped his nature, it was not to deceive, but to escape, as Hans Pfaall to the Moon or Arthur Gordon Pym to the shrouded final figure at the Pole. He was perverse. Although the creator of a French sleuth of piercing insight, he committed his own crimes. He was a cryptographer and a hoaxer. He confessed of 'The Raven' and the 'The Gold-Bug': 'The bird beat the bug, though, all hollow.' And in his essay on 'Diddling', he stated that man's destiny was to diddle. He himself had all the ingredients – 'minuteness, interest, perseverance, ingenuity, audacity, *nonchalance*, originality, impertinence, *grin*'.

Moreover, the dead poet who possessed Pons was unstable and volatile. When he wrote that he was exchanging some words with a mummy, Poe declared: 'My life has been *whim* – impulse – passion – a longing for solitude – a scorn of all things present, in an earnest desire for the future.' So his imitator Pons discovers his own inconsistencies on the trail of his *alter ego* as far as the Montparnasse Cemetery. There he finds the tomb of the decadent French poet Baudelaire, sculpted with a corroded double face, as if he were what he claimed, Poe's 'likeness – his brother'.

Yet why did the French think the American a genius, when his critics at home derided him as a fraud? Pons believes that the Parisians admired Poe's mental fight to overcome his dreadful passions, as in the Age of Reason before the Terror and the guillotine with heads in baskets. Dealing with Poe's powers of creation, Valéry summed him up: 'the demon of lucidity, the genius of analysis and the inventor of the newest, the most seductive combinations of logic and imagination, of mysticism and calculation; the psychologist of the exceptional; the literary engineer who studied and employed all the resources of art.'

Indeed, Poe did pioneer modern science and detective fiction, the thriller and the horror story. The only other American writer in the 19th century to alter literature in such a staggering and magnificent way was Walt Whitman. Yet Poe's greater capacity to conjure up new genres lay in his paranoia and persecution complex. 'Is it any wonder that I was driven *mad*,' he wrote, 'by the intolerable sense of wrong?' Imagined harms were inflicted on him, while he called his genius a mental disease. 'The works of such genius are never sound in themselves and, in especial, always betray the general mental insanity.' Yet such imbalances enabled him to vault the hurdles of traditional tracks to reach the byways. His supreme follower Jules Verne would even write a sequel to *Arthur Gordon Pym* and an account of a Voyage to the Moon.

As for the detective story, one of Poe's contemporary critics did recognize a talent hardly noticed before except in the novels of James Fenimore Cooper, the creator of the Western:

> *Induction, and a microscopic power of analysis, seem to be the pervading characteristics of the mind of Edgar Poe. Put him on any trail, and he traces it as keenly as a Blackfoot or Ojibway; give him any clue, and he unravels the whole web of mystery; never was bloodhound more sagacious in scenting out a murderer; nor Oedipus himself more shrewd in solving an enigma . . . He is a hound never at fault, a moral tightrope dancer never thrown from his equilibrium; a close keen reasoner, whom no sophistry detracts – nothing foreign or extraneous diverts him from his enquiry.*

The extent of Poe's influence on the cinema and in the comic and monster magazines embraced all. He walked again as Vincent Price in the Roger Corman films; he was echoed in the terror stories of apparitions from Bram Stoker to Stephen King. Poe had unlocked the doors to the supernatural, and he had lain the threads through the labyrinth of the beyond. As D. H. Lawrence wrote of him: 'He was an adventurer into vaults and cellars and horrible underground passages of the human soul. He sounded the horror and the warning of his own doom. Doomed he was.'

Naturally or unnaturally, Poe predicted his own end. In his squib, 'Never Bet the Devil Your Head', he reflected, 'He was a mad dog, it is true, and it was a dog's death he died, but he himself was not to blame for his vices.' These were his actress mother's fault for flogging him left-handed, so driving into him a quota of wickedness. Yet in his Bible, still preserved in his Fordham cottage, he marked in the Book of Job: 'I loathe it: I would not live always. Let me alone, for my days are vanity.'

As Pons is told, 'all biography is autobiography'. When he begins to dissociate himself from Poe, he suffers the fate of 'The Facts in the Case of M. Valdemar', who is mesmerised into a living death for several months and decomposes into a liquid mass. Once Pons feels that he is cured, he loses any sense of self and latches onto his analyst. And so Dupin, turned from a detective into a criminal mind-bender, sets up his patient's terminal heart attack in a *grand guignol* hoax as shock therapy, not a route to the mortuary.

This book is said to be written by Ernest Albert Pons, with Andrew Sinclair appointed as its Literary Editor by the executor of the Pons Estate, Dr Charles Dupin. By identifying himself wholly with Poe at the beginning of his papers, then by divorcing himself from the poet's character, Pons has provided a new solution to the *process* undergone by biographers during their long years of study – the initial attraction to, the following revulsion from, and the final synthetic verdict on another obscure person, who may often impose his style and thought upon the effort to describe him.

A critic of this endeavour in the *Sunday Telegraph* has called it 'a fantastical mirror game. Certainly, (the author) makes a good case for the hypothesis put forward by Dupin, that all writing is untrue by virtue of the selective process. He may even have managed to break down the barrier between fiction and biography.'

Andrew Sinclair
London

August 15, 2013

THE FACTS IN THE CASE OF E. A. POE

To
DUPIN
for his peculiar analytic ability

Contents

1	Another Case for Dupin	7
2	The Enchanted Garden and the Death Pit	21
3	I Fled In Vain	36
4	The Ragged Mountains	49
5	A Gold Bug Better	59
6	To Be Appreciated You Must Be Read	78
7	The Fall of –	99
8	Driven Mad	114
9	Death is the Final Conspiracy	128
10	Night and Fog	145
11	The Return of the Raven	158
12	MS. Put in a Bottle	164
	Editorial Notes	174
	A Short Bibliography	177

Nobody is more aware than I am that simplicity is the cant of the day – but take my word for it, no one cares anything about simplicity in their hearts.

EDGAR ALLAN POE

I

Another Case for Dupin

'Perhaps the mystery is a little too plain,' said Dupin.
EDGAR ALLAN POE in 'The Purloined Letter'.

My name is Edgar Allan Poe.

In the morning, I cannot use my name. We all need an alias to hide ourselves during our working hours. Like professional highwaymen, we must put on masks and cloaks for our daily robberies – sometimes called our salaries. We assume our disguise at that superfluous and nasty meal, breakfast, after we have said our grace:
For those we are about to deceive, may the good Lord make us truly careful.
Then between the cereal and the non-fat milk, we pick the fluff off our dark suit.
Then between the bacon and the decholesterolated egg, we adjust our quiet tie.
Then between the Sanka coffee and the saccharin, we compose our mouth to sip, but never suck.
Then we leave for work, the impostors of the day.

Outside my apartment, which is more of a retreat than a home, the streets are always a weir or an abyss. I have, indeed, moved up from the Brooklyn flats to the heights overlooking Manhattan Island, from the melting pot that never mixed us to the tower block that hardly protects us. Yet my fears have moved with me. I cannot pass a group of black boys waiting under the broken doorways without being Whitey again, held up against the high school wall for a nickel and a dime – 'Gimme yo' lunch money, motherfucker' – and I gave, I always gave.
Even then I knew it was not robbery. The *schwartzes* were per-

secuted even more than we were, or so my mother told me. I was only paying the tribute a born liberal must pay for his undying guilt. But now I hurry along by the curb far from the walls – so cautious that I have not been mugged in ten years – yet I still cannot shed the fear of the black boys I envied as a child – so terrible and truant, so fearsome and free, so – can I say it? – *black* as midnight against my pale terror.

I do not have to work. That is another pretense of mine to pass the time of day. I am rich enough to live off the income my mother left me, but to admit it – to confess to being a dandy and a drone – that is impossible among the circle of my schoolfellows who have made the long march across Brooklyn Bridge to the flip side of the Chrysler Building. They are all editors now or commentators, aspiring to be pundits, forgetting that they are mere bandits of the language their parents did not know. And solitary though I am by nature, I cannot withdraw totally from the world. People may be speaking of me – they will be judging me – and we always say the worst of those we do not see. Evidently, a missing person must be indulging in crime, vice or suicide if he dares not show his face to his friends.

So several times a week, I must take the subway under the river to my editorial office – a courtesy term for my cubbyhole. I am an advisor on the Decadents to publishing houses and reviews – the new Descartes of the self-dramatic dead – the modern Machiavelli of the intrigues of the Mauve Decades. Whenever there is a new book on Lord Byron or Edgar Poe or their later French imitators, the cry goes out for Pons – and the work is read by me. Pons is the name on my passport – Ernest Albert Pons. But what is a passport but an official lie, which enables us to cross an artificial frontier?

On this February day of the year of 1979, only one manuscript lay on my desk awaiting my criticism. It was one of those worthy dissertations, all flatulence and footnotes. Its title was meant to titillate – *The Maelstrom is the Message: Chaos and Continuity in the Works of Poe, Baudelaire and Rimbaud*. But the contents merely provoked a world series of yawns, punctuated by nods of recognition. The author had rearranged his twenty sources in a laboured pattern and had called it scholarship. It might have passed in academe, but never in Gotham.

The real crux of a book is the relationship between the author and subject – their correspondence or their difference – their appreciation, truce or hostility. Yet the average assistant professor hardly ever dares to discard the anonymity of shuffling facts or the security of quoting a greater authority than his own. We never know what he thinks, but we only see his stitching together of snippings from better minds. And if we have already read everything there is to read on the subject, we chiefly appreciate the occasional rogue who plagiarizes with panache and calls it originality. We despise the usual researcher in search of tenure, who embroiders the work of others with his *petit point*.

'Ernest,' Tilly said, pushing her bobbed hair and nose round the door. 'I never knew you were here.'

'I am,' I confessed, rising gallantly to my feet, looking for the way out as Ms Zimmerman came into the room, a white envelope in her hand, her beige suit as well-cut as my own. 'I will disappear if you like. Be my absent guest.'

'As you're here, this won't be a surprise.'

She gave me the envelope, which I hardly dared to touch. I felt the familiar pit open in my stomach as I glanced at Tilly's brilliant and swerving eyes. I was meant to flirt with her and live another lie – that I was the only middle-aged bachelor in the office block because I had loved too many ladies and could not settle for one. Not to flirt with Tilly proved me a gay – to flirt too much made me seem to propose – and I did not think Tilly would refuse a hint from me. But to flirt and flirt – what a tedious game!

'Open it,' Tilly said, fixing me with a lustrous stare, bright with adrenalin drops.

I slit the white envelope and pulled out a heart-shaped red apple with a hole in it. When I opened the greetings card, a green worm on a spring bounced up at me with a message ballooning from its mouth:

You are the apple of my eye.

Another message on the card told me what day it was:

Will You Be My Valentine?

'Oh, Tilly, thank you,' I said warmly. 'I had forgotten this day of revelation when all shall be known!'

Tilly offered me a cheek to kiss but as I bent forward, she turned up her mouth to mine and smeared me with her carmine lips.

'Will you?' she asked.

It was a full frontal, and I have always preferred the lateral and the devious.

'Wait and see,' I said. 'The day is far from over. I shall visit a card shop that I know and pick out my message to you.'

'Is that a trick or treat? I know you, Ernest.'

'A treat. I swear a treat for your eyes alone.'

'So you will be my Valentine?'

'That was the name of Poe's foster mother,' I said, side-stepping with my nonchalant erudition. 'Frances Keeling Allan *née* Valentine. He loved her totally.'

'As you love pretending that you are Poe.'

'I never pretend,' I said. 'I proclaim.'

The resemblance is striking. Poe and I both have black curling hair, which I also part into two raven's wings on either side of my broad brow. We have the same liquid grey eyes, which I have brought up from their natural dark colour through the tint in my contact lenses. And we both have a slim moustache along with the pallor of the man who meditates ceaselessly and the quick step of the searcher after truth in a false and vulgar world.

Tilly still refused to see me as I appear. She viewed me in the image which suited her.

'Then you'll come back, Ernest, and give me my Valentine and take me out for a drink?'

'Nothing would give me more pleasure, Tilly, but you know it's my day for Dupin.'

'You don't need a shrink, you need a close friend – '

Not too close, I thought, edging away from Tilly, who was pressing forward with her breastworks.

' – Someone who relates to you as you truly are, Ernest – to the great human being you will not allow yourself to be – that warm caring person I know lies deep down inside you – '

Tilly was making the same mistake Pickett made at Gettysburg. Her uphill charge against my resistance broke on the edge of my desk. The way to the door was clear. I had to get away for a long time. It was she or I – and frankly, I preferred myself. The office was too small for both of us. And she needed the job.

'Tilly,' I said over my left shoulder as I stalked out of the door, 'I must love you and leave you. Wait for my card.'

'I won't wait too long,' I heard her threaten behind me, as I strode towards the elevator. Sweet words – but I did not believe them. She would still be waiting even if I stayed away from my desk for a year, and she would continue her assault until I could resist no longer. I had to flee – or else accept my fate as a boy from Brooklyn who had to do what Brooklyn boys must do – and carry on the great chain of the living and the dead, baby after bagel until the last generation and the terminal cookbook.

I put my head in at the door of the editor's office, catching him at his mirror tracing on his bald forehead the line of the hair transplant he had already booked.

'I resign,' I said. 'Send on my salary after me.'

'We don't pay you, Ernie,' he said. 'We put up with you and give you desk space. How soon can you leave?'

'Now. Replace me if you can. Hire the disadvantaged. Fill your quotas. Feel free to show how unprejudiced you are.'

The editor groaned.

'Can't you stay, Ernie?' he implored. 'Tokenism is all a man can tolerate.'

'Never,' I declared. 'How can I stand in the way of another great human being – that warm caring person you need to work here?' Then I added the *coup de grâce*. 'You'll have to pay the new señorita a living wage, you know. And rip apart the washroom for her wheel chair.'

A promise is a promise, even to a Ms Zimmerman. But as I stalked through the dirty and drumming streets, wrapped in my long black Spanish cloak against the cold wind cutting along the avenues off the river, I could drop the disguises of the working day and become my private person, my true self – Edgar Poe. I passed the twin pinnacles of the World Trade Center, from which an Italian trickster had recently hurled down a mighty monkey, an electronic idiot called King Kong, which had been inflated from the original murderous ape in the Rue Morgue – made monstrous only through our fear – a nightmare more than an orang-outang – gnashing its teeth and flashing fire from its eyes. But now all is oversized and shown – and only our heads are shrunken with our imagination. God rest you, Edgar, in your pauper's grave and my present soul!

Another skyscraper of black glass and sandy slabs had obliterated the brownstone boarding-house where Poe and I had first brought our dear wife Sissy in 1844. They had welcomed us at 130 Greenwich Street with a supper piled up like a mountain, large slices of everything – wheat bread and rye bread, cheese and elegant tea-cakes, great dishes of ham and cold veal. Now the card shop I was seeking stood at street level under the pillars of the gigantic building above, and as I looked into its window, very, very dreadfully nervous I became. For I saw tell-tale hearts – great ones and small ones – hanging from wires, imprisoned on stands, or else racked in rows with red messages upon them:

— FOR YOU, MOM
— TO MY SWEETHEART
— FOR MY OWN DADDY BOY
— TO MY BETTER HALF — LET'S FACE IT, HONEY!

I still felt bound to buy my Valentine and entered the charnel house among the smiling shopkeepers. All around me gory plastic hearts lay bleeding, shaped as peanut bowls or cookie cutters – scarlet paper hearts for use as coasters for highballs – strawberry cream hearts and two pound crimson Cupid candy-boxes – woolly hearts to keep love warm and pincushion hearts for piercing. So strange a sight excited me to uncontrollable terror. Anything was better than this agony! Anything was more tolerable than this derision! I could bear their hypocritical smiles no longer! I felt that I must scream or die!

'May I help you, sir?' a voice accused in my ear.

'There is no help,' I cried, 'for the beating of the hideous heart!'

And so I fled the fearful spot without choosing my card, and hearing only the words of judgement sound behind me.

'Have a nice day.'

Across the way, temptation lay at the corner of old Cedar Street. A liquor store hung out its sign, its bright bottles clustering on their glass shelves in promise of oblivion. I entered and bought some Southern Comfort, sweet forgetfulness in a brown paper bag. I knew I must go uptown to see Dupin before I suffered another attack of those fears, those horrors unutterable, those phantoms of my first existence as Edgar Allan Poe.

I did not go directly to Dupin. It is not only the perverse that rules me, it is also the urge to explain – and confess. I knew that Dupin ate early like most Americans whose stomachs are keener than their brains, and as it was half-past twelve, he would not be in his consulting room. I was also too agitated to undergo that rational process which is my bond with Dupin. The modern fashion is to call it Psychotherapy, but I prefer to call it the Calculus of Probabilities. So I thought I would return to the realm of logic by visiting the site of another of the previous C. Auguste Dupin's famous cases, the lodging house of the beautiful cigar girl, Mary Cecilia Rogers, whom Poe and I had called Marie Rogêt to avoid the law of libel.

It was not far to walk there past the hustling windows of the traders who live off Broadway in the mean streets near the Fulton Market. Where Poe and I had once worked on the *Broadway Journal* now stood a store called Shoe City – journalism is mere legwork today. Nearby ran Nassau Street, where Mary Rogers had boarded before she had disappeared – to be found later upon the New Jersey shore, three days' drowned dead, her face and body mangled, a piece of her lace petticoat buried in the flesh of her neck, tied tight by a sailor's knot.

Poe and I had been clever then – for we had learned how diddling can be an exact science, and how to hoax the whole city of Gotham. Soon after the murder, we had printed the first two parts of our detective story about C. Auguste Dupin in the *Ladies' Home Companion*, suggesting that the murdered girl had been violated and strangled by her naval officer lover. But then, we had been undone. For a local innkeeper had made a deathbed confession that Mary had died in the inn during an abortion. So we had to delay our last instalment and hint at another solution in order to pretend that our detective Dupin had deduced this alternative all along.

As Charles Dickens once told us, stories are best when worked backward, when we know the end before we pen the beginning. Yet with the unfortunate girl hardly in her grave, new evidence had always been forthcoming, so that we had to turn and turn about C.

Auguste Dupin's powers of reasoning like a hare among hounds. Devil take a deduction from what is still happening – we're better off demonstrating what is truly dead!

When finally, full of nerves and Southern Comfort, I reached Dupin's place and was admitted to the presence, I had to conclude as always that he looked as nondescript as a man should whom I had selected from a telephone book because he was the only psychiatrist in Manhattan called Dupin. Poe had never delineated his detective friend who had lived by night, only the powers of his analysis and the frigid petulance of his periods of concentration. My Dupin, too, was indelibly forgettable for his bland cheeks and rimless glasses. He was not tall and not short, not thin and not fat, not bald and not hairy, not salt and not pepper. In fact, he was the perfect reduction of everybody else – except for his mind, which was uncommon after he had eaten enough to forget the cravings of the little stomach that pushed out his jacket buttons.

'Soft-shelled crabs,' he said to me before I could condemn him for having lunch. 'From Maryland. With a bottle of Sancerre from my family's firm. You should eat more, Ernest. I know you want to be cadaverous – but surely not a skeleton.'

'And you should eat less, C. Auguste,' I said, as I sat down in the high-backed chair I preferred to the couch. I was not yet ready to be laid out for a premature burial.

'My name is Charles Dupin,' he said sharply, his voice rising to that treble which I knew so well. 'Not Auguste: Just as your name is Ernest, not Edgar. Do we have to go through this routine every time you consult me?'

'Yes,' I replied. 'I come here because your name is Dupin just as my name is Poe.'

'Your name is Pons. Ernest Albert Pons.'

'E. A. P.,' I said. 'Edgar Allan Poe.'

'Pons,' Dupin said. 'Ernest Albert Pons.'

I relaxed and unbuttoned the top button of my black jacket with the high collar. There is something soothing in a little ritual, always the same like the schoolboys' games we passed on from class to class, when I was a child in England with William Wilson.

'Where are they?' I demanded.

'Do you insist?'

'I insist.'

'Well, as you pay me – '

Dupin went over to the oak corner wall cupboard which I had had installed in his dull consulting room. He opened it to show the treasures entombed within – the stuffed raven sitting on the marble bust of Pallas evermore.

'They are ridiculous,' Dupin said.

'They are I,' I replied. 'The ego, the self. I as Poe.'

'One of my other patients once opened this cupboard and accused *me* of insanity.'

'Of poetry, please.'

'I said I stuffed birds as a hobby. He had seen a film called *Psycho* and I lost a patient.'

'Alfred Hitchcock makes inferior versions of my original tales of mystery and the imagination.'

'Ernest, please – ' Dupin showed his impatience, his voice again rising from its rich tenor towards a treble. 'You have been coming to see me all these years, and you persist in your delusion. I won't dignify it with the name of obsession or psychosis. You know perfectly well you are not Edgar Allan Poe.'

'Yet you are Dupin!' I cried triumphantly.

'That was my father's name,' he said. 'So it is mine. I do not exist as a figment of your Edgar's imagination. Once again – and for the *last time* – '

Dupin's voice was shrill and harsh now. My stomach quivered with pleasure as my voice grew haughty.

'Dupin, I did create you!'

'You are Ernest Albert Pons. Born in Berlin, you fled as a child to Brooklyn with your family, which was originally called P-O-N-Z.'

'When my foster family changed their name,' I said, 'they deliberately tried to humiliate me. They merely changed the Z to an S. They could have added a D for dignity.'

'Then they would have been called Ponds like the beauty soap,' Dupin said. 'Pons is the Latin for bridge. Quite distinguished.'

'Not quite American,' I said. 'Anyway, they could have called themselves Allan, like Poe's foster family, and have made it easier for me to recognize who I am.'

'Your mother Bee was your real mother, not your foster mother. Her name was Pons, not Allan. And your father – '

'Ah,' I crowed again, 'my father! You cannot deny, like David Poe, he abandoned me when I was an infant!'

'He fought in World War Two like a few million other people – '

'And *disappeared*! Vanished without trace. None knows whether he is alive or dead!'

'He was posted missing in action – and after some years, he was declared officially dead.'

'That is not the same as *being* dead!' I cried. 'My father was a David Poe! He abandoned me to my childhood fate and nothing was ever heard of him again. For that reason alone, I am Edgar – '

'It is the only thing,' Dupin said coldly, 'that you have in common with Edgar Allan Poe except for your initials. Your mother did not die when you were an infant, but raised you on a pension and a legacy in Brooklyn. You were not raised as a Virginian gentleman, but as a Brooklyn kid – '

'Tormented in high school, made to feel alone – '

'Well, look at you!' Dupin said. 'Dressed in black from head to toe, your pants sticking to your skinny shanks, acting as if you had just come back from a funeral and were leaving for an encore! Now, you're meant to be mature, so you would have played it up even more at sixteen. What could you expect your friends at school to think of you?'

'I had no friends, C. Auguste! I had Edgar. I knew he was born again in me.'

'A normal case of transference,' Dupin said, 'in an only child without a father, who does not relate to his peer group.'

'Peers!' I exclaimed. 'There are no peers at Brooklyn High. There are *plebes* – rascals – '

'So you felt superior and isolated – and afraid. You refused to adjust to your environment and wanted to despise it. You discovered a false similarity with the case of the young Poe, so you adopted his *persona* – '

'He possesses me. I *am* he.'

'At first, it was a game, to make yourself distinct from your peer group,' Dupin continued, remorseless in his analysis. 'Then your mother died just after you had graduated, and in your grief – '

'So did Frances Valentine die, Poe's *second* mother – '
'Yes, it affected him and it affected you. In your grief and solitude, as I see it, your game became an adolescent fixation – a normal transference of your minor tragedy onto somebody else. Except that most of us, if we want a father figure, go to Christ or Marx or Buddha, not to Edgar Poe! You, however, soaked yourself in Poe, and through his life, escaped your own reality.'

'Poe entered me,' I corrected Dupin gently. 'Like Ligeia entered the body of the Lady of Tremaine.'

'You will agree that Poe was fastidious,' Dupin said drily. 'If he did want to return from the grave, why should he choose an obscure Brooklyn youth called Pons? You chose him, Ernest. He did not choose you.'

'How do we ever know,' I mocked, 'whether we choose or are chosen? It is the illusion of choosing at all that keeps us alive.'

'I'll buy that,' Dupin said. 'You chose to act out a fantasy life as Edgar Allan Poe – and unfortunately, you had a private income from your mother's savings and uncle's legacy. The rest of your family were wiped out, weren't they, in Hitler's death camps?'

I nodded at this past history.

'I did not inherit much,' I lied. 'Not enough to live like a gentleman should.'

'Too much,' Dupin replied, 'to live like the rest of us who have to work. And Poe, after all, had to work, as he never had a dollar to his name.'

'He had expectations, viciously disappointed.'

'Don't we all?'

Dupin put his finger ends together, then made a cat's cradle of his knuckles in the one gesture of his that was memorable to me.

'We've been through this all too often,' he said.

'It reassures me,' I said. 'I assert what I am.'

'Yes, but we do not progress. Remember, I am meant to heal you as well as hear you out.'

'I am perfectly happy to be Edgar Allan Poe.'

'You make no one else happy.'

'But I do not make anyone unhappy.'

'No, but – '

Here Dupin turned away and walked over to the raven in the

corner cupboard. Later, I would swear that there was the light of inspiration in its bold glass eyes. For Dupin turned back, excited and dominant, and again I felt the perverse thrill of the wish to obey and to deny at the same time.

'Ernest, listen to me,' he said. 'Either you will do as I say, or I will give you up as a patient.'

'I refuse both alternatives,' I said.

'I am the only Dupin in my business in New York,' he said. 'Therefore you cannot replace me. So listen!'

'If you insist – '

'We have no disagreement about your case except in our language. You say Poe possesses you, that you are Poe, born again – the President talks like that, so you are in good company.' I laughed, but Dupin remained serious. 'I say that you identify with Poe to escape your sense of inadequacy, of loneliness, of failure, of refusing to face up to the world. Well – prove me wrong!'

'You are wrong,' I said. 'There needs to be no proof. I know that I am Poe.'

'Do you?' Dupin asked with the hiss of the serpent. 'Do you know who Poe was?'

'I have read everything written by him a hundred times over and have committed much of it to memory. I have also read everything written about him, I believe.'

'But have you been where he lived? Have you seen what he saw? You say, he entered your flesh. He chose to live again as Ernest Albert Pons in our time. You know why you take this easy way out? It's because you are frightened of travel – you're scared to leave the city you claim to despise. I know that – you've often told me travel makes you so sick before you leave that your illness prevents you from going! Yet you are making your nervous condition the whole excuse for your belief that Poe came to you in Brooklyn.' Dupin's voice almost rose to a shriek as he seemed to solve my case. 'It's so arrogant! Poe *chose* to live your dull life here – and you know his without ever going where he went?'

Dupin was being disturbing. I could begin to feel the terror of his suggestion spread tremors of anticipation through my veins.

'Travel now is so vulgar,' I protested. 'All those fumes and sonic bangs.'

And yet as I spoke, I could see the advantage. I had left my token job that morning. I needed to flee the hot embrace of Ms Zimmerman – into the unknown!

'My proposition is this,' Dupin said coldly. 'Either you never come here again, or you find out who Poe actually was. You examine thoroughly every stage of his life, every place he visited. You return here periodically to report to me the facts in the case of E. A. Poe – and of E. A. Pons, who thinks he is one and the same man.'

So Dupin thought he had me between the pit and the pendulum. If I was pushed into falling into his trap, I would have to leave my safe Poe shrine on Brooklyn Heights for the terrors of the quest. If I refused, he would cut off our relationship like the torturer he was. Yet I could still be saved! He thought I would discover the differences between Poe and Pons. Fool! I would find more correspondences.

'You think I have avoided true research, Dupin. You think, if you force me to relive his life, I shall assert my own existence in my own age.'

'Yes,' Dupin said. 'If you look for Poe, you may find yourself. If you analyse him stage by stage, baby and child and man, you will also analyse yourself. The facts about him will disclose the facts about you – that you are not the same. You may then be able to remove yourself from him.'

'We will find each other even more,' I declared. 'He and I – even in the most absolute identity – *mine own!*'

'That's from "William Wilson",' Dupin said icily. 'I have had to read my Poe too in order to understand you. You may quote him and believe in double identities and split personalities – '

'He wrote that you too – the double Dupin – had a Bi-Part Soul,' I shouted at him. 'And an excited – or perhaps a *diseased* – intelligence!'

Dupin was not amused. His voice was as shrill as the sound of a whiplash.

'Ernest, if you truly search, exactly examine, dig deep, don't lie to yourself, and come back to me to analyse what you have found – then you may yet be free of him.'

'Never!' I cried – yet within me, a delirious possibility of danger maddened my brain. 'Where shall I go first?'

'I do not have to tell you that,' Dupin said, 'if you know as much about Poe as you claim you do. We will ignore Boston where he was born, because a baby's memory is necessarily limited, particularly if his cradle is the trunk of strolling players. So off you go to Richmond, Virginia, where you will arrive like Edgar Poe at the age of one, abandoned by your father, with your mother already dying slowly of consumption.'

'So I live through you, Edgar!' I declared, leaping to my feet and buttoning up the high collar of my jacket. 'Till now, thou hast lived through me!'

'They may understand your language better in the South,' Dupin said.

2

The Enchanted Garden and the Death Pit

> He was a sad dog, it is true, and a dog's death it was that he died; but he himself was not to blame for his vices. They grew out of a personal defect in his mother... Poor woman! she had the misfortune to be left-handed, and a child flogged left-handed had better be left unflogged. The world revolves from right to left. It will not do to whip a baby from left to right. If each blow in the right direction drives an evil propensity out, it follows that every thump in an opposite one knocks its quota of wickedness in.
>
> EDGAR ALLAN POE in 'Never Bet The Devil Your Head: A Tale With A Moral'.

They had put her on the edge of the churchyard near the iron railings that overlooked the rooming houses for blacks on the other side of the street. The spire of Old St John's Church, which climbed in three white pepperpots up to the salt-cellar below the cross, was tall enough to sprinkle its blessings over all the decent graves to front and flank and rear. Yet even the low sun could not make the spire's shadow reach the tomb of the actress, ELIZABETH ARNOLD POE, on the outskirts of the graveyard, where Christian charity had placed it on the frontier of holy ground, but not too close to the godly.

'Man doth not yield him to the angels, nor unto death utterly,' I murmured to myself, quoting the dying words of the Lady Ligeia, 'save only through the weakness of his feeble will.'

I was standing by the grave of Poe's mother, who was only twenty-four when she was buried in Richmond in the December of 1811. I knew well the facts about her end. Her actor husband had abandoned her in the same way as she had abandoned her elder boy William Henry with her father-in-law, 'General' David Poe, in Baltimore. She was caring for her second child Edgar and the infant Rosalie in her little cold rooms by the Indian Queen Tavern. She was also playing at the Richmond Theatre as long as she could stand upright and laugh in public, before she had to take to her bed in early October, never to leave it again for two winter months.

'Ligeia grew ill,' I confided to the pewter plaque of Edgar's mother, her bowed head engraved by an urn on her tombstone. 'The wild eyes blazed with a too – too glorious effulgence; the pale fingers became of the transparent waxen hue of the grave; and the blue veins upon the lofty forehead swelled and sank impetuously with the tides of the most gentle emotion.'

Like Ligeia, Elizabeth Poe wasted away into death, and charity took in the two infants left by the actress – took them to the cleansing of good Virginian homes. Edgar's legacy was the memory of her beauty and her sin – a miniature of her with eyes spilling half-over her face in too, too glorious effulgence – her sketch of Edgar's birthplace, on which she wrote to him that he should love Boston for ever – and a packet of letters, hinting at the reason her husband had left her, that Rosalie might not be his third child, but another strolling player's.

'Let me speak only of that one chamber, ever accursed,' I said to Elizabeth Poe's unquiet spirit, 'whither, in a moment of mental alienation, I led from the altar as my bride – as the successor of the unforgotten Ligeia – the fair-haired and blue-eyed Lady Rowena Trevanion, of Tremaine.'

Edgar's sister Rosalie had fair hair and blue eyes and a slow mind, while her brothers and her mother were dark and quick and bright. In that fearful society, which confused consumption with the curse of God and tuberculosis with the touch of sin, Rosalie seemed to be the angelic and awful replacement of Edgar's dark wild mother, forever lost beyond the grave – unless his will could drag back her spirit. Certainly, the Scots merchant John Allan thought so, when his childless wife Frances Valentine brought Edgar into their home to serve as the son she would never bear. He was to write to Edgar's elder brother that Rosalie was their half sister, then add in vicious piety, *God forbid that We should visit upon the living the Errors and frailties of the dead.*

Yet this was done in Richmond. Edgar Poe, now called Allan, grew up apart from his sister, who was raised with the two children of the nearby trader MacKenzie. When she turned out to be retarded, doomed never to grow mentally beyond the age of ten, the mother's sin seemed to have set her daughter's mind on edge. So the young Edgar lost his mother to death and his sister to idiocy, and lived as the pet of his foster home with a new father, who would not formally adopt him. He would always take a defiant pride in being the child of actors, playing his public life as if on stage, accepting in bravado what Virginian society condemned behind his back.

I still had something to say to Poe's mother in her grave. 'What was the final poem you wrote, Lady Ligeia? Did you not make your dying your last and best performance?

> 'Out – out are the lights – out all!
> And over each quivering form,
> The curtain, a funeral pall,
> Comes down with the rush of a storm –
> And the angels, all pallid and wan,
> Uprising, unveiling, affirm
> That the play is the tragedy, "Man",
> And its hero, the conqueror Worm.'

Another voice, another song intruded into my ears from the basement across the street, sunken below the level of the graveyard:

> ' – *My man had gone away –*
> *By the pillow, he left a note,*
> *Saying I'm sorry, babe, you got my goat –*
> *No time to marry, no time to settle down –*
> *I'm a young woman and ain't done runnin' round . . .'*

It was Bessie Smith singing the blues, the same black sure voice that once had sounded to the little Edgar in the Allan kitchen in that old slave city of Richmond of twelve thousand souls, half-bond and half-free, in the time of President Madison. The child had heard tales of haunting then, of phantoms and tree-devils, spirits from Africa and the dead risen again by voodoo and hallelujahs. And once he had gone riding behind his foster-mother's brother, and they had passed a deserted cabin, surrounded by the graves of dead pioneers. Edgar had struggled from behind Mr Valentine round to the front of the saddle and the comfort of his holding arms. He had been shaking with terror at the thought of the buried. 'They will run after us and drag me off,' he had screamed – and had spoken to the MacKenzie boy of his nightmares, when an icy hand had come and had covered up his face in the dark.

> *I'm a young woman and ain't done runnin' round –*
> *Some people call me a hobo, some call me a bum,*
> *Nobody knows my name, nobody knows what I done,*
> *I'm as good as any woman in your town . . .*

So the everlasting blues sang to Edgar and the grave of his mother, as I walked away through the crowd of other tombstones built in the shapes of beds or tables, triangles and pillars and stone tabs that seemed to be pulled halfway out of the churchyard grass. On the far side of Old St John's, I knew Sarah Elmira Royster's house stood, Poe's first and last betrothed, the maiden of the Enchanted Garden and severe jaw. There was not much for me to see across the stone slabs and iron railings – only a two-storey brick house with a mansard roof, sheltering behind a tree afraid to flower yet. Her family had taken her away from the young Edgar for the same reasons that John Allan would not make him his official heir – he was an actors' child, not quite respectable, in a small Richmond world where everything was so visibly judged in black or white. He could never be accepted as the gentleman he was raised to expect to be – so he played out the postures and excesses of his true inheritance.

I closed my eyes and whispered softly to myself the magic lines of the end of 'Ligeia', when her spirit returns through the corpse of the Lady of Tremaine, her raven hair replacing the fair tresses of her dead rival. 'Here then, at least, can I never – can I never be mistaken – these are the full, and the black, and the wild eyes – of my lost love – of the Lady – of the LADY LIGEIA.' And I seemed to see the full, black, wild eyes of Elizabeth Poe staring through her daughter's face behind my eye-lids, as I repeated the words of horror of her son.

Now I truly saw Ligeia's eyes, as I looked at the little medallion of Poe's mother, which she had given her infant boy. Her face was the same as his description of Ligeia – the gentle prominence of the regions above the temples, the raven-black and naturally curling tresses, the large and strange eyes with the slight irregularity of true beauty, the delicate outlines of the nose – 'and nowhere but in the graceful *medallions* of the Hebrews,' Poe had written of Ligeia, 'had I beheld a similar perfection.'

The little portrait on the wall was hanging in the old cottages which the Poe Society of Richmond had rebuilt to make a shrine for their neglected son – long after his death and his fame. His relics were placed barely in barren rooms – a travelling trunk, his dead wife's trinket-box and mirror, a walking stick and a pair of hooks for his boots. The very poverty of it all was true enough, the promise of that golden boyhood with the Allans set against the squalor of Poe's actual origins and career and end. Too great a divide, an abyss, a maelstrom, to make a poet settle for the safe verses of a Lowell or a Longfellow.

One lithograph on the walls showed the young Edgar's personal hell-fire. The night after Christmas in the same December as his mother's death, the Richmond Theatre burst into flames during her company's performance of *The Bleeding Nun*. Seventy-three people died in the blaze, including the Governor of Virginia, and more would have perished, had not a gigantic dark blacksmith been a St Christopher to the survivors. The lithograph showed the scenes of terror and death outside, the flames bursting through the theater roof, and the gentlemen and ladies throwing themselves from the windows. The disaster was the talk of Edgar's childhood, and the flames lit his lurid memories of his mother, so that later he would claim she had died in the holocaust, not of bright blood from her lungs.

I walked outside into the courtyard, where the Poe Society had made a false enchanted garden in memory of their man. I could not believe my eyes as I remembered the lines that headed 'The Domain of Arnheim':

The garden like a lady fair was cut,
That lay as if she slumbered in delight . . .

I saw in front of me a mere convenience, a silly fountain made like a large candlestick, some sad brick paths ambling between a little lawn towards a pillared shrine, covered with ivy, where the poet's bust was set on a tile stand, brooding darkly on such a pretty pretense of simulating the sexual splendours of his enchanted paradise, which he had laid out with beauty, magnificence and strangeness to suggest the handiwork of angels. His landscape garden was entered by a river gorge, the vessel imprisoned within an enchanted circle of ultramarine satin, in which substance and phantom shadow were the same, before the traveller was given a light canoe of ivory, stained with arabesque devices in vivid scarlet, and the use of a satinwood paddle so he could reach a huge rock with the hue of ages, overspread with the ivy, the coral honeysuckle, the eglantine and the clematis. Finally in the womb of a vast amphitheater entirely begirt with purple mountains, the whole Paradise of Arnheim had burst upon the view.

'Where is a gush of entrancing melody?' I asked the deaf bust of the poet. 'An oppressive sense of strange sweet odour? A dreamlike intermingling to the eye of tall slender Eastern trees – bosky shrubberies – flocks of golden and crimson birds – lily-fringed lakes – meadows of violets, tulips, poppies, hyacinths, and tuberoses – long intertangled lines of silver streamlets – and, upspringing confusedly from amid all, a mass of semi-Gothic, semi-Saracenic architecture, sustaining itself by miracle in mid-air; glittering in the red sunlight with a hundred oriels, minarets, and pinnacles; and seeming the phantom handiwork – '

'Pardon me,' a voice said, 'we can't see him.'

I turned. *They* stood there, a pair more sinned against than sinning, frightful to the naked eye in bright check pants and yellow Bermuda shorts, ghastly growths protruding from their paunches in camera cases, their eye-sockets black and horrible behind their sunglasses.

I glared.

They stared.

I glared some more.
They stared some more.
'We're from Akron, Ohio,' the thing with the blue-rinse hair said finally. 'Where are you from?'
'Atlantis, ma'am,' I said, ever the Southern gentleman. Then I added, 'Atlantis, off New Jersey.' I did not wish to surprise them.

The horrors of the Enchanted Garden were not yet done. Its real place, where the young Edgar had walked and wooed his Sarah Elmira, lay at the back of the new Public Library. It was a vile caricature of Edgar's dream, laid out like a rape victim. Under the shadow of the library wall, as yellow and bleak as a hospital, I had to walk along one spread leg of a gravel path towards an empty brick hole, meant to be a pond. No vast amphitheater here of paradise! In fact, the purple hills that begirt it were grassy pimples, set about with sickly linden saplings and benches as welcoming as coffins. I hurried down the other gravel leg as if from the scene of a crime, and found myself spitting out the lines to Elmira in wrath at the demeaning of the secret garden:

> 'Thou wast all that to me, love,
> For which my soul did pine –
> A green isle in the sea, love,
> A fountain and a shrine,
> All wreathed with fairy fruits and flowers,
> And all the flowers were mine!'

What had it made of Poe, this merchant city – so proud on its hills where the churches and the mansions stood, and the Capitol dome and the fortified tower blocks – so contemptuous in its valleys where the railroads and the turnpikes ran, and the tobacco and canning factories opened their workhouse doors to the black and white trash packed into the frame shanties below? The rulers of Richmond were now trying to prove by praise of Poe that they were not the general philistines he had known, although nothing had changed since John Allan had prospered there – *Thomas Bob, Esq., for many years at the summit of his profession, which was that of a merchant-barber, in the city of Smug.*

I walked in agitation to the Valentine Museum, where the flounces and frills of Old Richmond were preserved in polished rooms and empty costumes behind glass. The house itself was pleasing with a heart-shaped curling stairway to the upper floor, as elegant and graceful as Poe's foster mother herself, Frances Valentine, whose relatives had the style so absent from the penny-pinching homes of her husband, the long-nosed John Allan. He gave one exquisite object, however, to the Valentines – a Greek pot embossed with feathered Mercuries and griffons pulling Aphrodites and Homers crowned with laurels. It showed his secret quarrel with his foster child – he would be a bard too! *Gods, what would I not give*, he once wrote to a friend, *if I had Shakespeare's talent for writing! and what use would I not make of the raw material at my command!*

The raw material at his command had been Edgar Poe, not his pen. And the use he made of it was ambiguous. He looked after him well enough as a small boy, paying for a good schooling, using switches on him only when he deserved it, indulging his wife's love of her pretty Edgar in gold-tasselled cap and Nankin silk suits, so that he himself might have more time for his mistresses and bastard children, the seed of his own flesh.

Yet when Edgar was old enough to box and run and wrestle and swim six miles against the tidal James River like Byron across the Hellespont, then he was old enough to compete for the love of Frances Valentine, now estranged from her husband because of his infidelities. The youth stood his ground in front of John Allan, defending his own mother's memory and his foster mother's honour. This resistance brought out the mean side of John Allan, who cursed this charity changeling, who had become a dog in the manger and a poet in the counting-house. *The boy professes not a Spark of affection for us*, he complained to Edgar's elder brother, *not a particle of gratitude for all my care and kindness towards him. I have given him a much superior Education than ever I received myself.*

Displaced by Edgar in his wife's love and in his secret ambition to become a poet, John Allan could not even point to his own success as a merchant. Throughout the first fifteen years, in which he raised Edgar into adolescent rebellion and noble ingratitude, his own affairs steadily declined from prosperity to near bankruptcy. Then his uncle Galt died and, by the single signature on an old man's will, he became one of the richer men in Richmond, setting up house in a mansion on the corner of Fifth and Main Streets, where an agate lamp was always kept burning to light Edgar to his room.

This fortune of John Allan was the misfortune of Edgar Poe. In the years when the adolescent poet learned to oppose the values of the merchant and the philanderer and the righteous judge set over him, his foster father became wealthy and secure in the approval of his society – Thomas Bob Esq. in the city of Smug, satirized later by Poe as so generous to the young poet's needs that he would allow him a garret, pen and ink and paper, and a rhyming dictionary – supposing that he would scarcely demand more.

So the conflicts were instilled in the charity child – an orphan seeking the mother love he had forever lost – a fatherless boy finding his father figure rejecting him as a rival and enemy – an actors' brat, born to suffer and strut his time upon the stage, yet raised as the gentleman of means he would not be allowed to become – a Southern white child, haunted by the angels and demons of his black mammy's fears – and the rebellious adolescent of the Romantic Age with its impossible chivalries and ruined castles, its fair ladies and dark fantasies, its courtship on the edge of corruption.

Evening was drawing down, as I set off for the station and the long train home to see Dupin the following afternoon, so that I could report on my discoveries. The mystery of Edgar Allan Poe was no mystery. The solution was simple – as Poe's Dupin himself said, almost too simple to be detected. Know thyself! the Greeks declared – and knowing myself as well as I knew all the facts about Poe, how could I fail to find out the secrets of his boyhood? It was just a question of analysis – and of self-analysis.

I dozed on the train, rocking through the night. Dreams troubled me, the waking dreams that linger and overcast mere thought. I had left something undone in Richmond. I had not visited some unforgotten grave. Then in a vision – half-seen between sleep and thought – I saw myself – or was it Poe as I? – in my black raven's suit, standing by a tomb. And as I knew I was seeing myself again by the monument to Elizabeth Poe, another name was cut upon the stone, shocking me into wakefulness –

HELEN!

How had I forgot her, his first true love, the young mother of a friend, Mrs Jane Stith Craig Stanard, with her wide-lidded eyes and squashed full mouth, with the body of a statue and the grace of a Naiad, already sickening of a brain tumour when she met Edgar, then dying soon afterwards in raving dementia, gone gone forever like his mother before her.

I looked out at the grey dawn trying to creep through the smog over Philadelphia. Out there, a tall chimney stack tried to be an obelisk – and failed. I could not utter the famous lines to her, which I had thrust out of my memory because I knew them far too well. So my mind scuttled crab-like past the Nicean barks of yore, the glory that was Greece and the grandeur that was Rome, to a simile from a nobler time for the neon signs that signalled the passing of my monotonous train . . .

> *How statue-like I see thee stand,*
> *The agate-lamp within thy hand!*
> *Ah, Psyche! from the regions which*
> *Are Holy Land!*

'The psyche's got nothing to do with your feeble explanations,' Dupin said in his high voice. 'All I can see is your tremendous *ego*!'

Dupin was being intolerable. He was jealous that I had solved the mystery of E. A. Poe, not he. The case was already closed, and he considered it hardly open! I remained nobly silent.

'For instance,' he continued, 'did you actually speak to anyone who lived in Richmond? Did you ask other people what they thought about Poe? Before you judged the entire city, did you find out the opinions of any of the citizens? Or did you know it all in advance? Were you that grand?'

'I *was* Poe in our city of Smug – and I am no grander than he. Anyway, my dear Dupin, you are the original great detective who, given a few facts, can deduce the solution without even visiting the scene of the crime, let alone asking anyone for more evidence!'

Dupin seemed furious at my astute reply.

'The point of the therapy is for you to distinguish your personality from Poe's. You must give up the pretense that you are the same man.'

'I am that I am,' I said grandly.

'You're a fool, Ernest Pons – even more than Poe was. What did they say of him? Three-fifths genius and two-fifths fudge. You're all fudge!' Dupin paused for effect, then dropped his angry squeak to a confidential croak. 'You've read Marie Bonaparte's classic Freudian analysis of him?'

'Oh yes,' I said. 'She explains Poe and myself as psychopaths. Our infantile traumas made us impotent necrophiliacs.'

'You're not very fond of living women – or men,' Dupin observed. 'Who's that one you are always running away from? Tilly Zimmerman.'

'I'm not very fond of the present human race,' I countered. 'There's nothing wrong with my potency – if I should care to use it, though certainly not on Tilly Zimmerman. The point the dear Princess Bonaparte made was that Poe never recovered from watching his mother die. So his Ligeia and Morelia and Berenice and Madeline in the House of Usher are all consumptive decaying ladies that he brings back from the grave – his buried memories of his mother expiring in a squalid room like a tomb.'

Dupin twisted his fingers into a cat's cradle. He was intrigued at last.

'And how far do you take the Freudian analysis?' he asked. 'The Pit and the Pendulum, for example? Is the shrinking cell the closing hot womb of the mother? Is the pit her vagina and the pendulum the penis-scythe of Time?'

I began to laugh and Dupin laughed with me. He *had* forgiven me! My stomach eased. That was the way to a man's heart – to tattle about his trade rivals.

'Oh yes,' I cried, 'just as the orang-outang stuffing the daughter up the chimney in the Rue Morgue is really the phallus pushing the child back into the maternal womb! It is ridiculous to make too much of Poe's infantile fears, important though they were. He was certainly obsessed by his mother's death – and Helen's. Also his stories do show his revolt from his father figure, John Allan. Think of the suffocated old man in "The Tell-tale Heart", cut up and stuffed beneath the floor-boards! But I don't think hacking up the corpse is really the castration of the father in the Oedipal struggle – nor is the beating of the hideous heart an infantile memory of a sex attack on the mother! The Princess goes too far.'

'Do you remember,' Dupin asked, 'your father making love to your mother? In the same room as you – or noises through a thin wall? The thump of it – like a heart?'

'Of course not,' I said indignantly. 'There was once – ' Then I saw Dupin's stare. O serpent, trying to separate me from my Poe! 'My experience was the same as Edgar's. As infants, we did share our mother's bed at times, but we never heard or saw her making love to another man.'

'What was your mother Bee's regular boy friend to you?' Dupin added. 'Your John Allan figure? You once told me you spent years of your childhood blackmailing your mother into not marrying him. Every time she tried to make you accept him, you'd have a temper tantrum and really fall ill, so she had to nurse you and give him up.'

'That's not different from Edgar,' I said acidly.

'He was a healthy young man,' Dupin said. 'He excelled in sports. He led his peer group. You were terrible at everything except gymnastics – a solitary sport which nobody used to admire. Where he dominated, you were persecuted. You won't deny that.'

'You will not drive us apart!' I shrieked. 'I will not listen!'

'You will listen,' Dupin said. 'You will find out the differences between you and him. Look at them! He was raised in a racist slave society, where the young rich whites thought they were aristocrats, even if they were not. Poe's fear of being thought a charity child or an actors' orphan made him risk his life, excel physically, lead, declaim, exaggerate. You may quite resemble the older Poe, thin and pale and dark-eyed like a reject from *Dracula*, but not the younger one. Black boys trod on you on the way to put the ball in the basket! Nice Jewish girls called you a schmuck when you sent them dirty love messages. The only dates you got were blind ones – and they were really short-sighted! You told me how you always felt isolated, excluded, a mother's boy, only safe with her at home. The playground was your pogrom.'

'But my mother died too!' I cried.

'We haven't come to that part of our analysis yet,' Dupin said. 'We're going through Poe's life in order – and your own. From the very beginning to the end. Indeed, the next step will be truly traumatic.'

I felt my stomach slither loose. My bowels were jelly inside me.

'No, I'm not ready yet. Please, Dupin – '

'Look,' Dupin said, 'you simply have to take responsibility for your own life. Not put it onto mine or Poe's. Did he blame everything on his birth? Did he become a drunkard because it ran in the family? Could he only be a poet because he was haunted by his mother's death or sister's bastardy?'

'If you're a poet *damné*,' I said, 'you have to feel damned.'

'The point is, Ernest, no one is wholly damned by his birth. He is only damned if he thinks he is. It's an excuse for failure, not a reason for success. Many actors' abandoned children have lived long and fruitful lives. And some poets come from happy families and sell insurance to make their bread!'

'Not the poet who possesses me!' I shouted. 'Those are mere diddling rhymesters.'

'Even Poe's obsession with death,' Dupin continued remorselessly, 'was normal for the age. Life expectation then was half what it is now. People died in their homes, not in hospitals. It was only exaggerated people like Byron who made a *romance* out of it, visiting graves and all that. Dying was just another part of living then – we have stupidly chosen to exclude it and fear it too much.' His eyes pierced into mine. 'You don't like to think of *modern* deaths, do you?'

I disliked the way Dupin was in charge of the conversation. It was my case, was it not?

'We shall continue my analysis of the Poe problem early next week, when I have more material – '

Dupin threw in his bomb like the anarchist he was.

'I shall not be here,' he said. 'I'll be in the Virgin Islands.'

'You can't desert your patients!' I shouted. 'It's unethical! If you have to go, you must take me along with you. I'm very good on other people's holidays – '

'I am going with my wife. She will be the lady in the Enchanted Garden you described to me.'

'She'll find me very useful. I'll shop for her in the gift shop. I'll even take a separate room – '

Dupin gave me a cold smile.

'You're going to England, Ernest. You're going by boat. The Queen Elizabeth the Second leaves on Wednesday. I've booked you to sail on her.'

'There'll be a storm – I need months to pack – Dupin, you're a sadist!'

'We agreed on your therapy, Ernest. At the age of six, Poe went to Britain for five years with the Allans. He first went up to Scotland, then down to London and school in Stoke Newington. He *sailed* there! That is what you are doing. The trip will take you *months!*'

'Weeks!' I shrieked. 'You're doing this deliberately just to get away from me.'

I had to stand upright in my agitation. I found myself looking down at the naked spot on Dupin's skull, half-hidden by slick streaks of brushed hair. How could such a bald runt think he held any power over me? Yet he looked up at me, unafraid.

'I'm going to cure you of your childish dependence on two people – Charles Dupin and Edgar Allan Poe. In that order! So pack your trunks for England, Ernest. I'll be back by the time you're back to hear your report. I promise that.'

'I refuse to go!' I shouted. 'I categorically refuse!'

I found myself grasping Dupin by the shoulders. I shook them, then I hugged him. I had to stoop to do so. Then I suddenly saw myself as if Edgar were watching me. I let Dupin go.

'Calm yourself,' Dupin said. 'I am going on holiday, whether you like it or not. And you are going to Stoke Newington. Isn't that where your favourite split personality went to school, William Wilson? The story that *proves* you can have a double identity – be yourself and Poe, one and divisible?'

'That is true,' I said. And the image of Poe now seemed to stand before me, drawing himself up proudly before the mean presence of John Allan, throwing away a fortune because of a personal sense of honour, independent of those who believed he depended on them through interest or fear. 'I will sail over there – and do not expect me back!'

'Suit yourself,' Dupin said placidly. 'Have a good trip.'

I strode towards the door of the consulting room, then I stopped. A remark of that sly Dupin was troubling me.

'You said that this next step would be truly traumatic. What did you mean exactly?'

Dupin smiled with thin cold lips.

'If William Wilson was Poe's trauma, his split self and double life and shattered personality, what is yours? Where is the school you did not attend as a child? Where did your first friends end? What happened to the rest of your family in Berlin, your relatives?'

I felt the sweat break out on my forehead. Dupin was worse than the Inquisition of Toledo. Each interview swung the pendulum closer to my naked chest, each suggestion drove my shivering feet closer to the brink of the death pit.

'Why not look into your real self, Ernest Albert Pons?' Dupin insisted. 'Make a search for the buried figures *you* hide from your own consciousness.'

3

I Fled In Vain

> You have conquered, and I yield. Yet henceforth art thou also dead – dead to the World, to Heaven, and to Hope! In me didst thou exist – and, in my death, see by this image, which is thine own, how utterly thou hast murdered thyself.
>
> EDGAR ALLAN POE in 'William Wilson'.

Naturally I fell ill at the prospect of going away. I had always fallen ill, even when my mother had told me that we would spend the following day at Coney Island. The excitement of future pleasure – or a change for the worse – would affect my nerves. I would break out into a fever, which even hot tea with lemon and aspirin would not cure. And this time, that villain Dupin had gone to the Virgin Islands *without leaving a telephone number!* Torture could go no further.

So I had to pack in a sweat, shivering between so many dread choices – the nightshade cravat with my evening dress or the batwing bow tie? – the charcoal smoking jacket or the sable one? – the black Wellington boots *and* the black loafers, or one of them? – it was impossible! I did not even have my mother Bee to make up my mind for me – 'Ernest, I have put in all your wool vests, so cold you should not catch!'

In such an agony of indecision, I would often sink on to my knees in front of that wooden trunk, wrapped with iron bands, its lid as open as a waiting coffin. I would shake there, unable to move, until a greater fear would send me scrambling across to my bomb-proof front door. I would check its steel plate, riveted in place; its seven locks with jaws strong enough to snap any burglar's tool; its twin cross-bars and third backing bar that slotted into an iron hole a yard behind my entrance barrier. Yet what if some bandits were to ignore the obstruction and cut through the wall – while I was sent away across the ocean? They could loot at their leisure my shrine to Edgar Allan Poe!

I would then have to reassure myself – check my relics – be certain all was still there! My shrine room is cleverly hung with grey drapes, gathered at the top to droop apart like the wings of angels on either side of each portrait of Poe. There is no likeness of him of which I do not have the faithful copy – daguerrotype and etching and sketch – and even the lost Sully painting of him in the pose of Byron, which I have had forged by employing an artist to copy the original and add Poe's face.

Below each portrait, the nightlights burn on the little stone altars beside every mirror – those fateful mirrors of comparison, by which we know ourselves perhaps to be an Other! I often stand looking into each obscure glass, staring at my own curling dark hair, noble brow, sunken grey eyes, small moustache in a shadow on my upper lip. Perhaps I am a little *finer* in the nose and *stronger* in the chin than Poe – my diet has been better than his! Yet when I put my right hand in that Bonaparte gesture beneath the buttons of my black waistcoat, I can see *his* features superimpose themselves on the slight variance of my face.

For what did William Wilson see in that fatal mirror, after he had stabbed to death his double, his avenging conscience? Did he see his own reflection? 'Thus it appeared, I say, but was not. It was my antagonist – it was Wilson . . . Not a line in all the marked and singular lineaments of his face which was not, even in the most absolute identity, *mine own!*'

On this last sick day before leaving for Stoke Newington across the raging Atlantic Ocean, my eyes blurred until I could see Poe's face upon my reflection in the glass. Yet wink as I would, my vision would not clear. I could feel the salt tears falling down my cheeks. Damned Dupin! Damned fatigue! And Poe's face that was also mine in the mirror seemed to move its lips.

'Rosa,' he said, his name for Rosalie, his sister that was not.

'Rosa,' I said, my name for she who was as my sister, and was not.

I was compelled to do what I would not do. Some strange force dragged each foot one after the other to my portrait of Virginia Clemm – the child wife of Edgar Poe he called his Sissy. I looked at her face and saw only a little girl, turning away shyly with her round chin and pout and drowsy eyes under the dark slumber of her hair.

'No, no, get back!' I commanded my right hand, but it would not obey me! It seized the portrait of Virginia in blasphemy and undid its silver frame. Behind her lay a sepia snapshot of a little girl in a white dress like Virginia's, smiling and holding a skipping-rope in a park beneath some linden trees. She also had dark hair, longer and falling to her shoulders, and she would have had the pallor of Virginia, but that the yellowing of time had tinted her chubby cheeks into the hue of memory.

'Rosa,' I said, weeping. 'Rosa – '

I kissed my cousin's photograph, the playmate and love of my early Berlin days, and placed it behind the portrait of Poe's Virginia. Twice damned Dupin! He was wrong, and he made me err! Her fate, their fate, my kin and comrades in Berlin – it was all a fantasy! Had not Poe, too, believed his lies about his foreign travels, telling tales of great journeys to Paris and St Petersburg? I had never fled Berlin – for I had never truly been there! I am so sensitive to the suffering of others that my mistaken conscience was persecuting me – like the false William Wilson – into thinking that I had escaped the holocaust of the Jews. It was as the nightmare of some opium dream, and that secret likeness of the little girl – my Rosa! – she must be taken from an alien family album to prove the loss I never really had!

How the floating gambling saloon miscalled a liner ever was granted the name of a queen – and a queen of England too! – I shall never know! Imperial Throne, how thou hast stooped to survive! I may condescend royally myself, but I hope I never have to grovel.

I stalked the decks and lower levels of the pleasure palace between the staterooms, all differently decorated in garish colours of peacock and orange and swamp-bright verdigris. The builders had been malevolent enough to place glass doors between each clashing section, so that the poisonous decorations assassinated each other before the offended eye. This was no abbey of Prince Prospero, where the heedless thousand guests could gather together, fleeing the Red Death outside the walls. The Prince had decked his apartments also in different colours – one vivid blue, one purple, one green, then orange and white and violet and lastly black with window panes of deep blood. Yet he separated each new effect by a sharp turn, a dark corridor, a heavy tripod bearing a brazier of fire. So it should be! All bad taste is tolerable, if only there is time to recover between one shock and the next.

I prefer not to remember the voyage, the pitch and toss of the rolling sea, the interminable food that the stomach rejected and the mind avoided, the rough service of the young stewards freshly drafted from porting fish at Billingsgate. It is true, we skirted the maelstrom, sliding into no black spinning whirlpool which might sweep us round and round in dizzying swings and jerks. Only my descent into my deep dramamine dreams in my cabin sank me into such a wide waste of liquid ebony, from which no escape seemed possible to another day.

Once did I imagine that I was buried alive on that vast ocean on the boundary between Life and Death. Who shall say, as Poe has said, where the one ends, and where the other begins? I knew, or seemed to know, the unendurable oppression of the lungs – the stifling fumes of the turbine engines – the clinging to the death garments – the rigid embrace of the narrow house – the blackness of the absolute Night – the silence like a sea that overwhelms – the unseen but palpable presence of the Conqueror Worm – and I woke, drenched with sweat, gasping and striking out blind against the entombing walls – to find the air conditioning in my cabin had failed.

One night, an entertainment was promised, an exhibition of hypnosis. To reach the nether ballroom, I had to make my way through a gambling hell that would have rejoiced the cunning heart of William Wilson. Gowned girls used busy fingers to flick out the cards at blackjack tables or stood by the little maelstroms of the roulette wheels, round which the ivory peas bounced and skittered until they fell into the final number. 'Thirteen!' I heard a cry, and then, 'Twenty-two! Zero!' While I was watching, never did the pea pick a number where a passenger had placed his bet. The house won all.

Passing through the games of mischance, I reached the ballroom where the hypnotist would perform. I had long been interested, with Mr Poe, in mesmeric revelations to discover the nature of God and to arrest the death throes of our human state. Yet this hypnotist made of his black art a silly sport for jesters. He called out twenty willing clowns from the audience and made Hop-Frogs of the four most supine of them, buffoons at his command in comic gestures to make the mob laugh. He did not encourage them to speak of the nature of the divine, but made pretend that one was an astronaut talking to a Martian in a nonsense language. So low had sunk the quest for the high, that even heaven was degraded.

Finally, the hypnotist summoned a girl assistant and put her in a mesmeric trance, stiffening her body in a sort of *rigor mortis*. He then laid her like a marble slab between two chairs, her head on one, her heels upon the other. The Hop-Frogs were invited to climb upon her, jump on her, test her stern rigidity of stone. Yet so deep a muscular spasm kept her straight and stiff that she seemed a mummy-case in her own body. Then the hypnotist put his arms beneath her and released her from her trance, catching her as she sagged and setting her on her feet. She was no Mademoiselle Valdemar, preserved from dying for seven months by mesmerism, only to collapse upon release into a nearly liquid mass of loathsome – of detestable putrescence.

'You do not clap, sir,' a voice said by my side. It was the eager entertainments officer, worried that he had never seen me smile. 'It does not amuse you?'

I put my pale hand upon his braided jacket like a message from another world.

'It decomposes me,' I said.

He did not share my laughter, which was rusty from disuse and sounded like a death rattle.

The days on board I spent swathed in a rug upon a deck chair, sipping my *bouillon* tea, and reading 'William Wilson' again and again to prepare me for my investigation. It was Poe's only autobiographical tale, yet he mocked himself with it, exaggerating both his immorality and his condemning conscience, his violent swings between riotous living and remorse. Did he really believe that he inherited his self-will and his ungovernable passions? Did his Irish ancestors, the Poes, give him his remarkable, imaginative and easily excitable temperament? Did their weak will and weaker bodies, prone to the least illness, blight him all his life? So William Wilson stated of himself, but only to excuse his later villainies.

He also claimed his upbringing tainted him. Like Poe and myself, bereft of our mothers before we reached maturity, Wilson could say with truth: 'At an age when few children have abandoned their leading-strings, I was left to the guidance of my own will, and became, in all but name, the master of my own actions.' Adolescence in modern America is, after all, but a continued childhood, given the spoiling of the age of Dr Spock. And I was still a mother's boy when she left me forever at seventeen, to look after myself, who knew not how.

I do not resent her for it, for what can resentment do about death? I do resent her dominance of my every act. My mother Bee was John and Frances Valentine Allan to me – the master and the lover, the smiter and the spoiler, the smack and the caress in one hand, so that I was left defenseless in a desperate world and was forced to choose the best armour I knew to hide me from the mockery and the indifferent knives. Oh Edgar Poe, who revealed yourself in William Wilson, must I reveal myself in you?

The ship docked at Southampton, not Liverpool, although I sent word to the Captain that I would have preferred the second port, since Poe had landed there. The Captain did not deign to reply to my note. Courtesy is dead. Southampton itself was a trifling city, neither new nor old, of no significance to me, so I took the Boat Train to London – and on my way, I debated the question – To Scotland or not?

Poe, of course, made much of his schooldays in Irvine in the heart of the Burns country with its weird castles and ghost-walks in Lord Kilmarnock's mansion and Brig crossed by Tam o'Shanter in person. But all that was Scotch mist and faeryland. The boy of six actually spent no more than a month with the Allan relatives in the north and, like all Southerners, knew Sir Walter's Scotland, whose fantasies of chivalry were far more appealing than the wet place itself.

Anyway, what had I to do with the banks o' bonnie Doon, or the banks o' bonnie Doon to do with me? I was only haunted by the Loch Ness Monsters of the Catskills, who used to come dripping out of the beauty parlor five feet tall and ditto sideways with pink curlers in their hair. Also, if I took the train to Scotland, I would be another week away from Dupin, and I *needed* him. So I quoted aloud Poe's lines from 'The Lake' and cut short my pilgrimage:

> 'In the spring of youth it was my lot
> To haunt of the wide world a spot
> The which I could not love the less –
> So lovely was the loneliness
> Of a wild lake, with black rock bound,
> And the tall pines that towered around.'

'Very nice, sir,' the inspector said, who was blacker than my mood and suit. 'Would that be Rod McKuen? Your ticket, please.'

Once I had arrived in London, accommodation proved difficult. Knightsbridge looked like a *casbah*, Sloane Street like a *souk*. Yet I did manage to place myself in an anonymous room in the Carlton Towers, a mere block away from the school where Poe had gone to learn under the Misses Dubourg. He had learned so well that he made one of them a laundress and a witness in the murder case in the Rue Morgue! Nothing else survives of his stay at their establishment except a school bill, charging 'Master Allan' among other things five shillings for medicine and ninepence each for explaining the Catechisms of the Church and of the History of England. So young Edgar was drilled in the Anglo-Saxon God and the Kings and Queens of England too, from William the Conqueror to silly George the Third, who had let his America slip through his fingers.

Yet this was trivial stuff. I hate travelling because of all the details and delays. The porters and the cabmen do not seem to recognize the quality I possess, only the size of my slender wallet. It took me an hour of rebuffs to find out where Stoke Newington was, and another two hours to penetrate the traffic, which deliberately placed itself in our path all the interminable way there. Where were the gigantic and gnarled trees, overarching the carriage road, beside which the ravens croaked and flapped their wings? They were translated to supermarkets and tobacconists, Boots' Chemists and W. H. Smith's, with only the telephone wires overhead and the grumble of the aeroplanes leaving Heathrow.

As for Stoke Newington itself, it was as far removed as Poe's own description of his schooldays in 'William Wilson'. He had changed a true Georgian mansion into an Elizabethan labyrinth behind massy walls, he had turned a boys' playground into a prison yard, he had transformed a youngish sporting principal into the Reverend Doctor Bransby, who ruled with sour visage and draconian rod over his gothic schoolroom. If Poe had made a monster from his teacher and a mystery of his ordinary school, time had made of Stoke Newington the epitome of nothing. Everything in it was reproduced by every suburb around it, until North London seemed to prove Einstein wrong, that infinity could exist upon earth in the brick boxes without end on the way to Cambridge.

Poe had sent his William Wilson there too, after his education at Stoke Newington and Eton. Yet his revels and orgies at Cambridge did not interest me – they were but exaggerations of Poe's brief stay at the University of Virginia – the next stage in my analysis. What mattered now was my alienation from my sad surroundings. I could not feel in this drab Stoke Newington any identity with the young Edgar at his school nor any correspondence with William Wilson. *He* might have had a double, made by his self-hatred to condemn his dissipations, whose singular whisper grew into the very echo of his own. But I found the regular raven's croak of Poe, that sounded in my inner ear, had fled me in the noise of car exhausts and foreign voices. In North London, I did not know myself in his experience, and I found I was a stranger in a place I would not be.

I resolved to leave immediately for New York and risk the aeroplane, which could take no longer than the three days' flight across the Atlantic of Poe's balloon-hoax – Mr Monck Mason's Flying Machine! I directed my cab driver to take me to the Charing Cross Road in the last hope that I might rescue something of value from the antiquarian booksellers there. All the journey, I raged silently against the perfidious Dupin for his success in separating me from my shrine to Poe, my memories and my memorabilia. He had distracted me from my *alter ego*, he had sent me like Hans Pfaall or Arthur Gordon Pym so far on an absurd voyage that I had lost the moorings of my former self. So I damned Dupin to the fate of Eugene Aram, the murderer and usher of the Stoke Newington school, whose ghost was said to haunt the place in Poe's time, and whose clever logic at his trial had not saved his neck from the gallows any more than Dupin's wit would save him from my wrath.

The bookshop in St Christopher's Place was cold and fusty with that smell of folio decay that is the perfume of the book-lover. The proprietor had the aroma of his stock in trade, his clothes like wrinkled dust-jackets, his skin foxed with blotches like old pages, and his manners an essay on ancient etiquette.

'May I help you, sir,' he offered. 'My aim is yours – to satisfy your needs – and thus my own.'

'Poe,' I declared. 'Edgar Allan Poe. Anything uncommon on him, anything at all. You see, I am – ' I hesitated, feeling both my caution and my confidence return. It would not do to let out my secret too early. 'I am – an *amateur* of Edgar Poe, as the French say.'

'I have the very thing for you,' the bookseller said, and burrowed in a pile of volumes behind him, coughing at the leather dust he roused, and emerging with a thin folder of green morocco.

'The original prints *ex libro*,' he said as reverentially as a priest, 'of Aubrey Beardsley's four illustrations from the *Tales of the Grotesque and Arabesque* – or *Mystery and Imagination*, as you please.'

I opened the folder with the same piety and looked over each etching one by one. They were as mint as innocence and as decadent as William Wilson. Here a horned woman showed her breasts above a black stomacher with imps' faces strung about her loins, while leaning on a wide-hipped world-weary Pierrot, and looking for Prince Prospero in the Masque of the Red Death. Here again the Black Cat sat in white outline against the night upon the white hair of his victim, whose eyes were closed against the certainty of his fate to come. And here Roderick Usher was enthroned in profile and in gloom, wearing a black frock coat and white cloak, waiting for his sister to come back from the dead. Then, fourth and last, the naked ape strode across the boudoir curtains in the Rue Morgue, one earring pendant and obscene in his lobe, bearing the lifeless daughter in his hideous grasp – the beast within us that Poe would loose and Dupin would track down.

'Yes,' I said, 'I only have the book. How much are these originals?'

'Fifty pounds,' the bookseller said. 'Or a hundred dollars, shall we say?'

They were ridiculously cheap. In New York, I would have gladly paid a thousand dollars. The bargain almost repaid my fare. I took out my wallet and found a single large note and gave it to the man. Yet greed – or was it the irrepressible Imp of the Perverse? – then drove me on. I could not let well alone.

'You have more?' I inquired.

'Sir, things come and go,' the bookseller said. 'I have nothing else exceptional. You have the Arthur Rackham illustrations of Poe's Tales?'

'The mint folio edition,' I crowed, 'and two other copies, just for *reading*!'

'Then please to leave me your name and your address. And if something special comes my way – '

My name? What name should I give? To say the truth, that I was truly Poe resurrected, would be absurd, although the four Beardsleys had put me again in mind of him. Yet – if I did so, I would scare the man. He would think me mad and sell his treasures elsewhere, unless I spent hours on tedious explanations. I must give my modern *alias*.

'Pons,' I said. 'Edgar Allan – ' I corrected my deliberate mistake with a charming smile. 'Ernest Albert Pons.'

The bookseller was silent. He put his face closer to mine, so that I could see his remaining hair was dark, his nose was fine and his foxed skin was pale, although webbed with wrinkles as if his features were almost mine in caricature on some parchment cracked with age.

'Pons?' he said. 'Ernest Albert Pons?'

I nodded mutely.

'Was Beatrice Ponz your mother? Ernst your father, Ernst Ponz from Berlin.'

So swift the pendulum swung from ease to despair! The dreadful questions of the Inquisition had discovered me again in this English haven. This bookshop was the hidden pit of my avenging conscience!

Deny him – I could not.

'Yes,' I said. 'My mother told me so – but I – I do not remember.'

'You managed to escape as the S.S. were taking us away. We prayed for you in the trucks – and you did reach America, after all. But Uncle Leo and Marta, and your cousins Mordecai and Rachel – '

'And Rosa?' I heard myself ask. 'What of her?'

'You do not know?'

'I do not know I know.'

'You do not wish to know?'

'I – I wish to know.'

'All dead. In the camp.'

'And you alive?'

'I was the gravedigger,' the bookseller said among the leather bindings of the past. 'I dug the death pits and I covered them over with earth. There were so many and – I have forgot.'

'I have forgot too,' I said.

'Yet we must remember.'

'Yet we must forget.'

He put his fingers on my face. Cold they were, as they traced my cheeks like tears.

'Ernest Albert Ponz,' he said. 'You lived too. Shall we meet again?'

I gave him my address at my hotel, telling him to call me in the morning. I fled that night on the last aeroplane to New York. And in the high limbo of the flying machine, suspended between the dark heaven and the hell on earth, I did not – I could not believe that I had truly met my other self – my William Wilson from my Berlin days, my *doppelgänger* and my conscience from the childhood I would not admit.

Was Dupin right? Had I begun to investigate my own past? Transfer my analysis of Poe to myself? Or had I only met a phantom of fatigue, a nightmare from my unconscious conjured from the alien ground of Europe?

It must be so, I thought, to ease my mind – then saw the Beardsley folder, as obvious as Poe's purloined letter, in the rack in front of my seat.

Dupin had a disgusting tan upon his face and the backs of his hands – straight from a bottle, of course, although he would pretend it was acquired naturally. I have never understood why white people want to turn brown, while brown people want to turn white. I shall stay the paleface God made me. So I did not allow Dupin time to brag, before I began my complaint.

'You *tortured* me, Dupin. Or rather, you made me torture myself. You knew, if I returned to Europe, all those horrible memories would come back. And as for Poe at Stoke Newington, it must have been purgatory for him – even at the age of eight!'

I then proceeded to speak about the bookseller and his identification of me. Dupin listened with a superior smile.

'Are you sure,' he asked, 'you were not talking to your reflection in a mirror? You are a solitary man, and you do talk to yourself. This wasn't a case of your guilt surfacing, because you escaped the holocaust – and most of your Berlin friends did not?'

'No, no,' I cried, flourishing the Beardsley folder. 'I have proof! He sold me this.'

'I do not doubt that,' Dupin said. 'But did you have the conversation you report to me?'

'Absolutely – ' I declared. Yet as I spoke, I knew I could not swear to it. Memory is such a charlatan. The mind diddles with past truth. Every witness in a court of law is forsworn, for we all dandify what we have done.

'It does not really matter,' Dupin said. 'The great thing is, you have begun to admit to your past, your guilt, your fears. And they are yours, not Poe's. That is real progress. And on this trip, you talked to somebody, made a human contact – even if you fled from it.'

'I fled in vain,' I said, echoing the words of William Wilson. 'That conscience travels with me.'

'The fate of the Jews,' Dupin said, 'travels with us all. It is part of our dark inheritance – the sins of old Europe which even the New World cannot escape. Still, Ernest, you should be pleased. The analysis goes forward.'

'I am tired,' I said – and found myself weeping. The tears were warm and uncontrollable. 'I am sorry, Dupin – I simply can't – can't go on with it – '

'You will go on,' Dupin said. 'You cannot stop now, just as you begin to confront your real self and leave the *persona* of Poe. You must go to the University of Virginia next – face up to his self-destruction and his fight with his father figure.'

'I can't! Dupin – please – '

'You must, Ernest. Here!'

He handed me a silk handkerchief that was worse than an eyesore – it would have spoilt vistas. It was volcanic red, spotted with purple sores.

'Keep it,' Dupin said kindly. 'When I saw it, I thought of you. Anyway, we should all try to encourage native arts and crafts.'

'Not witchcraft,' I said. I could not bear to put the loathsome thing to my face, which I wiped with the back of my hand. 'I suppose I shall have to go on.'

'Good,' Dupin answered, rubbing his brown hands together. 'I knew you would.'

'You know nothing!' I cried. 'Nothing at all. This whole analysis is entirely artificial. There are any number of ways of treating me, and you chose one so curious – '

'Nonsense,' Dupin said. 'You know the old saying – you should make the punishment fit the crime. Well, a psychiatrist should make the case fit the patient. Your delusion is that you are Poe. So we are using Poe's own method – *the detection of the mystery of who he was by a logical process between Dupin and yourself* – to free you from your delusion.' Here Dupin put on the pleased smirk he always used before delivering a bad aphorism. 'We are setting a Pons to catch a Poe!'

I failed to laugh, but found my composure quite returned. I stood up, folding the obscene handkerchief into smaller and smaller squares before depositing it in the middle of Dupin's couch, immediately infecting it with the bubonic plague.

'This object,' I said, 'is far more in need of medical treatment than I am.'

'Pick it up,' Dupin said. 'It reminds me of you.'

4

The Ragged Mountains

> In the greenest of our valleys
> By good angels tenanted,
> Once a fair and stately palace –
> Radiant palace – reared its head.
> In the monarch Thought's dominion –
> It stood there!
> EDGAR ALLAN POE in 'The Haunted Palace'.

No doubt of it, Thomas Jefferson was the C. Auguste Dupin of the United States. He applied logic even to the wilderness. What other man would put a grid pattern across the whole American west, stamping little boundaries across a virgin continent with a waffle-iron? And who else would build a university like Poe's palace before it was haunted – its main quadrangle shaped like a lying body, flanked by the limbs of student rooms, topped by the head of the Rotunda, where the monarch Thought's dominion had its own Pantheon of three egg-shaped cerebra for hatching inspiration and a master library in the crowning dome of its skull.

My soul was uplifted like the young Poe's on arrival at seventeen, to see such order laid upon the rocky valley of the Rivanna River below the Blue Ridge and the Ragged Mountains. Such consciousness writ large on the turbulence of nature! The white classical columns running along the West and East Ranges with their Doric and Corinthian and Ionic Pavilions, overlooking the serpentine walls about the careful mazes of the backing gardens. This was truly the landscape of man's proper soul – and if anyone could set such a gentle rule upon his own body, what liberty of spirit he would have to wander his chosen walkways!

I knocked at a door under the colonnades. It bore the name of

Thomas Eggleston Blake III. A lanky youth, all bones and protuberances and fair floppy hair, answered my knock. When I asked him the way to Poe's old room, he kindly offered to show me there himself. 'It's no problem, sir,' he protested – and became my Vergil and my Ariel across the serpentine gardens to Poe's student room, still preserved in roughly the same state in memory of him, a founding student and the most famous of them all.

It was Room 13 in the West Range, a monkish barren cell with a Latin plaque at the door:

EDGAR ALLAN POE

MDCCCXXVI

DOMUS PARVA MAGNI POETAE

Small dwelling, great poet, indeed! I dismissed my guide, thanking him for his Southern courtesy, and stared through an iron grille at the ever-open door. There was an old grate, the ashes still within it as though Poe had just left the room – a small desk and a cane chair and a truckle bed from the Allan home – the only genuine article, for Poe had burned his sticks of furniture on his last night at the University to keep himself warm. A wash-stand stood there, too, with china bowl and pitcher – and a Bible, sneaked in to suggest the salvation of the poet's soul. In fact, he would have had his illustrated Byron, from which he had copied engravings in charcoal sketches to hang on his bare walls. The noble radical English lord's books had sold to those first wild students at Jefferson's 'Academical Village' at the rate of five to one of any other author.

Titled bandits, many of Poe's companions would have liked to be – and rowdy young gentlemen they were. Poe's ill fortune was to be sent to the first liberal university in America, when its democratic founder had insisted that the students were to make their own rules – and fail to govern themselves. Some of them arrived with servants and pointers and blooded horses and fowling pieces, others with open purses to play Loo or drink unlimited 'peach-honey', the local brand of moonshine. If half the students came to study, the other half were there to waste the days and nights away. The only obligatory lectures were between seven and nine in the morning – and a gentleman could sleep through them, if one of the six foreign professors did not force him rudely awake.

Poe's second misfortune was to be poor – and also able to pass himself off as the heir to a fortune. John Allan was deliberately mean with him, sending him to the new university with too little to pay for his bed and board. So Poe was compelled to borrow, ashamed to beg for more, and looked to gambling to supply the difference. His credit was good as the apparent heir to the Allan wealth, so the merchants would supply him – and the money-lenders of Charlottesville, the local town. To repay them, he played cards and lost and plunged deeper into debt. In his later excuse to John Allan, he claimed that he joined the gentlemen outcasts because he had no money, and therefore no choice:

> It was then that I became dissolute [he wrote] for how could it be otherwise? I could associate with no students, except those who were in a similar situation with myself – altho' from different causes – They from drunkenness, and extravagance – I, because it was my crime to have no one on Earth who cared for me, or loved me. I call God to witness that I have never loved dissipation – Those who know me know that my pursuits and habits are very far from any thing of the kind. But I was drawn into it by my companions. Even their professions of friendship – hollow as they were – were a relief . . .

To a young man among his university friends, much of love from home is money in his hand. Poe found himself seemingly ignored by the Allans and his betrothed – his love letters to Sarah Elmira Royster were intercepted, and she was married off to the rich older Shelton. So Poe took to drink because his companions drank. He did not like it for the taste, but for the upsetting of his equilibrium. The other students would watch him drain a dram of toddy in a gulp, which would make him so excited he would need no more. With that one glass of liquor, he would talk the whole night through or play cards maniacally in his room in 'Rowdy Row'.

He seemed to carouse to lose, as if the fever of the spirits and the gambling debts made him feel more the American Byron, supreme among true gentlemen – and forgetful that he was a charity child and an actors' orphan. In bravado and bold companions, cards and egg-nogs, he found oblivion and brief belief that he was the young man of his own pretensions.

From the near frontier, violence also attacked the Academical Village. Poe's first letter back to John Allan told of local Grand Juries trying to indict his refugee companions, and of assaults with pistols or teeth that resulted in a fellow student losing pieces of flesh from his arm as big as Poe's hand. Savagery and the wilderness lay over the Ragged Mountains and the Blue Ridge, and in the ungovernable young men of passion. Even Poe had to use his fists to fight.

He excelled easily in his classes, particularly in his declamations in French and Latin, and somewhat in Italian and Greek. He had a capacious and capricious memory, and an inherent sense of phrasing and style, so that he could launch into eloquent monologues and hold even his professors with the amount of his apparent knowledge. In fact, there was something of the grandiose and the glib in his gifts.

He studied from time to time, particularly the Romantic Poets, Byron and Shelley and the overrated Tom Moore, and after them, Coleridge and Keats and the earth-bound Wordsworth. Among the novelists, Walter Scott naturally led the way with Dickens and Disraeli, Washington Irving and Hawthorne following in their wake. As for the essayists, he would turn to Lamb and Hazlitt and De Quincey, the opium eater, who made a romantic fashion of his drugged dreams. And there were the great ones – Shakespeare and Milton and Pope – quite enough for the education of a Virginia gentleman who wanted to be a poet at leisure.

At seventeen, Poe was among the best scholars at the fledgling university – just as he was among the best gamblers and drinkers in 'Rowdy Row'. He needed everything in excess – without discrimination – and he did not have the means to pay for it. His pockets were empty, his constitution was weak. One drink would make him half-insane with nervous excitement, a small loss at cards send him plunging after its recovery into ruin. When he owed two thousand dollars, John Allan drove two days from Richmond to quarrel with his foster son and remove him from the university after less than a year there.

Wealthy though he was now, Allan would not settle Poe's debts. There was more than righteousness in it. He knew Poe condemned him for his adulteries and his bastard children, and he wanted to punish the young man's double standard of behaviour. So he forced

Poe to flee from Charlottesville and the arrest warrants of his creditors – despised by his gentlemen friends for not paying his gambling debts – the actors' brat showing his true colours – what could one expect? Allan had his revenge on his charity child, and Poe had his lifelong complaint about being raised to expect what he was not born to have.

> *Did I, when an infant,* [he wrote to Allan] *solicit your charity and protection, or was it of your own free will, that you volunteered your services in my behalf? . . . Under such circumstances, can it be said that I have no right to expect any thing at your hands? You may probably urge that you have given me a liberal education. I will leave the decision of that question to those who know how far liberal educations can be obtained in eight months at the University of Virginia. Here you will say that it was my own fault that I did not return – You would not let me return because bills were presented to you for payment which I never wished nor desired you to pay. Had you let me return, my reformation had been sure . . .*

So is all reformation sure – as long as we are prevented from having to try it!

I cannot pretend I wrote all these notes about Poe at the university – or even thought about them – at the door of Room 13 in the West Range. I had taken the volume of his early letters with me and I read them that day before I tried to commit my analysis to paper for my report to Dupin. Yet it is, after all, characteristic of writers as sensitive to our surroundings as Poe and myself, that we should pretend that thinking actually comes to mind in the spot which logically conjures up the ideas.

Of course, thinking is not so. A pattern of facts and inferences is put together at random and only becomes coherent during the real act of writing, which *takes place* later and far away from the site where the thinking is said to have occurred. It is the oddity of my quest for the personality of E. A. Poe that I must seek out the spots which he visited in order to ferret out the secrets of his wayward nature. Thus my journey itself must influence the art of my presentation – and my analysis be a kind of odyssey.

Like Poe, I took a walk that afternoon upon the Ragged Mountains. I knew well Poe's story about them – his tale of the melancholy Bedloe with eyes either luminous or vapid, filmy and dull like those of a long-interred corpse. Bedloe, in the same way as Poe's favourite De Quincey, was addicted to morphine, which he took every day after breakfast, in order to increase his perceptions on his rambles in the mountains. On the day of his great adventure, when he met a hyena and saw a vision of his past existence as a British officer serving under Warren Hastings during the Benares riots, he was walking through a dim misty day of Indian summer. All the scene about him had an indescribable and delicious aspect of dreary desolation, while . . .

> the morphine had its customary effect – that of enduing all the external world with an intensity of interest. In the quivering of a leaf – in the hue of a blade of grass – in the shape of a trefoil – in the humming of a bee – in the gleaming of a dew-drop – in the breathing of the wind – in the faint odours that came from the forest – there came a whole universe of suggestion – a gay and motley train of rhapsodical and immethodical thought.

That was not my vision, after eating canned clam chowder and crackers and coffee for lunch. I walked along a marked ramblers' trail with folksy signs, telling me how not to stray into the small woods. I was no sole adventurer like Bedloe in a virgin wilderness, but one among tens of thousands in a State Park. My thoughts were certainly immethodical enough, but hardly full of rhapsody, because I could find nothing delicious in the dank trees, many of which were wrapped in curious cocoons of grey gossamer, as if looted by gigantic silkworms or else shrouded in their premature decay.

After his vision in the Ragged Mountains, Bedloe had fallen ill. His sinister physician, the mesmerist Templeton, had applied leeches to bleed him better. One of these happened to be the poisonous black sangsue of Charlottesville, so that Bedloe died by mischance or intent. I personally did not hang my hand in any forest pool to try the deadliness of the local bloodsuckers – unlike a Chinese apothecary I once knew, who would use his fingers as udders to feed his medicinal leeches daily.

Again, I began to feel removed from my old identity in the Ragged Mountains, now tamed from their gothic solitudes – the only hyena voices to be heard came from transistor radios, howling like wild beasts to the wolf chorus of electric guitars. If I was truly the reincarnation of Edgar Allan Poe, as Bedloe was of the British officer Oldeb, I doubted that I would die the same death, poisoned by drink and thugged at the polls of Baltimore. And I had to admit, the idiocy of Oldeb being spelt Bedlo in reverse – thus *proving* the reincarnation – was as silly as my belief that I was Poe because my initials happened to be E.A.P. *Set a Pons to catch a Poe,* that smirking Dupin had said, and in the Ragged Mountains, he seemed right.

I sat that evening off campus in Charlottesville in POE'S UNLIMITED SALAD BAR, where tee-shirts of the poet were on sale, showing him hovering on wings over the Rotunda in 100% Pure Cotton, machine washable too – a sad sartorial end for a man who liked to play the dandy. I was trying to arrange my notes about Poe amid the jabber of the students and the jangle of their forks digging into their ecological dinners. As I wrote about the dead poet, I found myself polishing my sentences as artfully as he used to rewrite his poetry, an exercise in choosing the apt word or repetitive phrase. And by that action, I was removing his personality even further from my own, by setting down his doings in a place and time I only knew by hearsay and reconnaissance.

There was even an *excitement* in improving my analysis, so that I forgot the babble around me until somebody sat down at my table. I looked up to tell the stupid youth to go away and saw Thomas Eggleston Blake III smiling at me in an inviting way. Was this a gay approach? Were student morals here still sunk so low?

'Pardon me, sir,' the boy said, 'but – we have a bet – '

'Gambling on campus?' I said. 'I thought that was forbidden now. Of course, in the wild days when the university began – '

'It's that, sir,' the boy declared. 'My friends and I – ' He indicated a group of lounging students, all staring at me from a nearby table and laughing to each other – 'We were betting on what sort of an actor you were.'

'An actor – I?' I bridled at this remark, but was secretly pleased at the recognition – as Poe had been, although he would not admit to it.

'Yes. We can see you've got on the costume and make-up of Poe – Method Acting obviously – and you've come down here to get the feel of his life – '

An acute boy with powers of recognition. The American educational system was not entirely dead, if it still had a few such brilliant exceptions!

'That is, if you're in a play or something, and I've bet against that!' Here Thomas Eggleston Blake III laughed like a hyena, his brightness gone to brutishness. 'I think you're advertising something – like Poe's pep pills or Edgar Allan's applesauce! Or you're the stooge for Candid Camera, and we're meant to approach you and make fools of ourselves – ' Here the foul child stuck out his tongue and set his eyes agoggle before pointing at a hole in the wall and shouting, 'I know you're there, Candid Camera. So y'all come out, do you hear!'

I could see myself in his eyes, a grotesque caricature of Poe, a buffoon and a Hop-frog of my own making. I rose trembling to my feet with the last strength of my dignity, and gathered up my notes.

'I am no actor, boy,' I said, 'but a writer too. And any resemblance to Edgar Allan Poe is entirely a coincidence. We are not alike and you are mistaken. You lose your bet.'

I deferred my next visit to Dupin in order to write the words of this chapter, making a sort of novel of my visit to Virginia. I worked on it for a week, polishing it to a professional standard. For once, my solitariness seemed to have a purpose. A writer has to be alone – it is the test of his trade. Only when I had to go to bed did the nightmares come – a grinning youth with a bony face under his floppy hair was pushing me – dressed as I was in a Pierrot costume with a comic mask on my face – into a plague pit of horrors, where the scabrous dead gibbered behind me.

As a mark of immolation and recognition, I wore round my neck Dupin's fearsome handkerchief from the Virgin Islands. It gave a dash to my black outfit, although I looked as if my throat had been cut and had gone gangrenous. Dupin whistled to see my attire – then whistled again when I put the typed pages in his hand.

'I shall not speak,' I declared. 'Read these – concentrate – and inwardly digest.'

He read my pages and nodded his head as he returned them to me.

'Remarkable,' he said. 'More literary than case history. You've really told me something about Poe – quite removed from yourself. Aren't you satisfied?'

'Yes,' I said. 'It's proceeding quite nicely. Tell me, Dupin, are you satisfied? Am I nearly myself again?'

'Not nearly,' Dupin said. 'It is good that you are giving up your confusion between Poe and yourself. Good that you are writing a biography of him as well as the diary of your own feelings. But the two are still mixed up. You switch from one to the other – and in the Ragged Mountains, you are still trying to slip back into his body like Bedloe into Oldeb.'

'But I wrote that was a silly idea – '

'You wrote that *later*, as you admit. You may have thought differently in the mountains. In fact, you wrote the whole episode in Virginia *after* the student had insulted you. Perhaps the shock of seeing yourself as a figure of fun through his eyes made you reinterpret all you had done before.' Dupin paused. 'How many of these pages are justifications after the event – invented to prove the fiction that you no longer identified yourself with Poe *before* your traumatic time in the salad bar?'

Dupin was clever, damned clever. Perhaps I had interpreted my quest to Charlottesville backwards from the ghastly encounter in the restaurant, when my young Vergil had turned out to be the very devil. But by writing and rewriting it for a week, I now believed my version. My words were the witnesses of my memory.

'It's too late, Dupin,' I said. 'Those pages are what I think happened in order. They are my evidence.'

'Then we will live with them,' Dupin said, ' – and go on. But may I suggest a change in your working method?'

'You may *suggest* anything at all,' I replied with *hauteur*.

'Suppose you were to write at a distance *from yourself* as well as Poe. Suppose you referred to yourself as *he* just as you refer to Poe as *he*. Drop the "I", drop the ego! Think of yourself as dispassionately as you would think of the hero of another writer's novel.'

Dupin stared at me, trying to mesmerize me into doing the impossible.

'I cannot!' I cried. 'It would be untrue.'

'All writing is untrue,' Dupin said. 'In any given book, the author must select so few of the facts that he must show bias or even lie, since he must eliminate all other possible truths and facts which he has not the space to set down. So if all writing can only be a better or a worse fiction – plunge! Revel in it! Make it an artifice of art! Flaunt your craft! Write of yourself – Ernest Albert Pons – as *he*!'

It was horrifying, Dupin's suggestion – part of the urge to anonymity of the mass society. Yet there was something in it, as there always was in that imp of perverse logic!

'I promise nothing,' I said, 'but I may try.'

'Good for you again,' he said. 'Now your next step is to be off with Edgar into the Army. West Point and the Gold Bug! It should be fun. And, Ernest, remember – ' His loathsome smirk appeared again. 'Sartre said that the great problem for a new writer is to distinguish himself from his hero – to separate the "I" of the author and his personal judgements from the "he" of the hero and his given judgements. This is particularly difficult in biography. To be objective is humanly impossible. So I put it to you – ' Dupin paused again, now covering his smirk with his smartness. 'All good biography is, in a sense, autobiography. You cannot know more of your chosen subject than you know of yourself. You must feel with your victim, understand what he understood, empathize absolutely. So – who knows? – your delusion about being Poe, your living imitation of him, your soaking yourself in all he wrote and said – why, it may prove a blessing. You may be the first to penetrate his many disguises – and analyse totally his complexes!'

'I already understand Poe utterly,' I said. 'I know his secrets, but – I have never organized that knowledge with my Dupin!' I felt I should make a concession to the fellow who, after all, had to feel he was contributing something to me so that he could pocket his huge fees without guilt. 'I will try, however, to improve on my new art. Biography as autobiography – I shall invent it! Know thyself – and thus know *him*!'

On this line, Ernest Albert Pons left the consulting room, striding with the erect grace of Edgar Allan Poe.

5

A Gold Bug Better

> Circumstances, and a certain bias of mind, have led me to take interest in such riddles, and it may well be doubted whether human ingenuity can construct an enigma of the kind which human ingenuity may not, by proper application, resolve.
>
> EDGAR ALLAN POE in 'The Gold Bug'.

Boston was a continual earth tremor, made by man. Its rebuilding had cracked the continent, so that the San Andreas Fault had split sideways and now ended under Beacon Hill. The crashing of the old structures, the grinding jaws of the mechanical scoops lifting the rubble, and the war-whoops of the riveters in the hands of the Iroquois on the high steel girders, made the dusty air sound with permanent catastrophe. As the new skyscrapers were rising over the refurbished old warehouses round Durgin Park, the recent ones were already beginning to fall in glass guillotines from the John Hancock Building, which the mob avoided in high winds, trying to keep its neck from summary execution.

Ernest Albert Pons was as unsettled as the city. If he took any detour from the odd oblong of Boston Common, he risked bumping into a dump-truck or a concrete lump fallen from the sky. He found no correspondence between his shattering surroundings and the Boston of long ago, which Elizabeth Arnold had sketched for her son, telling him to love it as *the place of his birth, and where his mother found her best and most sympathetic friends.*

Poe's exile from Richmond had been stage-managed by John Allan. With his wife Frances Valentine slowly dying and unable to defend the young Edgar, Allan made life intolerable at home for him, hounded by creditors from Charlottesville and haunted by the contempt of his friends because he could not settle his gambling debts. Allan told everybody the reasons why Edgar could not return to university, until shame forced the young man to quarrel with his foster father and run away to make his fortune.

His letter of leaving to John Allan was plain enough, written in the March of 1827. He said that he was being denied the education that he had been led to expect. He had overheard his foster father say that he had no affection for Edgar. He had been ordered to quit the house and stop eating the bread of idleness. 'You take delight,' he reproached John Allan, 'in exposing me before those whom you think likely to advance my interest in this world – You suffer me to be subjected to the whims and caprice, not only of your white family, but the complete authority of the blacks – these grievances I could not submit to: and I am gone. I request that you will send me my trunk containing my clothes and books – '

Much of Poe's later life was to consist of requests for his trunk to be sent after him. His first address as a runaway was at the Court House Tavern, where he took the *alias* of Henri le Rennét – *renaît*, the born-again Poe – or *renié*, the denied Poe – who knows what French pun he had in his mind? Allan sent him no money for his journey, but he borrowed some and took a boat to Boston, where he tried to find his mother's old friends and perhaps to work at her profession. But the theater companies there would not take the young Virginian – and dreams of Byronic glory still burned in his skull. So he had his first pamphlet of poems published with the last of his money, and volunteered for the American army under the name of Edgar A. Perry.

(*Dupin, I must break into my detached journal and biography now, to tell you something you forget. Poe took an alias, using the same initials, E.A.P. So why should I not take the alias of Poe, having the same initials? Also that first edition of his 'Tamerlane and Other Poems' – it is too ironic! Here is young Edgar, alone and starving in the hard city which his mother told him to love – and he has to join the army to help pay for an edition of fifty copies of 'Tamerlane'. One copy was sold at an auction sixty years ago – it fetched $11,600 – only four copies are known to exist! So I myself can only possess a facsimile in my own poverty. It is too much!*)

'Tamerlane' is the poem of a young rebel and would-be Byron.

The hero is proud and independent, a lover of beauty and a hater of compromise with the rabble-men. Yet more prophetic and haunted are the lines in one of Poe's short poems to his dead mother – and foster mother, soon to die.

> The spirits of the dead, who stood
> In life before thee, are again
> In death around thee, and their will
> Shall then o'ershadow thee – be still.

So Edgar A. Poe became a published poet and a volunteer soldier at the same time in the city of his birth. So bitter was he about his adopted city of Richmond, so determined to deny the unforgiving John Allan, that 'Tamerlane and Other Poems' was claimed to be written 'By A Bostonian', while the recruiting officer was told that Edgar A. Perry was a clerk from Boston, aged twenty-two. The new recruit was assigned to Battery H of the First Artillery at Fort Independence in Boston Harbor – the scene of the sketch by Poe's mother. In the barracks there, he suffered the self-denial and brutality of military discipline, and, as young men can do, he learned to absent his spirit from the monotony of the everyday. In the fall, his battery was ordered to Fort Moultrie on Sullivan's Island off Charleston, the leading city of South Carolina. He sailed there in the brig *Waltham* and remained there for thirteen months, marooned off the Deep South.

(*If you think, Dupin, that flying from Boston to Charleston is amusing, I would condemn you to life imprisonment at Logan Airport, where nobody can tell where they are or who they are in that utter nonentity and purgatory of international flying, in which everything is both similar and alien – an insupportable time of lingering on a dull part of earth before the foul fear of leaving the ground. I know Poe in his 'Balloon Hoax' made his flying machine land in South Carolina at Fort Moultrie itself, but he was only inventing it – he was not doing it – suffering the long tedium, only broken by the horror of taking off in an aerial coffin!*)

In his scarlet oblong box marked Mustang, which he hired from a firm he miscalled Hearse, Ernest Albert Pons drove from Charleston Airport towards Sullivan's Island. He skirted the city and made for Mount Pleasant, where he found himself irresistibly drawn to *The Gold Bug Restaurant And Lounge,* which stood near a huge billboard advertising – BIG NUMBER ONE IS TOUGH ON TERMITES. It certainly was tough, because the scarab on the yellow plastic sign outside the restaurant was a mere black beetle – nothing to do with Poe's brilliant gold death's head.

Once inside the place, Ernest A. Pons ate a shrimp cornucopia, which came from the generous hands of a fat black cook, who was no Jupiter to threaten him with a stick and a beating. On the jukebox, alas, the tunes wailed for his estrangement from time past, although Poe would have responded to some of the song titles:

> *Year of the Cat*
> *Time in a Bottle*
> *A Fifth of Beethoven*
> *Muskrat Love*
> and *Only Sixteen*

Virginia Clemm had been only thirteen when Poe had married her.

E. A. Pons drove on the causeway across the brown marsh to Sullivan's Island, which was an overbuilt suburban strip all the way to Fort Moultrie on the south-west point. The only hint of the tale which Poe set there was a sign – DON'T BE A LITTER BUG. Pons parked his oblong box outside the fort, now become a national monument to coastal defence throughout the centuries. Inside the museum, he found a photograph of the poet Poe hanging among the generals who had commanded the fort – a place where Poe would have liked to be, except he was also alongside the likeness of the patriot Seminole Chief Oceola, an Indian whom he would have despised as a torturing Bugaboo or Kickapoo.

On the low walls of the fort outside, the cannons which Poe had used were pot-bellied iron tubes, mounted on wheeled carriages. They could fire a hotshot or an explosive canister a mile across the approaches to Charleston Harbor. Once they had repulsed the British General Clinton's assault in 1776 – and who knew when they would not be needed again against foreign attack or civil strife? Poe only learned to fire them in practice and lounged away the hours in the stone barrens of the barracks, while inveigling the artillery officers into promoting him through the quartermaster's stores to the rank of sergeant-major, all the time hinting at wild escapades to help Byron's ghost in the Greek War of Liberation – and claiming wealthy relations in Virginia.

Proving himself by his promotion, he wrote home for his release from his five years' engagement in the army – something which needed John Allan's permission. His first letter received no answer, and his second repeated his pride in what he had made of himself. He had to have Allan's consent to his discharge, and so he had to appeal again to that father figure who did not love him and thought him degraded, even by his present contact with enlisted men.

> *There is that within my heart* [Poe wrote] *which has no connection with degradation – I can walk among infection and be uncontaminated. There never was any period of my life when my bosom swelled with a deeper satisfaction . . . My father, do not throw me aside as degraded. I will be an honour to your name . . . If you determine to abandon me – here take farewell – Neglected – I will be doubly ambitious, and the world shall hear of the son whom you have thought unworthy of your notice.*

Poe had no answer by the time his battery was transferred back to Fort Monroe in Virginia near his foster home. Pons, too, had no answer to his own shrinking from the boot camp, where he had been drafted for seven weeks of humiliation, before chronic pneumonia and athlete's foot had made the military grant him an honorable discharge. How had the poet from the rich Allan household ever survived the crude shouts, the continual cursing and the cruel tortures of the barrack room? It broke Pons in less than two months, while Poe had survived it for more than two years in magnificent inner isolation.

Was it only a genius for supreme detachment – or was it a need for order to be imposed on a wayward nature? Was it also a desire for military glory – to be a Bonaparte or a Lafayette or even his own Byron, dying in glorious failure? These were good reasons for Poe to serve, until he had become bored of garrison duty and desperate to live the life of a poet. But for Pons, the only reasons he could dodge his draft were his puny body and his feeble will.

Leaving Fort Moultrie, Pons drove off after the one thing that distinguished him from the weaker Poe – his gold-bug that he managed with such care – his small fortune that kept him free to pursue the poet, so long pursued by want of gold himself. Pons stopped in the little town to buy a newspaper and check the price of Krugerrands – rising satisfactorily again in price after the administration's idiocy in selling some of the bullion stored in Fort Knox. But when America had a lunatic government of Dr Tarrs and Prof. Feathers – claiming to be economists and running an annual deficit of thirty billion dollars – what could a prudent man do but follow the gold-bug and keep it in the bank!

Poe's gold-bug had only been on deposit in his head, when he was walking through the wild myrtles of Sullivan's Island, which were to set the scene for his cryptographic story about Captain Kidd's buried treasure. Of course, the writer Poe had distorted the truth about the place to heighten his effects, bringing in cliffs and ravines, a table-land and huge tulip-trees on nearby Long Island, now called the Isle of Palms. Pirate legend and tropical trees had inspired the young soldier's memory to make this a fit location for his solitary mastermind Legrand – but Pons only found stray myrtles near the spot of Legrand's hut and few sea-shells on the beach that had escaped the picking fingers of summer visitors. There were bugs enough, biting at hands and neck and cheeks, but these were contemptible midges, none as large as a golden hickory-nut with two jet black spots and a grinning mouth upon its back – and twin long antennae to frame the oval portrait of a skull!

Instead of a piece of parchment sticking from the sand to show where the pirate's hoard was hidden, Pons found seventeen Hershey wrappers, fourteen ice-cream cartons, nine cigarette packs, three Kleenex boxes and a sanitary napkin. He held up some of them to the heat of the sun, but no invisible writing appeared on them – only a Free Offer for more Kleenexes, if he were to tear off the label and buy three more boxes. As for finding a skull nailed to a tulip-tree on the Isle of Palms across the inlet, he could only see more summer houses with tiles nailed to their roofs – and one decorative French-style weathervane of a copper cockerel. If he dropped a Krugerrand through the eye of that bird, it would only land on the iron cover of a sewer pipe.

Pons drove away, his own gold bug more secure in a safe-deposit box in the Chase Manhattan, where the sympathetic magic of the falling dollar would make it rise in value without his digging for buried treasure. He drove west toward the interior in search of some wild place, where Poe's dream would not have been despoiled to make neat homes for those blind to all except comfort.

To me, at least, the presence – so Poe wrote in 'The Island of the Fay' – *not of human life only, but of life in any other form than that of the green things which grow upon the soil and are voiceless – is a stain upon the landscape – is at war with the genius of the scene.*

Pons had heard of the Okefenokee Swamp in Georgia – and thought a piece of the Paradise of Arnheim could be found there. So he rolled in his oblong box on wheels past long avenues of aged oaks hoary with Spanish moss, which led toward some old plantation mansion, spared the flames of Sherman's advance or Metzengerstein's mad arson before his own holocaust on his fiery steed. Somewhere on the rim of the swamp, he found a Holiday Inn, which might lock him up for the night like Poe in Moyamensing Prison. On the battlements of that place, a white female form had appeared to Poe and had told him how to escape – and so one appeared to Pons, the waitress in her white overalls, serving his breakfast Danish and coffee.

'The swamp, suh – ' she said, ' – yew go left an' head right on till yew fall in – an' mind yew come visit with us all again.'

Pons hired a private metal swamp-boat to take him through the secret waterways of the Okefenokee, a vast peat bog of trembling earth as unsafe as the land which held the House of Usher above the black tarn. Ebony water, stained by cypress bark, stood below the bearded branches of splash-pine and blackgum, so jet and lurid in its unruffled luster that the watcher gazed down with a shudder, seeing the inverted images of self and boat and ghastly trees in the brilliant night of the surface – and as he moved on, he knew his shadow had drained away into the pitchblend flood, leaving his substance to make the blackness more black, as in the Island of Fay . . .

So I sat in the bows of the boat on the borders of water and earth, spirit and flesh, death and life – with a black Charon poling me silently into the underworld. Watching each grass, bush, scrub or sedge repeating its shape in perfect shadow, draining away into another being on the shining ebony of the surface, then – then I felt apart from my own body in my reverie, as if I were going with my shade to merge in the translucent swamp. Yet on the sudden, we burst out of the cypress arches into a clearing of bright water-lilies, and Charon spoke and ended my enchantment.

'Yew see them there skulls on the tree – '

I looked and saw, indeed, what Pons had not seen on Sullivan's Island – three skulls nailed to a branch – one of a bull, one of a stag, and one perhaps of a man –

'They's six-inch nails through them an' they's come from the slaughterhouse, not the Seminoles – '

'Drop a lead weight on a line through their right eyes,' I said, 'and you'll find treasure sunk in the swamp.'

'More like Marlboro Country,' my Charon said, 'than a swamp legend to me – but the folks all want it, so they sees it, don't they?'

'Just what I was looking for,' I said and fingered the lucky Krugerrand I keep in my breast pocket for the day the muggers get me. It will buy them off from killing me . . .

Returned from my loss of self into the weary flesh of Ernest Albert Pons, he ordered the boatman to return. With the spell broken, the man seemed to take a perverse delight in pointing out the loathsome alligators of prodigious size, which were lazing on the mudbanks or cruising with a ripple and a ridge of eyes above the surface, expecting a visitor for their dinner. There was a chill in the air now, and Pons was not amused – just another tourist, really, in another tourist attraction. At the landing place, indeed, a ranger fed a herd of white-tailed deer behind plate-glass, making a shopwindow of the wilderness.

As Pons drove north toward Virginia, he thought of Sergeant-Major Perry (or Poe) arriving at Fort Monroe as Frances Valentine Allan lay dying. Poe had foretold his second mother's death – and in that heartache of precognition, he had also come to know a terrible truth about himself. In the poem of his military days which he had called 'Romance', he had written:

> *I could not love except where Death*
> *Was mingling his with Beauty's breath –*
> *Or Hymen, Time and Destiny*
> *Were stalking between her and me.*

In later life, he had hated such a cruel self-analysis so much that he suppressed the lines. Yet he had only loved what he was doomed to lose – Elizabeth Arnold Poe, Mrs Jane Stith Stanard, Sarah Elmira Royster Shelton, and now Frances Valentine Allan.

The message that she was dying had reached Poe too late – and he had his regimental duties. He had begged leave of absence and had taken the stage-coaches to Richmond, fretting at the delays for changing horses as much as Pons fretted at the garages that fueled his oblong box on wheels. Poe had arrived in Richmond even after the burial, although he did find the grieving John Allan ready for a reconciliation – he bought his foster son a suit of mourning clothes.

In Shockoe cemetery, Poe had thrown himself prostrate upon the newly dug earth that covered his second mother – who herself lay near the grave of Mrs Stanard. The death of those he loved seemed to be a fate in his life. He could easily think it such, even in that age of early mortality.

At home, however, he had persuaded John Allan to help him in gaining his discharge from the army, in order to go to West Point and become an officer. It was a compromise, but a reasonable one. Allan could not deny his foster son, who had proved himself a good soldier, the chance of rising to be an officer and a gentleman again – and Edgar would be leaving Richmond and his suspicion of Allan's bastard families for a four-year course on the faraway banks of the Hudson River in New York State. If a military career no longer interested Edgar, he could buy himself a breathing-space before engaging himself again – and did.

Pons reached Richmond again himself by road, but he did not stop to see the sights for a second time. It was not part of this stage of his analysis. He kept on driving north, for Poe had gone there after securing his discharge with Allan's permission and finding a substitute, Sergeant 'Bully' Graves, for the sum of seventy-five dollars, one-third in cash and two-thirds by note of hand. Poe had not, unfortunately, mentioned this new small debt to Allan, who was now supplying him with the occasional draft for a hundred dollars or so.

There was no need to stop in Washington, where Poe had presented his letters of recommendation to become a West Point cadet, so Pons drove on to Baltimore, where Poe had proceeded to find his flesh and blood – his brother William and his aunt Maria Clemm with her young children, Henry and Virginia, who were all living in a small house in Mechanics Row on the pension of the paralysed widow of Edgar's grandfather, 'General' David Poe. If his wealthy foster home had rejected him, perhaps he could stay in an attic with his own poor kind.

Pons could also say that he was welcomed in Baltimore. Gingerly steering his oblong box through the blight and decay that is now called an American city, he came upon a new Holiday Inn and Civic Center, surrounded by strip clubs for out-of-town visitors. He checked into the fortress tower of the hotel – and noticed that the management took no responsibility if grave-robbers were to steal his tomb on wheels from the underground parking cemetery. After his dinner, he decided to prove himself still a man in the place where Poe had first began to love his cousin and future wife, Virginia Clemm, then only eight years old. So Pons left the Holiday Inn to hunt among the nearby bar girls.

There was a delicious terror to be felt in this act of sexual courage. To be a bachelor now was difficult, without being accused of homosexuality or impotence. To choose to be alone was not good enough, although God knows he had never met a woman he could bear to live with for more than a week – he had not *chosen* to live with his mother Bee before her death, after all. So – to remain solitary – to form no attachment – and to exist for an hour or two in the delight of risk – Pons cruised the hard bars of strange cities.

In the wasteland of incomplete urban renewal, the girlie clubs flaunted their signs between derelict houses and bare parking lots. The choice was heady:

- THE INTIMATE AND EXCITING CLUB TIC-TOC – *Open Every Nite* – GIRLS, GIRLS, GIRLS!
- CLUB HAREM – *3 Shows Nitely* – *Continuous Entertainment* – NO ADMISSION!

– ROMANTICA LOUNGE WITH GO-GO GIRLS!

And behind black plate-glass doors, on which a bare houri was etched in white, the FAMOUS COPA SHOW BAR AND LOUNGE! Its posters of naked lifesize women climbing out of huge cocktail glasses promised even more – MAJOR CREDIT CARDS HONORED – *Ladies Invited* – and also – *We're at the COPA* – *Where Are You?*

Where, indeed, was E. A. Pons? What was he doing there? How could he refuse such an invitation? The answer was – very easily. For he had just seen down a side street a dim doorway and a lighted sign, which merely advertised *The Black Pussycat*. The spirit of perverseness seized his soul, as it had Poe's hero who had hanged his ghastly pet. For it *is* one of the primitive impulses of the human heart – one of the indivisible primary sentiments which give direction to the character of man! As Pons pushed open the door of the *Pussycat*, he whispered to himself, 'Who has not, a hundred times, found himself committing a vile or a stupid action, for no other reason than because he knows he should *not*?'

There is little to tell, for in places such as Baltimore, money buys what it can pay for. Pons drank the house champagne and asked the fading lady, who buzzed under her beehive hair, to provide him with *Another* – as *young* as possible – if not a *child*, for that was now too dangerous with the law – then a girl formed like a child, who would dress in a white child's dress, and do what she had to do for him. He paid the procuress fifty dollars for her services and the champagne – and paid a thin dwarfish pale creature eighty dollars for her services and twenty for the rent of the room. She played the part well enough – in pinafore and lacy cotton drawers – chattering in a high voice and doing exactly what Pons asked. But once she had used her little mouth and hands to give him the release he sought without the fear of catching some disease, he felt his perverseness change to disgust. Why was he present at this degrading farce, from which he was utterly detached?

His melancholy lasted through the following morning, and he could not pursue the quest for Poe. He arranged to return to the Inn for the following stage of his analysis in Baltimore. He would treat Poe's two longish periods there as one, broken by his eight months at West Point and the end of his military fantasies. The deaths of Poe's brother and his grandmother – his love for his third mother figure, his aunt Maria Clemm, and her child Virginia – these would focus the next scrutiny of his life.

Disgust still led Pons to drive directly back to Dupin and New York. Otherwise, he would have made the detour to the gates of West Point, which even now commemorated its unlikely cadet on a stone doorway into the library. Pons had a photograph of the inscription there, which quoted one of Poe's favourite remarks from Sir Francis Bacon: *There is no exquisite beauty without some strangeness in the proportion.*

Poe had been strange enough as a cadet there, claiming falsely to be the grandson of the famous local traitor Benedict Arnold as well as of the Revolutionary Quartermaster 'General' David Poe – and playing grotesque jokes on his friends, on one occasion pretending that a bristling and bloody dead gander was a severed head. He had had to play Hop-Frog again in swallowtail coat and shako hat, enduring the bullying of sergeants and of the upperclassmen who hazed the *plebes*; but he had seen service, was older than the other cadets, and had published two books of poems by now, *Tamerlane* in Boston and *Al-Aaraaf* in Baltimore. Yet even with this superiority, his self-control and physique had been giving way under the strain of the incessant and intrusive discipline with its list of thirty-three DO NOTS, of dull military studies and the companionship of mere boys – and of the bad news from Richmond.

John Allan had married again, not the mother of his new set of twin bastard children, but a woman from a prominent family, twenty years younger than himself. He had encouraged her to want nothing to do with his foster son, who had only come into the Allan home because of the love of his dead first wife – and he soon saw to it that his second wife would provide him with his first legitimate heir of his own flesh and blood.

His caution had always stopped him from adopting Edgar Poe legally – and now he was glad of it. He seized on an excuse to cut the young man out of his life. Poe had lied to him that he had paid 'Bully' Graves in full to be his substitute – and worse – he had sent Graves a letter saying that Allan always shuffled off his requests for the remaining fifty dollars – and was not often very sober. This indiscreet letter was sent by Graves to Allan, who paid the fifty dollars and severed himself from his foster son. He made this clear to Edgar at West Point, who could now see that he was unlikely to inherit any of the Allan fortune or to receive future help from Richmond – unless he caused so bad a scandal that it would harm the Allan name. As he had only become a cadet to please his foster father, he resolved to leave West Point by failing to obey orders. He was a beggar there, anyway, as he had been at the University of Virginia, because Allan would send him no money, while his pay was only ninety cents a day:

The same difficulties are threatening me as before at Charlottesville – Poe wrote to Allan – *and I must resign . . . I have no more to say – except that my future life (which thank God will not endure long) must be passed in indigence and sickness – I have no energy left, nor health . . .*

Allan did not reply to this self-piteous letter, but scrawled a comment on it:

I do not think the Boy has one good quality –

Poe's next desperate plea for help remained unopened for two years, before Allan read it and commented then that it was the

. . . relict of the Blackest Heart and deepest ingratitude alike destitute of honour and principle. Every day of his life has only served to confirm his debased nature – suffice it to say my only regret is in Pity for his failings – his Talents are of an order that can never prove a comfort to their possessor.

Allan was shrewd in his final judgement. Poe was talented enough to persuade the commandant of West Point to allow the cadets to subscribe seventy-five cents each from their pay – the price of a copy of Poe's third volume of poems. With such a subscription, Poe could easily arrange for its publication in New York. Yet his talent for arranging the appearance of his writing made him give up the relative comfort of West Point for the starvation and illness of solitude in the city. When his refusal to obey orders led to his court martial and summary dismissal, he left West Point before the due date on a steamboat down the Hudson River. He was wearing a second-hand suit, a cadet's overcoat and a battered hat, and carried along his old tin trunk, full of books and manuscript. He collapsed in New York with a suppurating ear, but rose from his supposed death-bed to see his poems through the press, dedicating them:

TO THE U.S. CORPS OF CADETS

He did not ask what they would make of 'Israfel' or 'Lenore' or 'To Helen' or 'The Valley Nis' – Sin spelt in reverse! What was certain that West Point's only poet had flown the coop to try to join his beloved heavenly spirit, whose heart-strings were a lute:

> *If I could dwell*
> *Where Israfel*
> *Hath dwelt, and he where I,*
> *He might not sing so wildly well*
> *A mortal melody,*
> *While a bolder note than this might swell*
> *From my lyre in the sky.*

In one last Byronic fantasy, Poe wrote to the commandant at West Point, asking him for a recommendation to Lafayette so that he might go to France and beg an appointment in the Polish Army in its fight for independence. He received no reply. West Point had done enough in paying for the printing of romantic poems, which it had believed to be barrackroom ballads.

'An improvement,' Dupin said. 'A definite improvement. You intrude far less on Edgar Poe – except for three vile interruptions!'

'Vile is who vile does,' I said lightly, taking back the pages of this chapter of the analysis from him. 'This account is only for you, Dupin – for an audience of one. I do not intend to pay for its publication like our hero. So if I insert two paragraphs addressed directly to you, they are mere glosses – marginalia – like those ghastly comments added by John Allan on the bottom of Poe's appeals to him!'

'That does not excuse your reverie in the swamp, when you refer to yourself as "I" again – not Pons!'

'That was true art! What I wrote consciously in my text showed what I felt unconsciously in the Okefenokee – '

'Bad writing!' Dupin said remorselessly. 'And bad for your analysis. The point is to take yourself out of the narrative and only call yourself Ernest Albert Pons, as if he were a stranger to you. That will give you a double distance from Poe – '

'Like the reverse image of the trees in the waters of the Okefenokee – '

'Nothing of the sort. In fact, I want you to do something even more difficult when you return to Baltimore and cover his five years there. Remove yourself completely! Write only of Poe there – only a biography of him! Cut yourself out! Abolish yourself – the final solution!'

I could look past Dupin's talking skull to the stuffed raven sitting on the bust of Pallas in his corner cupboard. With all Dupin's pecking at me, I could well believe that he was the bloodless shadow of that bird of prey!

'I will try again to do what you say – *evermore*,' I croaked. 'But I am surprised – I would have thought my episode with the child whore in Baltimore would have been revealing.' I paused to look at the evident curiosity in Dupin's eyes, glinting behind the double vision of his glasses. 'I was bold to write about that!'

'Did you write the truth?'

'Of course.'

'All of it?'

'The important things.'

'I asked, all of it?'

'Nearly all. The artist must select – you said so – '

'Ah,' Dupin said unpleasantly. Then he added, 'Aha!' Things were looking bad and became worse when he put his fingers together in that damned cat's cradle of his. I knew he would dig into my moment of weakness – and perversely I had brought up the subject. The horror of modern times is that most people are only interested in other people's sexual failings, which are used to explain everything about them. Once we were gratified by the Heavenly and Ethereal – now we grab after Havelock Ellis!

'Firstly,' Dupin asked, 'was she actually a child? Or just pretending to be one?'

'I don't know,' I replied. 'And I didn't want to know.'

'You're meant to be analysing yourself – looking for the truth – '

'I would remind you, Dupin, that committing a sexual act with a child is worth ten years in the penitentiary. I did not want to risk that, so I did not want to know definitely if she was a child. Equally, I did not want to know if she was actually over the age of eighteen – that would have ruined my illusion. So I did not know how old she was – or pretended to be – and in the dark, she passed for eight.'

'Did she undress? Was she made like a woman or a child?'

'No. I asked her – to lift up her pinafore – drop her drawers briefly – but I could hardly see – she had no breasts, I'll swear to that – '

Dupin did not respect my embarrassment, but continued to harass me.

'I didn't know Baltimore was so sophisticated,' he said. 'They provide for every taste – they recruit the very young. I suppose after the films of *Taxi Driver* and *Pretty Baby*, every tiny girl wants to go on the streets to get into the movies – and every starlet wants to have the silicone taken out of her breasts, so she can be flat-chested and pretend to be ten again.' He paused, as he always did when he had been clever and wanted appreciation. 'But, Ernest – one thing I must know – what did you *call* her?'

I did not answer. He was too shrewd for me.

'Tell me, Ernest. Was it Virginia? Or Rosa?'

I tried to control myself, but heard the sob break in my throat.

'Devil – ' I whispered.

'Or was it both names? Did you call your little whore Virginia for Poe and Rosa for your own guilt – for your own dead lost love?'

'Poe also had a retarded sister he called Rosa,' I said weakly. I knew it was not much of a defence, but it was the best I could manage. 'Even when she was fully grown, her mind was like a little girl's. It was perfect for my grown whore, pretending in a pinafore.'

'You're so predictable, Ernest.' Here the fiend Dupin smiled in his superior way. 'You're a classic case. It will probably go in the textbooks as the *reductio ad absurdum* of the double *persona*. You called her Rosa because you could pretend to be Poe, while working out your own guilt for leaving that little girl to die in Berlin – and have it off, too!'

I hung my head. The Inquisitor had me between the pit and the pendulum again – and I was paying him for this torture! Each session cost me a hundred dollars – and all for my pain!

'I called her Virginia too,' I wailed. 'Both names!'

'Only to pretend again that you were acting out Poe's perversity, not your own – his guilt, not yours. And one other thing – did you only *call* her Rosa and Virginia. Or did you do more?' Again he paused, raising the stiletto. 'Did you mark her, perhaps?'

I shrieked. How did he know? Was Dupin a spy, who dogged me like a shadow? Was he, indeed, the rational part of my own brain, who observed me in my folly and degradation? Was he my remorse?

'How did you know, Dupin?'

'I deduced it,' Dupin said icily, 'which is my role in your fantasies, is it not? Also you are, as I said, very predictable. Your little Rosa in Berlin, your first love – she would have been tattooed with a number in the death camp, before she was killed. The Nazis would have marked her.' He glared at me without mercy. 'You marked your girl too.'

I was struck dumb again. The monster! He was now comparing Albert Pons with Adolf Hitler! That was one *persona* I would not adopt after Allan Poe's!

'With my ball-point pen, I – I – '

'Go on.'

'Under her pinafore, I wrote on her thighs – '

'Her inner thighs?'

I nodded, still whispering from loss of breath.

'On one thigh, *Rosa* – I inked – on the other, *Virginia* – '

'What did she think of that?'

I recovered my courage and my voice.

'She was not paid to think!' I shouted. 'Nor apparently are you!'

Dupin still had my measure. Nothing could crack that icy temperament or cool tone.

'I also noticed in your pages, Ernest, your feeling of superiority to Poe over money matters. You wrote that gold did not *bug* you because you had some, while it did bug him!' I sneered at Dupin's little joke, which was even worse than my own feeble puns. 'The Krugerrands you wrote of, how important are they to you?'

'They keep me independent.'

'Really? I know you don't have to work – but how rich are you exactly?'

'That is a question no gentleman ever answers,' I said with disdain. 'Also no psychiatrist has the right to ask it. As long as I pay my fees promptly, which I do – '

'I can ask that legitimately,' Dupin said, 'if it has a bearing on your case. I am playing Legrand now – you are merely the simple friend he mystifies on Sullivan's Island, while he actually solves the problem of where the treasure is buried. I am the cryptographer of your case – which you fail to understand! If you have a gold-bug – and evidently you do – I must solve its secret location in your psyche. Do you think gold is your mother's milk, your impossible dream, or your shit? Seriously – tell me, how much money do you have? And how much do you care about it – and hoard it?'

I was silent. Dupin had a point. He always had a point. He was a human porcupine. No, that was too noble for him – he was a sea-urchin!

'About half a million dollars,' I confessed unhappily. 'A pittance.'

Dupin smiled. Did I catch a gleam of greed behind his rimless lenses – or was it merely pleasure or interest?

'All wealthy people pretend to poverty,' Dupin said, now kindly. 'They are afraid somebody will come along and take it all away. Then they would have to work for a living – what a dreadful thought! What have you done with your money, Ernest?'

'Trebled it, since I began managing it,' I said with pride. 'And I have bought up the best Poe collection in private hands.'

'I said, what have you *done* with it? Have you used it for anybody else's good? I'm not a moralist – '

'I know that!'

'But you do seem rather tight with your gold – some would call it constipated. I'm not sure your meanness is something to feel superior about. Poe himself mocked the business mind. Perhaps he threw everything away and wasted it, but that may be better than being a Scrooge – '

'You've had ten thousand dollars off me over the years!' I shrieked. 'And now you call me a Nazi and then a Scrooge!'

'You pay your accounts,' Dupin said. 'I never said you were not an honest man in the way of business. But I don't have to admire the way you refuse to use your fortune for anything except your own selfish interests. You have a very fearful personality. So I can understand that, in your lifetime – '

Here the devil paused again to insinuate himself into my mind like the adders writhing through the eyes of the grinning masks on the temple of Persepolis – which Poe likened to the habit of intense and continual thought.

'If you should die suddenly, Ernest – like Edgar Poe in Baltimore – '

I found myself trembling. What was the intolerable man suggesting?

'It can happen, you know,' he continued. 'Death can happen any day as you cross the street – '

I knew I had made a fool of myself by telling Dupin I was quite rich, although to be a millionaire under the Internal Revenue Service is to exist one step from the poorhouse. *He wanted to get his hands on my money!*

'Are you threatening me, Dupin?'

'Oh, Ernest, don't add paranoia to your false *persona*. I know Edgar Poe often thought he was being persecuted, but usually when he was drunk or drugged. You are neither, I hope – '

'Absolutely not!'

'Then make a will like everybody else. Don't keep on putting it off because it reminds you that you will die – like everybody else. In fact, I think part of your need to act as Poe is that you can forget your own fear of death in his false personality – thereby evading it.'

I gasped at his terrible acumen.

'Don't you go on being clever, Dupin, *at my expense!*'

'You know I'm right, Ernest, so don't try and resist me. You're so afraid of dying that you even had to call your hired car "an oblong box" – Poe's words for a coffin. I found that trick of yours irritating to read. Why can't you call a car a car?'

I rose to my feet. This was the first time that I had been given the chance of a parting shot – so I had to be prepared to leave.

'Because a car *is* an oblong box,' I said. 'Drive on a highway one day! A car *is* a coffin on wheels. Don't you ever read the news? Fifty thousand Americans every year die in road accidents – and change one oblong box for another!'

6

To Be Appreciated You Must Be Read

> You ask me in what does this nature consist? In the ludicrous heightened into the grotesque: the fearful into the horrible: the witty exaggerated into the burlesque: the singular wrought out into the strange and mystical. You may say all this is bad taste. I have my doubts about it.
>
> EDGAR ALLAN POE replying to a criticism of 'Berenice'.

In Baltimore, it was a time of doubt and beginnings, plague and meteors, small magazines and little to eat. Edgar Poe moved back into the attic at his grandmother's house in Mechanics Row, which he shared with his drunken and drugged brother William Henry, who was dying of tuberculosis as his mother had. Alcohol eased the pain in his rotten lungs, as did the morphine in laudanum and opium. Poe again found himself in a mean room, watching his closest kin through a slow dying – and seeing the common remedies against misery and their effects – and then living through the inconsequence of the final burial in 1832, when one city newspaper briefly referred to the interment of W. H. Pope.

Without Maria Clemm in her Puritan cap and ample black dress to beg food and stretch the little widow's pension and comfort her beloved nephew, Poe would have never had the time to develop his prose and poetry. There are few details of his early years in Baltimore that are not legend or else based on one unreliable source. He is said to have courted a girl called Mary Devereaux, become drunk one night with West Point friends, declared that she was his wife in the sight of heaven, and whipped her uncle with a cowhide before she broke off the affair – a romantic myth told by her to a magazine reporter thirty years after Poe's death. He is also said to have visited Richmond to beg John Allan not to disinherit him – to have burst in on Allan's second wife, terrifying her – and to have fled when he heard the limping approach of his foster father, already dying of dropsy – but in a letter of April, 1833, his last appeal to John Allan, he wrote that it had been more than two years since Allan had assisted him – sending him money to keep him from jail for guaranteeing his brother's debts – and more than three years since Allan had spoken to him.

Another legend, then! For this was a legendary time, in which Poe began to write his legendary tales – and as the saying goes, when there are no facts, print the legend!

When Poe came back to Baltimore, there was also a plague of cholera which killed tens of thousands in the city and inspired him later to write 'King Pest' and 'The Masque of the Red Death'. In the first story, he put the plague in London: *where, amid the dark, narrow, and filthy lanes and alleys, the Demon of Disease was supposed to have had his nativity, Awe, Terror, and Superstition were alone to be found stalking abroad.* In the second story, he told of Prince Prospero's riotous castle, in which finally *Darkness and Decay and the Red Death held illimitable dominion over all.*

Both his mother and his brother had died of the red death of tuberculosis, and Poe feared it as the red plague of his time even more than cholera. There were portents enough to have satisfied the grandeur that was Rome – on 13 November 1833, a rain of meteors put torches to the night sky and made it brighter than the sunrise, as if these were the signs and wonders of the end of the world. And so Poe could be inspired again in 'Eiros and Charmion' to write of the destruction of the earth by a comet – *the final holocaust for the whole human race, not just the Jews* – in universal delirium, a wild lurid light, an intense flame, a brilliant and all-fervid heat brighter than angels, and *thus ended all.*

In that attic in Mechanics Row, other visions came to Poe, interwoven with those he loved and those who lived and those who died. The growing love of his fantasies was his plump pretty cousin Virginia, half-child and half-girl on the edge of puberty, laughing at him with her radiant teeth, loving him in the semi-conscious adoration of adolescence. He wrote 'Berenice' and 'Morelia', in which he mixed his horror of his mother's and his brother's death with his increasing obsession about the last of his close flesh and blood, whom he might hope to hold to him. In 'Berenice', the hero is called Egaeus – a Latin version of Edgar – and it is written in the first person 'I' – *something which better writers avoid*! Egaeus declares that misery is manifold and wretchedness covers the earth, then he demands how he has derived from beauty a type of unloveliness. He comes from an ancient family and is very learned, although ill from a morbid irritability and addicted, body and soul, to the most intense and painful meditation. Yet Berenice, *his cousin who grew up with him*, is full of light-heartedness and joy:

> Oh, gorgeous yet fantastic beauty! Oh, sylph amid the shrubberies of Arnheim! Oh, Naiad among its fountains! And then – then all is mystery and terror, and a tale which should not be told. Disease – a fatal disease, fell like the simoon upon her frame; and even while I gazed upon her, the spirit of change swept over her, pervading her mind, her habits, and her character, and, in a manner the most subtle and terrible, disturbing even the identity of her person! Alas, the destroyer came and went! – and the victim – where is she? I knew her not – or knew her no longer as Berenice!

So Poe confused his love of Virginia with his horror of watching his brother, like his mother, change his identity as he lay dying. It was not so much a prophecy that Virginia would also die slowly before his eyes, but a sense of mortality beneath the childish flesh. He gave to Berenice something of grandmother's disease, a sort of paralysis called catalepsy, which induced a trance of death-in-life. He then extended the fearful to the horrible by making Egaeus marry Berenice, although she was already transfigured by her disease. His morbid fascination fixed itself on her teeth, shining out at him from her thin and shrunken lips. He pulled the teeth out of her jaws when she lay in her tomb, but she came back from her cataleptic swoon, all bloody-mouthed like Elizabeth Arnold and William Henry Poe in their coughing deaths.

So Poe put together his love of his living kin with his horror at his dead family. In 'Morelia', he was more explicit about the identity of somebody passing along the great chain of the living and the dead through another of the same flesh and blood. Again he wrote of the hero as 'I', and he stated, 'the notion of that identity which *at death is or is not lost for ever* – was to me, at all times, a consideration of intense interest; not more from the perplexing and exciting nature of its consequences, than from the marked and agitated manner in which Morelia mentioned them.'

He sought legitimacy for transferring his love of his mother and foster mother to his aunt Maria Clemm – who took on their *identities* after their deaths – and for replacing his love for Jane Stith Stanard and Sarah Elmira Royster with a feeling for his small cousin Virginia. Through this belief, his need to love a mother figure and a romantic object remained constant rather than fickle – death or marriage or absence transferred the identity of his same passion to another person. So it was for Morelia, who was made to die in childbirth – only for her child to die also when named Morelia by her father –who, burying her in the family tomb, could find no trace of the body of his wife, now passed wholly into her daughter.

These stories of morbid fantasy might have been intended to appeal to the sensibility of the South, which revelled in tales of fair young ladies, dying and reappearing supernaturally. Yet they were exaggerated beyond the call of the market by the dreaming and the drugs taken by the young writer. There was good reason for the Baltimore years to be lost without much incident. Poe's health was beginning to give way; he feared to die early like his mother and brother of hereditary weaknesses; and he had been taught the relief of taking opium.

Despite those who would defend Poe, the evidence of his opium habit is strong. His cousin Miss Herring declared that he hardly ever touched a glass of wine in Baltimore, but his periods of excess were caused by the free use of opium, which Maria and Virginia Clemm did their best to conceal. The stuff cost little, was mixed into most medicines, and needed no prescription. Many writers of the day were addicted to it, De Quincey and Coleridge, Elizabeth Barrett and Wilkie Collins – and Charles Baudelaire, who read Poe to discover the same dark intense visions which came from a pipe-bowl or a small black bottle.

In other morbid stories of mixed love and death, Poe usually made his hero his *alter ego*, who used opium. In his lament for his mother, 'Ligeia', 'I' the hero became 'a bounden slave in the trammels of opium, and my labours and my orders had taken a colouring from my dreams'. It was the same for Roderick Usher, whom Poe described as if he were commenting on his own reflection in a mirror, and then added that Usher spoke like an 'irreclaimable eater of opium, during the periods of his most intense excitement'.

The most open confession of his drug habit was given in the first magazine version of 'The Oval Portrait'. The paragraph was significantly cut out later from his collected tales, as he strove to hide his habit. In this very short story about the life portrait of a girl, who died during the sittings to give it life, the hero was again called 'I', and the missing paragraph of great length told of 'I' using a packet of opium to reduce a fever:

> I sought and found the narcotic. But when about to cut off a portion, I felt the necessity of hesitation. In smoking, it was a matter of little importance how much was employed. Usually I half-filled the bowl of the hookah with opium and tobacco, cut and mingled, half and half. Sometimes when I had used the whole of this mixture, I experienced no very peculiar effects; at other times, I would not have smoked the pipe more than two-thirds out, when symptoms of mental derangement, which were even alarming, warned me to desist. But the effect proceeded with an easy gradation, which deprived the indulgence of all danger. Here, however, the case was different. I had never swallowed opium before. Laudanum and morphine I had occasionally used . . .

Poe cried wolf too much to be describing the habits of other people. Should he be censured for such indulgence in order to calm the nervous instability which he had inherited? Drug-taking was not prohibited. There was nothing illegal in his abuse of self – and in seeking his inspiration, as Coleridge did for 'Kubla Khan', in his pipe-dreams. Yet these also increased his morbidity. A verdict on him can only be not proven – what stimulated him, destroyed him – what eased him, slowly increased his torment – what he used, used him up.

When he was lucid and inquiring, as he certainly was when he was writing, Poe gave rational explanations for the plots taken from his nightmares and inner demons. He could turn out burlesque stories of the grotesque such as 'The Duc de l'Omlette', who faced up to the Devil, and 'A Tale of Jerusalem' about two Jews who were given a Roman gift of a pig. In these productions of strict logic, the humour laboured like a wind machine. Yet in another of his first stories, 'Metzengerstein', his attempt at pure Teutonic horror in the manner of Hoffman rode with the fiery horse into the blaze of total catastrophe.

By this time, he knew he had to earn a living from his stories, although his best effects came from his unconsciousness. He was deliberately turning away from the mystical musings of his boyish *Al-Aaraaf* to the secret cupboards where mankind locks up its skeletons. He knew he had an audience there, because everybody had hidden and common fears – of the returned dead, of being buried alive, of a crime being discovered, of mere perversity. Fear was inherent and popular – and Edgar Poe seemed to have a multitude of fears. As he wished for fame for his more mystical works, he took to terror to please the crowd. *To be appreciated*, he wrote of 'Berenice', *you must be read*.

He had originally come to Baltimore with literary hopes. He had already published a book of poems there, while his dead brother knew many of the small magazine printers and publishers. But he could not find a market for his horror stories except for 'Metzengerstein', until he submitted six stories from his *Tales of the Folio Club*, all written out in fair Roman script and bound together, for a fifty dollar prize offered by the *Baltimore Saturday Visitor*. The judges unanimously named him the winner, preferring the 'Ms Found in a Bottle' to his other masterly tale of vertigo, 'A Descent into the Maelstrom'. One of the judges, John Pendleton Kennedy, became his supporter and friend; another left a description of the young writer:

> He was if anything, below the middle size, and yet could not be described as a small man. His figure was remarkably good, and he carried himself erect and well, as one who had been trained to it. He was dressed in black, and his frock coat was buttoned to the throat, where it met the black stock, then al-

most universally worn. Not a particle of white was visible. Coat, hat, boots, and gloves had evidently seen their best days, but so far as mending and brushing go, everything had been done, apparently, to make them presentable. On most men his clothes would have looked shabby and seedy, but . . . Gentleman was written all over him. His manner was easy and quiet, and although he came to return thanks for what he regarded as deserving them, there was nothing obsequious in what he said or did.

His features I am unable to describe in detail. His forehead was high, and remarkable for the great development at the temple. This was the characteristic of his head, which you noticed at once, and which I have never forgotten. The expression of his face was grave, almost sad, except when he became engaged in conversation, when it became animated and changeable. His voice I remember was very pleasing in its tone and well modulated, almost rhythmical, and his words were well chosen and unhesitating . . .

Poe's effect on other people was studied. He wanted to impress as the dandy and the poet and the aristocrat – *and his example can serve to influence all those who feel themselves much the same!* Poe now moved to a brick two-storey cottage at 3 Amity Street, taking along his paralysed grandmother and her pension, his aunt and his girl cousin – her brother had run away to sea, leaving Poe as the sole man in the household. The cottage is still preserved in what is now a black slum quarter of Baltimore, totally enclosed by one of Franklin D. Roosevelt's housing schemes under the Works Progress Administration. In these Edgar Allan Poe Homes, the poor live poorly and without hope of fortune – as he did. All around them are the decaying mansions of the city's former splendour, Carrolton and Carey and Calhoun Streets; but these wide avenues and pleasant squares, these large porticos and plinths now offset mere tenements for the refugees from the tobacco field and the cotton patch. Faded glory and degraded grandeur hold illimitable dominion over all, like the guise of the Southern gentleman that Poe wore threadbare.

'Men, such as Edgar Poe,' a Northern literary lady once said, 'will always have an ideal of themselves by which they represent the chivalry of a Bayard and the heroism of a Viking, when, in fact they are utterly dependent and tormented with womanish sensibilities.' She said this to sneer at Poe, when it was to his credit. He knew, above all, the abyss between a man's fear and his pretensions, defended by his pride. He reached out for more than he was able to perform, thus stretching his capacities to the edge of genius. In professing the impossible, he achieved the extraordinary – *and so should each man choose to mime a greater than himself, in order that he may improve his defects through another's identity.*

Poe believed in phrenology, the psychiatry of the time – and just about as scientific! His protruding brow and his skull, full of bumps, was proof to him that he had genius inside his head, just as his loss of his mother early is now proof to the Freudians of his infantile necrophilia, not to mention his impotence – and his exalted Southern sense of chivalry and superego is further proof to the Jungians of the power of myth over his personal life. The curious thing is that he wrote a story called 'Mystification' about a certain Baron von Jung, who loved to deceive and exercised over the whole of his community a pervading and unaccountable influence! 'He contrived to shift the sense of the grotesque,' Poe wrote of von Jung, 'from the creator to the created – from his own person to the absurdities to which he had given rise.' A duel of honour, indeed, von Jung managed to reduce to the terms of a fight between two baboons – and doubtless he would have made the same reduction of the duel between a psychiatrist and his patient!

Need more be said? Poe believed in phrenology and mesmerism as we now believe in Freud and Jung. Each age has its absurd idols, which only proves the necessity men have to believe in something – in anything at all! If an analysis of Poe can be done, it can only be done in universal terms – in a common language that will outlast the clinical jargon of this time. In the 'Ms Found in a Bottle' and 'A Descent into the Maelstrom', for instance, Poe needs no psychiatric vocabulary to describe his sense of going under financially, his vertigo at his social fall, his sinking into opium dreams and drowning in nightmares, his knowledge that all efforts were useless, that he was powerless to affect his fate.

In the writing found in a bottle, the author was again 'I', a man of such education and method that he could detect the falsities of current intellectual superstitions. His doomed ship carried cases of opium before its final plunge into the supernatural sea, where *at times we gasped for breath at an elevation beyond the albatross – at times became dizzy with the velocity of our descent into some watery hell, where the air grew stagnant, and no sound disturbed the slumbers of the kraken.*

The porous Spanish ship that rescues him from his wreck is imbued with the spirit of the Eld and grows in bulk like the living body of a seaman. It hovers on the brink of eternity, without ever taking the final plunge into the abyss. *The crew glide to and fro like the ghosts of buried centuries; their eyes have an eager and uneasy meaning; and when their fingers fall athwart my path in the wild glare of the battle-lanterns, I feel as I have never felt before, although I have been all my life a dealer in antiquities, and have imbibed the shadows of fallen columns at Balbec, and Tadmor, and Persepolis, until my very soul has become a ruin.* And finally, in a reverse image of the red amphitheater in the heart of the Paradise of Arnheim, the ghost ship is sucked into the bowls of the earth in a white polar whirlpool surrounded by a gigantic amphitheater of ice. *The ship is quivering – oh God! and – going down!*

Such words need no explanation of a psychological kind. They defy analysis because they are a self-analysis! By his words ye shall know Poe! No biographer can dare to describe his state of mind better than he did himself. They can only hope to discern parts of their own identity in his, as if they were Morellas of his posterity – Berenices of his afterlife – dregs of his opium bottle –

To return to Poe in Baltimore – a description of the physical facts. He heard of John Allan's death in Richmond – in the will, he was left nothing at all. Even Allan's bequests to his bastard children were set aside after a long law suit by his righteous widow. Poe could no longer hope for a piece of a fortune, he had now to depend on his own slender resources. He made a myth of it, naturally, claiming that he had chosen disinheritance because of his own Quixotic sense of the honourable – of the chivalrous. 'The indulgence of this sense,' he wrote to one of his later literary loves, 'has been the true voluptuousness of my life. It was for this species of luxury that, in early youth, I deliberately threw away from me a large fortune, rather than endure a trivial wrong. It was for this that, at a later period, I did violence to my own heart, and married, for another's happiness, where I knew that no possibility of my own existed.'

Of course, Poe was lying after the event with the careful hypocrisy that most people call a good memory. He had not thrown away the Allan fortune, which Allan had left to his own flesh and blood as most fathers do in the end. As for marrying his cousin Virginia Clemm, which he was shortly to do, he did it from a desperate need to keep his little family near him – not for her sake, but for his own. In the demeaning days of poverty in Baltimore after his grandmother had died at last in the July of 1835, taking her pension to her grave, Virginia and Maria Clemm supported Edgar with their sewing and begging for charity, before his urgent appeal to John Pendleton Kennedy made him a regular contributor to Thomas White's new magazine, the *Southern Literary Messenger*, and then secured him the post as its assistant editor in Richmond, where he was forced to return at the end of the year.

His separation from Virginia and her adolescence made him marry her. He loathed living in boarding houses, even as a literary lion in a forgiving Richmond. Sarah Elmira Royster was still Mrs Shelton and fled his approach. His respectable cousins in Baltimore, the Neilson Poes, saw Virginia reaching the age of thirteen and imagined sexual advances from their unstable cousin Edgar. They offered to adopt her – and Edgar wrote to Maria Clemm a letter of utter despair at the possible loss of the only security and acceptance he had known in his adult life.

> *My dearest Aunty,*
> *I am blinded with tears while writing this letter – I have no wish to live another hour. Amid sorrow, and the deepest anxiety, your letter reached me – and you well know how little I am able to bear up under the pressure of grief. My bitterest enemy would pity me, could he now read my heart – My last my last my only hold on life is cruelly torn away – I have no desire to live and* WILL NOT. *But let my duty be done. I love,* YOU KNOW *I love Virginia passionately, devotedly. I cannot express in words the fervent devotion I feel towards my dear*

little cousin – my own darling . . . You both have tender hearts – and you will always have the reflection that my agony is more than I can bear – that you have driven me to the grave – for love like mine can never be gotten over. It is useless to disguise the truth that when Virginia goes with Neilson Poe that I shall never behold her again – that is absolutely sure. Pity me, my dear Aunty, pity me. I have no one now to fly to – I am among strangers, and my wretchedness is more than I can bear. It is useless to expect advice from me – what can I say? – Can I, in honour and in truth say – Virginia! do not go! – do not go where you can be comfortable and perhaps happy – and on the other hand can I calmly resign my – life itself. If she had truly loved me would she not have rejected the offer with scorn? Oh God have mercy on me! . . . What have I TO LIVE FOR? Among strangers WITH NOT ONE SOUL TO LOVE ME . . .

He added a postscript, which asked Maria Clemm to kiss her daughter for him a million times, then spoke directly:

For Virginia,
    My love, my own sweetest Sissy, my darling little wifey, think well before you break the heart of your cousin. Eddy.

Baudelaire thought that Poe's craving for his young first cousin both excited and repulsed him. There was a Byronic feeling of incest and the forbidden; there was a perverse sense of corrupting the immature and the innocent – and yet – there was also a nobility in protecting the dependent and the loving, while it was a Southern tradition that purity and fidelity were only to be found in very young girls. Most people prefer the worst explanation for any action – something which Poe called the schoolboy philosophy of a La Rochefoucauld – but in Poe's own case, he took a child bride from a mixture of motives, which he did not care to examine, and from which we cannot select a dominant one.

He summoned her and her mother to Richmond, where she played with his retarded and suspect sister Rosalie, one half-grown and one fully grown, both childish in their rompings together. A marriage soon took place at a simple ceremony, and Poe began to educate his young Virginia with her chalk-white face that never seemed to change from wax to rose. All the money he could save from his salary and Maria Clemm from her housekeeping was used to teach Virginia French and music – and even algebra. They lived as brother and sister for two years before he became a husband to her – and there was sexuality in their love, which Poe described in the language of the Flower Children of our last, our lost decade. He had always seen a woman's body as a perfect garden, and in 'Eleonora', he painted a childlike, brightly-splendoured hashish dream of awakening love.

First he – appearing as 'I' again – wrote that for some fifteen years, he had wandered only hand in hand with his young cousin Eleonora in the Valley of the Many-Coloured Grass. Then one evening by the River of Silence:

> We had drawn the God Eros from that wave, and now we felt that he had enkindled within us the fiery souls of our forefathers. The passions which had for centuries distinguished our race, came thronging with the fancies for which they had been equally noted, and together breathed a delirious bliss over the Valley of the Many-Coloured Grass. A change fell upon all things. Strange, brilliant flowers, star-shaped, burst out upon the trees where no flowers had been known before. The tints of the green carpet deepened; and when, one by one, the white daisies shrank away, there sprang up in place of them, ten by ten of the ruby-red asphodel. And life arose in our paths; for the tall flamingo, hitherto unseen, with all gay glowing birds, flaunted his scarlet plumage before us. The golden and silver fish haunted the river . . . And now, too, a voluminous cloud, which we had long watched in the regions of Hesper, floated out thence, all gorgeous in crimson and gold, and settling in peace above us, sank, day by day, lower and lower, until its edges rested upon the tops of the mountains, turning all their dimness into magnificence, and shutting us up, as if forever, within a magic prison-house of grandeur and of glory.
>
> The loveliness of Eleonora was that of the Seraphim; but she was a maiden artless and innocent as the brief life she had led among the flowers. No guile disturbed the fervour of love which animated her heart, and she examined with me its inmost recesses as we walked together in the Valley of the Many-

Coloured Grass, and discoursed of the mighty changes which had lately taken place therein.

Given the time, Poe could not have been more explicit about the sexual explorations of the virgin garden's inmost recesses and the change into womanhood. He was growing in confidence now, for he had tied his flesh and blood to him by love and dependence. His salary as assistant editor of the *Southern Literary Messenger* was enough to keep his household – some six hundred dollars a year, rising to eight hundred. He increased the subscription list of the little magazine seven times over by his horror stories and his swinging attacks on the cliques which controlled the literary opinions of New York and Boston. He himself had failed to make an impression on the two harsh and envious cities, and now that he had his own platform in the South, he could expose their malpractices and avenge their disdain for his early poems.

The Knickerbocker clique was particularly vulnerable. It puffed the productions of its members and reviled the works of outsiders – except from England, the source of most books published in New York, because Congress had failed to pass an international copyright law and thus American publishers could pirate all British books without payment to the author. Poe found himself a critic born and became the first American critic of importance, acclaim and notoriety.

His standards for poetry were romantic and intuitive: a critic of sensibility knew by instinct how to discern the great from the good, the ordinary from the vulgar. As for prose, Poe despised the *one vast perambulating humbug* of the clique-ridden North, in which publishers arranged for good reviews through small groups of their authors and friends who controlled the leading magazines. Poe lashed such puffery and made many enemies above the Potomac, yet he himself could puff the verse of literary ladies from gallantry and of Southerners from sectionalism.

For all that, he refused to praise an American writer merely because he was an American. He lauded originality and loathed the colonial sin of imitating successful English authors. He hated moralism in prose or essays, he insisted on Beauty as a standard in itself in poetry. And above all, he asked for each book to be studied and analysed on its own merits – however much he might himself fail occasionally to be impartial.

The proprietor of the *Southern Literary Messenger* admired and envied, feared and judged his brilliant assistant, who had made his little magazine the most famous in all the South. Removed from the Baltimore attic of his poverty, Poe had given up the solitary refuge of opium for the social pleasures of alcohol. Occasionally, he would drink too much and disappear from his desk for days on end. Thomas White dismissed him once, then took him back after an apology. Yet he could not resist preaching to his brilliant, erratic and charismatic young editor.

'If you go to a tavern,' White wrote to Poe, 'or to any other place where liquor is used at table, you are not safe. I speak from experience. You have fine talents, Edgar – and you ought to have them respected as well as yourself. Learn to respect yourself, and you will very soon find that you are respected. Separate yourself from the bottle, and bottle companions, forever!'

That was not Poe's nature, who sometimes found the plots for a manuscript in a bottle. He had a weak head for drink, but he needed the occasional release of alcohol for his headaches and his depressions, his fears and his nervous lethargies. He either worked in a frenzy of energy or slumped for days in weakness of body and spirit.

He did not choose to return to the *Messenger* for long. A financial slump, caused by Andrew Jackson's trust in paper money and wildcat banking, stopped some issues of the magazine from appearing. Poe thought that he had established his literary reputation and had begun to write his first and only novel. He parted from White, who was fearful of the reputation which Poe was inflicting on his little magazine. So Poe sailed again to New York to try his fortunes there.

He failed for a second time, although Maria Clemm and Virginia kept him making efforts there for eighteen months from the income of a boarding house which they ran. The economic slump had ruined most of the New York magazines as well; but Poe was enabled to complete his novel about another *alter ego*, Arthur Gordon Pym, and to arrange with Harper's for its publication as a book. Underrated by the English-speaking world to this day, it is undoubtedly the greatest metaphysical tale of a shipwreck, masquerading as an adventure story, to be told between *Robinson Crusoe* – a favourite boyhood book of Poe's – and *Moby Dick*.

It is full of Poe's sense of paradox and hoax, detail and horror, both cryptic and philosophic, wrought and wild. Since the first chapters had already appeared in the *Southern Literary Messenger*, and since Poe now wished it to appear as the true story of the voyage of Arthur Gordon Pym, the novel opens with a forged apology from Pym, that he regrets having allowed Poe to tell the beginning of his story, that he is now taking up the pen himself, and that his own style will easily be recognizable from Poe's! In fact, it is not, although another editorial note appears that Pym has unfortunately died, leaving his narrative incomplete.

The book is not important as a literary trick or an imitation of a genre, but for its mixture of the supernatural and the actual. Poe deals in a modern manner with the unspeakable details, usually omitted from stories of shipwrecks. He describes cannibalism in gruesome detail – *Having in some measure appeased the raging thirst which consumed us by the blood of the victim, and having by common consent taken off the hands, feet, and head, throwing them, together with the entrails, into the sea, we devoured the rest of the body, piecemeal* . . . His death-ship outdoes that of Coleridge in 'The Ancient Mariner'; for all upon it have perished by pestilence, and the only one grinning and waving at the castaways is being eaten by a gull, which pecks at his guts and jerks him about like a ghastly puppeteer. As Pym, Poe also recurs to his favourite terrors, burying his hero twice in *living inhumation*, which produces the *supremeness of mental and bodily distress*; making Pym dress up, as if in 'King Pest', as the putrescent victim of the mutineers in order to shock their leader to death; and insisting on the fear of falling, this time down a cliff, which Pym's perversity makes him do deliberately with *a desire, a yearning, a passion utterly uncontrollable.*

Yet the true genius of the novel lies in Poe's dialectic of black and white, and his discussion of language as labyrinth. Poe's common Southern fears of black treachery and revolt – Nat Turner had already struck in Virginia – and his ambivalent obsession about the enticements of shadow and of night, conspire to make him create a despicable tribe of black savages in Tsalal (La Last spelt backwards!), the terminal subtropical island in a strange warm patch of the Antarctic. There is no white at all in the colours of Tsalal – even the water is the consistency of purple gum arabic and the natives have black teeth. White is abhorred by them and fit only to be eliminated along with the Europeans and their ship. Only Pym and his strange dwarfish Indian companion, Dirk Peters, escape the massacre through the forgotten messages of inlets and channels, cut into the cliffs by previous civilizations, as if into *the very rock of language on which all writing depends to tell a tale at all!* A final editorial explains that Poe himself did not know that these mysterious characters spelt in Ethiopian script, *To be shady*; in Arabic letters, *To be white*; and in Egyptian hieroglyphs, *The region of the South*.

This masterpiece is misunderstood because of Poe's device of inserting long passages of nautical detail, such as how to lay-to a sailing ship in a storm, or even an intolerable log-book many chapters long of an exploration through the South Seas. Yet this is the essence of taking the reader easily from the everyday to the eternal. Defoe does much the same in *Robinson Crusoe*, setting out the endless housekeeping lists of his hero, so that he can hide his other purpose, the explanation of how a man's soul may survive in a solitary state – a question that perplexed even Aristotle.

Poe's reach was even further – towards the penultimate explanation – a vast shrouded human figure in the polar ice, the keeper of the gate of the final mystery of light and darkness, life and death, which Pym will meet and will not describe because he has perished before his book is done. Only through the particular may we grope towards the infinite on earth.

If I were not named Ernest Albert Pons or Edgar Allan Poe, I would announce myself as in the opening sentence of this book –

'My name is Arthur Gordon Pym,' I announced myself to Dupin, after returning to New York and writing my Baltimore chapter, which ended so brilliantly in setting the stage for my entrance here.

I did not, however, impress Dupin, who ignored me until he had finished reading my pages, alternately nodding and shaking his head as though he had a tic and a toc.

'You advance like a crab, don't you,' he declared. 'From the point of view of psychiatry, there is a great deal to be said for your progress. But if you want me to savage you like Poe as a literary critic – ' He paused to watch me squirm, and, like the jesting Pilate, did not stay for my answer. 'Your moralism is outrageous, and Poe wouldn't have stood for it for a moment. You may have technically eliminated yourself from the text as "I" the author – except for your last dramatic effect, so you could come in here and announce yourself as Arthur Gordon Pym – but really, Ernest, how dare you flatter yourself that you are in any way better than Poe as a writer!' He leafed through my pages as though through an indictment in court. 'Look at what you said of Berenice! "It is written in the first person 'I' – *something which better writers avoid!*" It was *I*, Dupin, who told you to avoid it – '

'You're using "I, Dupin" too,' I pointed out nastily. 'You're being egoistical now.'

Dupin squeaked in fury at me.

'Leave me out of it! We're talking about you.'

'About me,' I said. 'I mean – I.'

'About you as "I"! Don't be clever with me, Ernest, or I'll drop your case.' Dupin was waving his little arms around, quite like a pair of raven's wings, only he was chirping like a canary which has seen a cat. 'You cannot write a biographical analysis of somebody who is thought to be a genius – and feel superior to your subject. Poe hated moralism – you admit this, and then you judge him! You cannot thrust your values into an account of him, which is all we have agreed you should do. Any judgements must appear to grow out of the facts in the case, not out of your arrogant head.'

'I thought I was most impartial about his taking drugs,' I countered. 'I did not condemn. I said it was both good and bad – and not proven.'

'You hid your judgements there by writing contradictory statements and asking yourself questions you did not answer. You also did say Poe took opium regularly, which a lot of authorities deny. That is certainly a judgement! And – ' Here Dupin put his stiletto expertly into my back – 'how can a man who lives on Librium and Valium object to a man who takes opium now and then?'

It was a dirty thrust, but I replied with the enemy's own weapon – even though I did need a tranquilliser, right then!

'You told me, Dupin, that selection of the facts implied judgements – that biography was impossible – it was always an autobiography through somebody else – '

'Yes, but your value judgements must seem to be objective, although they cannot be. You must not throw in your own guilts as you do. Look at your comment on "Eiros and Charmion" – ' He found the place in the brief that I had written to condemn myself. 'You add to your description of the comet destroying the earth – *"the final holocaust for the whole human race, not just the Jews"* – and you underline it as if it were a quotation of Poe's! That's a literary crime! You are putting your comments into his language, his style, and his pen. It's terrible writing – and dishonest!'

'I thought I was here for analysis,' I replied stiffly, for I was proud of that apt aside. 'Or was your doctorate in Literature?'

'I should charge you double,' Dupin said. 'You're getting a free course in creative writing as well as an analysis.'

'I believe in creative writing no more than Poe did,' I noted. 'One is born to be a writer – or one is not.' I paused for effect this time, while Dupin's mouth dropped open in disbelief of what he knew I would say. 'I was born!'

'Your mother would back that,' Dupin said. 'But a writer – you?' He laughed unpleasantly. 'I have published two psychiatric monographs and a horde of articles – yet I do not claim to be a writer.'

'Because they are unreadable?' I suggested.

'Because it is not my profession! Yet I have published my work frequently, which you have not. And what you are writing is certainly unpublishable – except as material for a case history. If I am incidentally teaching you creative writing – and if it can't be taught, as you suggest, then tens of thousands of people are going to be out of work and will boil you in oil for saying so! – I am teaching you to express yourself better and so improve the quality of your self-analysis. If your words become clearer, hopefully your thoughts will become clearer, and you will be cured quicker. And hurry the day!'

I had never seen Dupin so exasperated. For the first time, the brilliance of my analysis seemed to be affecting him and not myself. I smoothed the crimson wings of my new butterfly tie, which showed how far I was fluttering away from my old *persona* Poe – who always wore black up to his Adam's apple!

'You must admit,' I said, 'if I judge Poe, even if I feel a little superior, I do remove myself further and further from his identity.'

'To where? And to what?' Dupin almost spat the questions at me. 'You have begun to question the value of the very things you are trying to do. And that way leads to a nervous breakdown! Your absurd attack on psychiatry – your idiotic comparison of it with phrenology – what a childish way of trying to insult me and all that we are trying to do together!'

Now I could see the reason for Dupin's irritation. My little barbs had got under the great man's skin.

'I thought they were rather apt,' I said. 'Pointed, don't you think?'

'Apt for what? A graffiti? *Shrinks should have their skulls examined.* And pointed for what? *All psychiatrists are pointy heads!*' Even I laughed at these absurdities. 'Ernest, I agree with you that we are in the infancy of psychiatry, but it has cured tens of millions of people of their mental ills, which phrenology certainly did not. More than that, nearly all Americans believe in one kind of psychiatry or another. And if you were true to Poe *as a thinker of his time*, you would admit that he would have believed in psychiatry now just as he believed in phrenology then – *and with much more cause*. It might have cured him too!'

I was silent, while Dupin, seeing his advantage now, changed his tune.

'Come on, Ernest,' he said with dreadful kindliness, 'you'll only lose my sympathy along with everybody else's, if you turn a healthy beginning at being independent of me into a childish attack against the very thing that is curing you – and also the greatest discovery of our age, the inquiry into the common disturbances of the human mind.'

'And the ways to manipulate it,' I said. 'In Russia, you know the psychiatric wards are sometimes used to treat the rebellious as insane.'

'This is not Russia,' Dupin said. 'We only treat the insane.'

'How do you know which is which?' I asked. 'Think of Dr Tarr and Prof. Fether! The madmen were their own keepers – the early Laing in charge there would contradict no fancies in their brains and insisted on running the place on a soothing system of total tolerance.'

'Yes,' Dupin said, 'but you will also remember the end of Poe's story. The madmen rebelled and introduced a new regime of total oppression of their old masters. Their lunatic government was one of tyrants and torturers, because they were insane – because they had no treatment – *because they refused to be told by experts what to do in order to be cured!*'

I must say, Dupin's powers of logic were greater than my own – or rather, his powers of presentation and persuasion.

'All right,' I muttered. 'I won't question the values of my analysis any more – '

'Good,' Dupin said. 'Then we will deal with the last piece of arrogance in your pages on Poe in Baltimore. Again, as a psychiatrist, I think your impertinence and new sense of your own worth is no bad thing – but as an intelligent man, how can I accept that you – the obscure Ernest Pons – can challenge a century of American critical opinion and put *Arthur Gordon Pym* beside Defoe and Melville! How do you know you are right, when nearly every expert is against you? Didn't Poe himself call it a silly book?'

'Only after it had been attacked by silly critics,' I said, before adding with nonchalant humility, 'It just happens to be what I think about it. And I have a right to my opinion, just as a critic has a right to his.' Then I counter-attacked. 'When Poe got his platform on the *Messenger*, he had never studied to be a critic – then suddenly discovered that he was born to be one – and is now recognized as the first important American critic!'

'I preferred you, Ernest,' Dupin said icily, 'when you confused your personality with Poe's. Now that you wish to rival him as a writer and as a critic – and call all of us professionals wrong – '

'Not you,' I said hastily. 'No – no longer you! Just the Knickerbocker knife-pushers, the Gotham gutterpress, the New York literati – '

'It's lucky you'll never publish this, Ernest, or you'd find yourself more unpopular than Poe. He was able to defend himself at least, but nobody's going to make you editor of a magazine – '

I was waiting to drop my little bomb – for was it not Dupin who had taught me the tricks of the anarchist?

'Who says I will never publish this?' I declared. 'Poe published in New York – and so shall I!'

'Keep your folly private,' Dupin advised me. 'You're too thin-skinned to take the sort of criticism you'll get.'

All advice from psychiatrists is a recommendation for compromise or cowardice, so I rejected Dupin magnificently.

'I shall now take *my* holiday,' I declared. 'Once I have covered Poe's six years in Philadelphia – City of Unbrotherly Love – I am retiring to a Landor's Cottage by the Five Finger Lakes – to write up the first chapters of this analysis from the time it was begun, when I came to you after seeing the Tell-tale Hearts in the Valentine shop.'

Dupin looked at me with disdain. He was probably calculating that he would lose some seven hundred dollars from the weekly sessions I would miss with him while I was away working at my manuscript.

'If you think that will help you in your case,' he agreed without enthusiasm. '*You* must be the judge – '

'Of myself, I will be.' I rose, victor at last over him I surveyed. 'I shall not call you until I have done!'

As I strode towards the door, the villain Dupin stopped me in my tracks with an expert bullet in the back of my new confidence.

'Did you remember to draw up your will?' he said.

7

The Fall of –

> I intend to put up with nothing I can *put down*.
> EDGAR ALLAN POE

> The simple truth is, that the mortification I feel in not being able to repay you, has been the reason of my not calling upon you.
> EDGAR ALLAN POE

Then as now, Philadelphia was a divided and agitated city. In 1838, it had a population of more than two hundred thousand and was the second in size in all the Union. Those who backed slavery had just burned down the offices of the *Pennsylvania Freeman*, while the local literary cliques were engaged in as internecine a war as in New York. Poe found himself, for once, on the side of the majority. As a Southerner, he defended slavery – he said that it made the master responsible and the slave faithful. He was also a Whig, who despised the abuse of democracy. In his amusing piece, 'Some Words with a Mummy', who was revived with an electric shock, he managed to make his ancient Egyptian put down all progress to date – the Pharaohs knew more about astronomy and as much about science – they had railroads to build the Pyramids and considered that the worst tyranny was the rule of the Mob. After hearing this, 'I' the hero became heartily sick of the nineteenth century in general, convinced that everything was going wrong.

Poverty and depression and friendlessness struck again at Poe. He took his little family to a wooden lean-to cottage of three rooms, then returned to his brooding and his writing. As he said of his Byronic hero in 'The Assignation' – 'To dream has been the business of my life'. He wrote perhaps the greatest of his visionary stories at the time, 'The Fall of the House of Usher'. Poe split himself between the characters of the narrator and of Roderick Usher – and both were in the grip of opium. The very House of Usher itself was compared to a morphine melancholy:

> I looked upon the scene before me – upon the mere house, and the simple landscape features of the domain – upon the bleak walls – upon the vacant eye-like windows – upon a few rank sedges – and upon a few white trunks of decayed trees – with an utter depression of soul which I can compare to no earthly sensation more properly than to the after-dream of the reveller upon opium – the bitter lapse into every-day life – the hideous dropping off of the veil. There was an iciness, a sinking, a sickening of the heart – an unredeemed dreariness of thought which no goading of the imagination could torture into aught of the sublime.

If the dark side of Poe was Roderick Usher with his huge brow and liquid eye and morbid madness, the good side of Usher was his last relative on earth, his twin sister Madeline, whom he buried alive almost deliberately. Most sinister of all was Usher's fantastic song and poem, 'The Haunted Palace', which reversed the good image of the maiden as a garden into the disordered brain as a ghost-ridden mansion.

> *But evil things, in robes of sorrow,*
> *Assailed the monarch's high estate . . .*
> *And travellers now within that valley,*
> *Through the red-litten windows see*
> *Vast forms that move fantastically*
> *To a discordant melody;*
> *While, like a rapid ghastly river,*
> *Through the pale door,*
> *A hideous throng rush out forever,*
> *And laugh – but smile no more.*

No other story of Poe's illuminated better his frequent nervous depressions and fear of madness. In his happier times, as when he wrote 'Eleonora', he could speculate that madness might be the loftiest intelligence – and that a disease of thought might provide more exalted ideas than the general intellect. Yet when he felt isolated and when opium was his only solace outside his wife and his aunt, he was sure that delirium would send him raving to the madhouse. In the grip of these depressions, he would not even go out at night for fear that his demons might trap him. As he maintained, the terror of his tales was *not of Germany but of the soul*. D. H. Lawrence was to agree – that Poe was *doomed to seethe down his soul in a great continuous convulsion of disintegration, and doomed to register the process*.

Yet he was usually sober and lucid and working to a strict regimen, when his black moods were not upon his back. He wrote a piece of hack work for fifty dollars, rewriting a textbook on sea-shells – and plagiarizing another book in the process. He was hardly surviving, however, or supporting his family, when an English comic actor called William Evans Burton invited him to help to edit his *Gentleman's Magazine*, working a two-hour day for ten dollars a week. *If you will cut your mutton with me, good*, Burton wrote to Poe – and Poe did.

Poe's sour and sado-masochistic humour of the period showed in three remarkable stories that are usually discounted – but were favourites of his own, as they made him laugh at secret fears. 'A Predicament' told of a man looking out of a clock tower, when the hour hand fell onto the back of his neck and slowly cut off his head – the literal Scythe of Time. As his neck was severed, the narrator's sensations were those of exquisite pain and extreme happiness. In 'The Man that Was Used Up', the handsome military hero turned out to be a mere torso, an *odd-looking bundle of something*, the rest of him being made up of mechanical parts superior to human flesh. Then in 'Loss of Breath', the narrator had his limbs broken, his skull cracked, and his ears cut off before being hanged and buried alive. At this point, Poe could even mock at his deep fear of living inhumation:

> I knocked off, however, the lid of my coffin, and stepped out. The place was dreadfully dreary and damp, and I became troubled with *ennui*. By way of amusement, I felt my way among the numerous coffins ranged in order around. I lifted them down,

one by one, and breaking open their lids, busied myself in speculations about the mortality within.

So Poe could laugh at himself and his terrors with a gallows humour. He could even make fun of his pennilessness in his one Tale with a Moral, 'Never Bet the Devil Your Head': – *'Poverty was another vice which the peculiar physical deficiency of Dammit's mother had entailed upon her son. He was detestably poor . . .'* Poe revealed himself as much in his humour as in his horror, and his burlesques of his fears were for his own relief as well as for the market.

The routine of being an editor again imposed an order on Poe, as had the artillery and the *Southern Literary Messenger*. He was punctilious in doing his editorial duties, assisting both the comedian Burton and a new proprietor, George Rex Graham, who soon bought the magazine. Poe worked the same magic as he had for Thomas White, increasing the subscriptions seven times over until *Graham's Lady's and Gentleman's Magazine* had a circulation of some forty thousand copies, and became America's first national journal.

Poe seemed to be a born editor as well as a born critic. However rarefied his own thinking could be, he had a flair for the popular – in puzzles as well as in horror stories. In addition to his tales of inductive logic, which progressed from his exposure of a man hidden inside Maelzel's Automaton Chess Player through his three stories with Dupin in the role of the rational detective, he invented a series called 'Autography', in which he claimed to discern the character of a famous author from his signature, and he also offered to solve any cryptogram sent in by any reader. He even won a hundred dollar prize from the *Dollar Newspaper* for his most successful short story, 'The Gold Bug', with its clever cryptographic solution.

On the money pouring in from new subscriptions, Graham became one of the more free-spending spirits in Philadelphia, while Poe reached a modest security, moving his family to the banks of the Schuylkill River near a new pagoda and buying a harp for his young wife. He was only rarely tempted to have a drink too much as he often had in Richmond. His defense against Burton, who accused him of tippling, is probably true:

'At no period of my life was I ever what men call intemperate. I never was in the *habit* of intoxication. I never drank drams. But, for a brief period, while I resided in Richmond, and edited the *Messenger*, I certainly did give way, at long intervals, to the temptation held out on all sides by the spirit of Southern conviviality. My sensitive temperament could not stand an excitement which was an everyday matter to my companions. In short, it sometimes happened that I was completely intoxicated. For some days after each excess I was invariably confined to bed. But it is now quite four years since I have abandoned every kind of alcoholic drink – four years, with the exception of a single deviation . . . My habits are as far removed from intemperance as the day from the night. My sole drink is water.'

Poe did not mention taking opium – that was his secret, and he did not seem to need it during his social years as an editor. Both the magazine's printer and proprietor were witnesses to Poe's sobriety and reliability. Graham found him always a polished gentleman and a thoughtful scholar, a devoted husband and a hard worker, and the soul of honour in his business dealings. Graham then added that this was in Poe's better days – but even in his worse ones, there was no writer to whom Graham would have more readily advanced money for future work.

Poe was, after all, one of the few American writers who was trying to live solely by his pen and occasional editorial jobs. There was no profit in printing his major works in book form – and they were pirated overseas. He did not receive a penny from the Philadelphia publication in two volumes of his *Tales of the Grotesque and Arabesque*, nor from the English reprint of *The Narrative of Arthur Gordon Pym*. To try and exist as a writer without any income except from his usual ten dollars a story for a magazine sale, was noble, admirable and foolhardy.

Yet Poe saw himself as an artist and gentleman. He did not want to compromise himself by engaging in a trade. He did, however, have one solution which could have made him as rich as he had made Graham. He wanted to find enough subscribers or capital to start his own magazine, first to be called the *Penn. Magazine* and then the *Stylus*. He was never to succeed in this ambition, which was fatal for his well-being, but fecund for his reputation as an artist *damné*.

Two running wounds began to bleed away his life, just as he seemed to have achieved some security. He met his William Wilson, his false Dupin! This trusted two-faced man of warped talent and total envy was a Baptist minister from Vermont called Rufus Griswold, who had created his own position of literary power by being an anthologist – and so the arbiter of what should be included in *Gems from American Female Poets* or *Poets and Poetry of America*, which was to run to twenty-nine editions. If Maria Clemm had replaced Poe's foster mother in his life, Rufus Griswold was to play the role of the new John Allan – the destroyer of hope, employment and reputation. For he saw in Poe's genius the originality he lacked – and thus he had to plot against the living evidence of his own inadequacy.

He began by replacing Poe as editor of *Graham's Magazine*. Poe walked into the office one day to find Griswold sitting in his editorial chair at a higher salary than he had been receiving himself. Because of a nervous collapse after his wife's sudden illness, Poe had often been absent from his desk early in 1842; but he did not expect Graham to supersede him. What was done was done underhand, although Poe continued to contribute to the magazine and to hope that he would start one of his own. As for Griswold, Poe both solicited his aid and suspected him, writing prophetically in an anonymous review on Griswold as an anthologist: *Forgotten, save only by those whom he has injured and insulted, he will sink into oblivion, without leaving a landmark to tell that he once existed; or, if he is spoken of hereafter, he will be quoted as the unfaithful servant who abused his trust.*

Virginia Poe's illness came on as inevitably as Eleonora's sense that the finger of Death was upon her bosom, as horribly as Madeline's reappearance in the House of Usher. Dressed in her usual white gown with her hair pulled back from the same huge brow and fine nose of her cousin and husband, she choked on a song she was singing and bright blood gushed out of her mouth. Poe went for the doctor; all thought she would die; but she recovered enough to begin the long slow lingering of Poe's mother and brother.

He found it too unjust a fate – almost too deliberate. It was the third time he had watched the ravages of tuberculosis, the changing of identity from the living to the dying – the waiting and the wasting were interminable – he could not endure the sickroom. Later he wrote a letter about his own breakdown:

> Her life was despaired of. I took leave of her forever and underwent all the agonies of her death. She recovered partially and I again hoped. At the end of a year the vessel broke again – I went through precisely the same scene. Again in about a year afterward. Then again – again – again and even once again at varying intervals. Each time I felt all the agonies of her death – and at each accession of the disorder I loved her more dearly and clung to her life with more desperate pertinacity. But I am constitutionally sensitive – nervous in a very unusual degree. I became insane, with long intervals of horrible sanity. During these fits of absolute unconsciousness I drank, God only knows how often or how much. As a matter of course, my enemies referred the insanity to the drink rather than the drink to the insanity . . .

It was this horrible never-ending oscillation between hope and despair that destroyed the end of Poe's own short life. George Graham noticed how devoted Poe was during Virginia's long sickness – he might have been nursing a first child as well as a wife. He had a sort of rapturous worship of the beauty that was fading before his eyes. The hourly anticipation of her loss made him *a sad and thoughtful man, and lent a mournful melody to his undying song.* If he could have such an effect upon a magazine editor, what should he do to the more sensitive? The disasters that overcame his own flesh and blood were so *repetitive* – their lives were so *short* – that these adjectives became principles of beauty to him. The romantic tale and the lyric poem were, to him, the facts of life.

In a famous review of Hawthorne's *Twice Told Tales*, which he praised for their originality and melancholy and restraint, Poe declared that the highest genius was expressed in the short rhymed poem, followed by the short story. As in life, brevity was the soul of beauty as well as wit. There was no virtue in length – a novel should also be brief enough to be read in a single sitting.

Without hope except of a Customs House appointment by the new Whig President Tyler, Poe watched over his dying wife and dwindling stock of furniture, which had to be sold off stick by stick. He was forced to move to the present Poe Museum in Philadelphia, a brick house in Spring Garden Street, which now bears an advertisement on its side wall: *Visit The House Where Poe Wrote The Raven*. He is supposed to have dredged the idea from Dickens's black bird Grip in *Barnaby Rudge* – its stuffed corpse now perches in the Philadelphia Free Library. After reading several serial episodes of the Dickens story, Poe detected the murderer in his best Dupin style, then added: 'The raven, too, intensely amusing as it is, might have been made, more than we see it, a portion of the conception of the fantastic Barnaby. Its croaking might have been *prophetically* heard in the course of the drama. Its character might have performed in regard to that of the idiot . . .'

Poe was to work on that counterpoint in his Spring Garden home – and to meet Dickens, when the Englishman came to Philadelphia. They talked over the loss to authors from the mutual piracy between America and England, and they said they would help one another – and Dickens did, after Poe's death, give money to the bereaved Maria Clemm.

Poe's usual Philadelphia companions did him little good, encouraging him into drinking and deliberate eccentricity when he could no longer stand the confines of Virginia's sickroom and his daily regimen in his garret study. As his poverty and his depression grew, his sprees became wilder and more notorious. An old friend, Lambert Wilmer, noticed that Poe was becoming subject to more and more vagaries and was going to destruction, moral, physical and intellectual. Certainly, the urge to self-destruction or the imp of the perverse controlled him during his eventual visit to Washington to meet the President and ask for his Customs House appointment.

When he arrived in the capital, he took too much port wine. By the time he was taken to the White House, he was incapable of seeing President Tyler. He then drank even more until his supporters and companions sent him home, worried that he had become the sport of senseless creatures who, like oysters, kept sober and gaped at his extravagances, such as wearing his Spanish cloak inside out. He returned to Philadelphia, however, pleased at being able to get back at all and apologetic for his misbehaviour in Washington. He still hoped for the appointment and thought *it would be a feather in Mr Tyler's cap to save from the perils of mint julep – and 'Port Wines' – a young man of whom all the world thinks so well and who thinks so remarkably well of himself.*

In the absence of a publishing or a university income, Poe could only hope to get a political job which might leave him time to write – both Hawthorne and Melville procured one, but Poe did not. He would work away in Spring Garden Street, trying to earn a miserable living from his stories and poems. He contributed to James Russell Lowell's new periodical, *The Pioneer*, some of his better writing, 'The Tell-tale Heart', 'Lenore', and his critical piece 'The Rationale of Verse' – yet when the magazine folded and Lowell could not pay him all, he was magnanimous with his fellow author even though he was desperate for the few dollars.

On one particularly pressing day, he took the fresh draft of 'The Raven' down to Graham's office to read it to him. Another famous magazine editor, Godey of the *Lady's Book*, was present, and they listened to Poe's remarkable and histrionic declamation of his repetitive poem about the ebony bird of ill omen from the night's Plutonian shore with its eternal croak of 'Nevermore'. Neither editor particularly liked or understood the poem, so a hat was passed round in pity, and Poe returned home with his best-known work and fifteen dollars of charity money.

So Poe became notorious and penniless despite his national fame as a writer, critic and editor. The trouble was that, as he said in his defence, his studies and literary life at home escaped the eye of the world, while his occasional drunken escapades with his friends made them think he was always in that state. He did not help matters by provoking his most dangerous enemy, Rufus Griswold, and attacking him openly at a lecture as an untrustworthy and limited man.

Poe was also indiscreet enough to accept an invitation to the fashionable resort of Saratoga Springs for the sake of his health as the public summer guest of a Mrs Barhyte – the first of a series of literary ladies with rich husbands, who relied on Poe to entertain their wives while they went about the business of making money.

Yet at home in the backbiting Quaker city, which knew all about Virginia's terminal illness, Poe seemed to be a callous philanderer.

In reality a devoted husband and dedicated writer at the time, Poe could well complain about the double vision of a gossipy society. In another of his underrated burlesques, 'The Spectacles', he gave his hero the same black hair and large grey eyes as himself – and the same passion for elegant women – but the defect of very poor sight and the vanity of refusing to wear even a monocle. At the end of the story, the hero found that he had married his own great-great-grandmother – so ridiculous were the make-up of society and the false eye-glasses through which it quizzed its members.

Poe's knowledge of his notoriety and his growing feeling of failure led to a form of literary paranoia. He revealed this to a novelist friend in 1844.

> As for these personal enemies, I cannot see that you need put yourself to any especial trouble about THEM. Let a fool alone – especially if he be both a scoundrel and a fool – he will kill himself far sooner than you can kill him by any active exertion . . . I have never yet been able to make up my mind whether I regard as the higher compliment, the approbation of a man of honour and talent, or the abuse of an ass or a blackguard. Both are excellent in their way – for a man who looks steadily up.

At any rate, the animosities of small men so bedevilled Poe in Philadelphia that he decided to assault the heights of New York for the third time with less than ten dollars in his pocket. He would return where he had failed.

In his country retreat on the Hudson River, Pons found both pollution and a form of paranoia. What had happened to the landscape that had inspired 'Landor's Cottage' – where every road was a work of art, and Poe's unpretending dwelling was arranged as part of a natural picture. The converted Dutch barn, which Pons had borrowed off a friend whose paintings occupied more space than inspiration, was a monument to knotty pine and the set-square. Nothing that a Swedish masseur's thumbs could chop or knead or harmonize into shape had been left unwrought. As for the highway that took Pons there, it passed Hamburger Heavens and Ice-cream Parlour Paradises, factories and smokestacks, all pouring out their effluent into the affluent, the air, the water and the earth.

So much for landscape as an action picture. Ignoring his surroundings, Pons set about writing the first chapters of his analysis, *The Facts in the Case of E. A. Poe*. He tried to recreate the certainty of mind which he had once had in his old identity as the poet. He tried to show the transition to the self-conscious writer and analyst, setting about the scrutiny of Poe's life – and of his own. And as he endured rural peace for the first time, with its infernal caterwaulings of birds and go-karts, cows and tree-saws, he felt that true solitude was a self-destructive thing, and Wordsworth was an ass.

His pride in putting down Dupin ebbed away. The superiority he had felt over Poe as a financial expert was illusory – he had only been honourable to his creditors because he had always been able to pay them with ease. His resolve to write more elegantly than his subject had written became more empty with each page that he tried to fill. And worse – far worse – during the long lonely evenings, in which he could only hope for the distraction of an assault by a Bronx gang on holiday or a demented Doberman off guard duty, he was forced to examine himself and ask the dark question – just who is Ernest Albert Pons?

The answer was, there was no answer. There was a small slight man who bore a resemblance to Edgar Poe – and even more to his terrors and ambiguities. Both men hated the horror inflicted on humankind by death and each other; but the fact was, Poe was far the braver man in trying to earn a living and support a dying wife, while Pons had tried to avoid all the bruises and engagements of his existence. It was not admirable. It was despicable.

Another foul truth struck Pons between genius and gizzard. Was he being another Rufus Griswold to Poe? Was he vilifying Poe's reputation, while pretending to be his sympathizer? Not out of envy, mind you – but out of his own defects, which would make him put down Poe's qualities. Many would defend Poe from the charge that he took opium – they would claim that he had invented the state of mind of his addicted narrators and of Roderick Usher. Was it because of Pons's own arsenal of pill bottles, his Libriums and Luminols, his Valiums and amphetamines – that he insisted upon Poe's dependence on drugs? Was it because he hardly ever touched alcohol himself – that he condemned Poe's occasional sprees? Did he judge Poe from the molehill of his rare virtues – and forgive Poe from the mountain of his defects – and force the poet to join him in his private failings?

Such thoughts made his depressive dreams return, breaking through the sleeping pills. The emaciated figures gibbering without sound – the scarecrows tumbling together into the open pit where the crows picked out their eyes – the puffs of lime blowing off the pocked corpses – and then – finally and repeatedly – the Poe-like fantasy of the plague-pits spilling over with bright red blooms, scarlet and flame and crimson roses springing out of the putrid limbs and covering over the crushed skulls, until they pressed down on Pons's eyes and filled his mouth with hot suffocation –

And he awoke, gasping –

One day, he could not find his grey-tinted contact lenses, and, groping for them, he found his eye-ball set against a monster – a thing of one bulbous sac and two deep sockets and twin febrile pincers, all set about with splint-thin broken legs. He started back in horror to see – a spider! And he remembered Poe seeing his vast Sphinx in his Hudson cottage, where he had withdrawn to avoid the cholera in New York. That monster had seemed to be the size of a shaggy ship of the line with a foul mouth larger than an elephant – and yet was only, without the distortion of the eye so close, one-sixteenth of an inch.

So we magnify the particular and inflate our personal problems into the fate of mankind. Pons became full of self-pity and disgust, but for once, he knew it was his own. He toiled on, the weeks shading into months, until his tale was done – the half of his analysis. As he was ending the work, he remembered Dupin's advice and sent for his lawyer to visit him upstate. He should draw up his will while he had the time.

Yet at the station halt, Pons could not believe his eyes. As he walked toward the train compartment, out of which his lawyer stepped onto the platform, he thought he knew the other man who stayed in his seat – the man to whom his lawyer was saying farewell with every sign of familiarity and complicity. It was Charles Dupin – he who had told Pons to make his last testament!

Yet as Pons moved forward to verify this conspiracy, the train moved off. And when he asked his lawyer if he had travelled with Dupin, the lawyer told him to keep his Poe mania to himself and concentrate on the clauses in his will.

'Were you on the train?' I asked. 'Are you in collusion with my lawyer?'

'You wanted to go on this rural interlude,' Dupin pointed out. 'You wanted not to see me for months. You wanted to show your new independence. Well – look at you! We're in analysis, not primal screaming! I would call your accusations a mild paranoia, if laymen like you did not always misuse the word.'

'You didn't answer my questions,' I complained. I could not tell whether Dupin was being evasive or authoritarian.

'They don't need answers. You should not have asked them. You suspect your own analyst!'

I would not let him get away with it.

'You already know what's in my will, don't you? And you're the one who told me to make it! You know the power you will soon have over my whole estate – you – Griswold!!'

Dupin shook his head, went over to the corner cupboard, and opened it. The bust of Pallas was gone – the raven flown!

'What have you done with them?' I shrieked. 'You kidnapper – '

'I thought you were making good progress until today,' Dupin said coolly. 'So I gave them to my cleaning woman. She thought they were something to do with voodoo and might be a conversation piece in Harlem. I agreed.'

'How dare you – I will not tolerate – '

'Ernest, throw away your crutches! You are already on your knees – and soon you will hobble! Then walk – then stride – then race! Or should I say – jog – '

A ghastly sort of revivalism had inflated Dupin's high voice so that it sounded like a choir out of tune – and even worse – his nauseating encouragement began to make me feel better. At least, he knew how far I had come – and he was not deserting me, however much I tried to make him into my persecutor and inquisitor.

'Did you like my written analysis to date?' I asked weakly. 'I mean, I did what I could – '

'Ernest, it *improves*. There is no doubt of it, your prose shows your mental improvement. The beginning is, of course, as confused as you were at the time when you could not tell your own identity from Poe's. But I must admit, this last account of Poe in Philadelphia is more than adequate. You hardly intrude at all – a few moralisms and too many dashes and exclamation marks – but otherwise, quite a sound and short account of the six years there and the breakdown of the man.' He paused after this mild praise to twist his fingers in that cursed cat's cradle of his. 'I had thought this stage of the analysis might lead partially to your own breakdown, which luckily you seem largely to have avoided – as he did not. He did recover, though. He had five more years to live, I think.'

'I have forty,' I said stiffly. 'Actuarially.'

'You will live to bury us all,' Dupin said, his voice more slick than the grease upon his cautious hair. 'Fear not and press on – and you will make history as the first patient who ever recorded in full the process of leaving his false identity to find his own true self.'

'You think I can – complete it?' I hesitated to ask the question, but I felt the need of reassurance, even though I knew I was giving Dupin back his power over me. 'The years of his perversity and his wife's death and his own – am I strong enough to *cope*?'

'With my help, yes,' Dupin said complacently. 'And don't think I didn't admire the acts of courage in your text – particularly your refusal to interject yourself into Poe's agony at watching his wife's long dying, when you too did so much to nurse your mother in those last three awful years of her cancer – '

'I do not want to think of that, Dupin!'

'Yet you did – and do,' Dupin insisted. 'I know the thought is always there, even when you try to block it mentally. You were brave to think it when you were writing about Poe – and not to write it. You were also brave to put down your nightmares of the death-pits full of roses. Your Rosa, of course – any fool can interpret that dream – you too! You are becoming *aware* of your guilt and your suppressions. You are grappling at last with your buried fears. Good – good – '

I felt my heart swelling to Dupin's praise – or was it heartburn? Really, I had misjudged the fellow. He had intelligence and even compassion, if he was not riding an intellectual hobbyhorse to death.

'It's good of you to say so, Charles,' I said. He knew I only used his Christian name if I was especially pleased. 'Perhaps you would join me in a gourmet dinner tonight.'

'Another night,' he said. 'I have some problems. My old family firm in Bordeaux, the wine merchants Comble, Dupin and Cie – there are a few troubles – '

I tried to be as magnanimous as my Poe.

'Let me help you!' I declared, patting my wallet in case it leapt from my pocket at my rashness.

'Even your sort of money,' Dupin said cryptically, 'could not solve this case – and I would never ask you for it.'

8

Driven Mad

Is it any wonder that I was driven *mad* by the intolerable sense of wrong?

EDGAR ALLAN POE

To show superiority and to achieve instant fame, Poe began by hoaxing New York City. He wrote a false aviator's journal, which described an Atlantic crossing by the balloon 'Victoria' from England to South Carolina in seventy-five hours. Banner headlines in the New York *Sun* promoted the deception:

> ASTOUNDING NEWS!
> *By Express Via Norfolk!*
> THE ATLANTIC CROSSED in THREE DAYS
> *Signal Triumph of Mr Monck Mason's* FLYING MACHINE!!!!

Poe had even placed the gothic English novelist Harrison Ainsworth on board as a reporter – and had carefully copied an authentic description of the flight of the balloon in Germany. A mob besieged the offices of the *Sun*, waiting for the following edition of the newspaper – and when the hoax was discovered, Poe's name was known again in New York in its ambiguous way.

The money for the article allowed Poe to send for his wife's mother and their tortoiseshell cat Caterina. For the sake of Virginia's precarious health, they went to live first at a farm and then at the old Brennan place on the outskirts of the city along the Bloomingdale Road. Poe was writing more of his intense short tales about his fears and selling them to the Philadelphia magazines such as *Godey's Lady's Book*. They were not his best work, but good enough: a story of detection called 'Thou Art The Man', in which the putrid corpse of the victim was made to spring out of a case of Margaux and confront his murderer: – 'The Oblong Box', which naturally turned out to hold the lovely young wife of an artist, driven frantic with grief, who refused to abandon her: – and 'The Premature Burial', which rightly ended with the hero giving up his *grim legion of sepulchral terrors which must sleep, or they will devour us – they must be suffered to slumber, or we perish.*

Although Poe was still dogged by poverty – and the mess of petty troubles that arose from that one trouble of poverty – he had time to play the hermit in earnest, see not a soul outside his family, and brood over two extraordinary poems, 'Dreamland' and the final version of 'The Raven', which took four years to complete. In the first poem, Poe revealed his true genius – his creation of a musical language which seemed to chime into every dreamer's perception of another world. He had the verbal gifts to sound out the mass fantasies of the unreal and the hereafter.

> *By a route obscure and lonely,*
> *Haunted by ill angels only,*
> *Where an Eidolon, named* NIGHT,
> *On a black throne reigns upright,*
> *I have reached these lands but newly*
> *From an ultimate dim Thule –*
> *From a wild weird clime that lieth, sublime,*
> *Out of* SPACE *– out of* TIME . . .

As for 'The Raven', its publication in the New York *Mirror* led to Poe's greatest popular success, even greater than that of 'The Gold Bug'. He had written the poem 'for the express purpose of running', and it ran all over the United States, so that 'the bird beat the bug, though, all hollow.' In his long essay, 'The Rationale of Verse', he explained the carefully-wrought arrangement of the repetitions and monotone of the piece; but this was a rational attempt to explain away the hypnotic power of his subconscious fears, translated through the hero's question to the black bird:

> '*Tell this soul with sorrow laden if, within the distant Aidenn,*
> *It shall clasp a sainted maiden whom the angels name Lenore –*

> *Clasp a rare and radiant maiden whom the angels name Lenore.'*
> *Quoth the Raven, 'Nevermore.'*

The truth was, the ungodly Poe had a terror that Virginia might die forever without the hope of a future meeting of souls.

To keep some food in the mouths of his little family, Poe had to work as an assistant editor on the *Mirror*, then later become one of the three editors and proprietors of the *Broadway Journal*. The cycle of his working – bursts of energy interspersed with bouts of lethargy – was interrupted by the daily routine demanded by the office. He was on his best behaviour at the *Mirror*, but he declined from grace as his power grew over the *Broadway Journal*.

His sporadic nature made journalism difficult for him. In one revealing letter, which he sent to James Russell Lowell, he showed that he knew his preferred habits well:

> I am excessively slothful, and wonderfully industrious – by fits. There are epochs when any kind of mental exercise is torture, and when nothing yields me pleasure but solitary communion with the 'mountains and the woods' – the 'altars' of Byron. I have thus rambled and dreamed away whole months, and awake, at last, to a sort of mania for composition. Then I scribble all day, and read all night, so long as the disease endures . . . I am *not* ambitious – unless negatively. I, now and then, feel stirred up to excel a fool, merely because I hate to let a fool imagine that he may excel me. Beyond this I feel nothing of ambition. I really perceive that vanity about which most men prate – the vanity of the human or temporal life. I live continually in a reverie of the future. I have no faith in human perfectability. I think that human exertion will have no appreciable effect upon humanity.

Yet that was the truth of only one side of his character – the philosophy of his solitude. With his duties on the *Broadway Journal* taking him daily to his desk there, he could no longer afford the time to walk the five miles each way from the Brennan house. So he moved Virginia and Maria Clemm and the cat down to Lower Broadway, then later to Amity Street in the district that we now call Greenwich Village. He became sociable again as he had been in Richmond. He was the drama critic of the *Journal*, so that he was frequently at the theater and at literary salons, particularly one in Waverly Place run by the formidable Anna C. Lynch. There many of the leading literary ladies met, including the portentous Margaret Fuller, Mrs Anna Cora Mowatt who wrote a play called *Fashion* – and the coy Mrs Frances Sargent Osgood, whose husband painted the portrait of Poe that hangs in the New York Historical Society.

Poe's Southern manners and mesmeric eyes – and the success of 'The Raven' – made him a darling of the literary ladies, whose flattery aroused his slumbering vanity, and whose intrigues were to destroy his smudged reputation. He was too gallant and too susceptible. He connived at his own downfall, even if he did not provoke it through 'The Imp of the Perverse', which he wrote at this time.

He particularly courted the rising star of English poetry, Elizabeth Barrett. To her, he dedicated *The Raven – and Other Poems*, which he sent to her with a new edition of his *Tales*; both books were published on the strength of his growing reputation. Miss Barrett was shrewd about her fresh admirer, commenting that his criticism of her poems was excessive, as if each paragraph had been written alternately by a friend and a foe, each stark mad with love or hate. As for the *Tales*, she saw his genius in making *horrible improbabilities seem near and familiar.*

That was his success in his most gruesome tale, 'The Facts in the Case of M. Valdemar'. It seemed to be a progressive and scientific story to a time which believed in mesmerism and galvanism as much as we now believe in telepathy and electric shock treatment. In the tale, a hypnotist kept a man on the point of dying in a trance for seven months, then ended the trance with the corpse ejaculating 'dead! dead!' while its whole frame shrank – crumbled – absolutely *rotted* away beneath his hands. Both in Paris and London, this story was held to be a literal account – Poe's most horrible hoax.

Its companion piece, 'Mesmeric Revelation', was more ethereal. The subject claimed that his trance revealed his death and ultimate life – he sleep-walked among the insubstantial angels – and never woke, ending his description of his other world *from out the region of the shadows*, which always spoke to Poe in the familiar accents of many thousand departed friends.

In the *Broadway Journal*, however, Poe seemed determined to attract the assaults of many thousand present enemies. He unfairly accused the rising Longfellow of the *moral taint* of plagiarism. For Poe to attack anyone for plagiarism after his textbook on sea-shells – or for a moral taint after his own reputation – was a form of suicide. Longfellow might forgive him, wisely remarking that Poe's savagery came from the irritation of a sensitive nature, chafed by his indefinite sense of wrong. But the hosts of minor *literati* in Boston and New York neither forgave nor forgot, particularly as Poe began a series of self-destructive acts that placed him in their jaws and at their pen-points.

If Poe was not being driven by his Imp of the Perverse, he was being goaded by his Angel of the Odd. During the hot summer of 1845, he seemed to have reached the summit of his power. Annoyed by Poe's egotism and vagaries, one of his fellow proprietors walked out of the *Broadway Journal*, accusing Poe of being a characterless character. The other proprietor soon sold out his share to Poe for a promissory note for fifty dollars, guaranteed by Horace Greeley. Thus Poe now owned a journal, although it was far from his desire – a heavyweight and occasional *Penn. Magazine* or *Stylus*.

Yet this expansion of power was fatal to Poe. As a critic, he often mistook – in his friend Lowell's words – a phial of prussic acid for his inkstand. As a proprietor, he printed and replied to the coy love-poems addressed to him by Mrs Osgood and some of her literary rivals, notably a Mrs Ellet, who had little looks and less quality. In this way, Poe sowed the dragon's teeth and added the compost for them to feast upon.

He was more penniless than ever – what money he made went into his ailing journal, which did not secure enough advertising to pay its costs. He might be able to publish the young Walt Whitman's 'Art Singing and Heart Singing'; but he confessed to a friend, *the Devil himself was never so poor*. Virginia was again critically ill, and he took to drinking too much in his despair, provoking more scandals than in Philadelphia because he was now in the public eye. His Southern friend, the poet Dr Chivers, met him one day as drunk as an Indian, boasting of his love affair with Mrs Osgood and threatening to assault a rival editor. Chivers took him home to his Broadway apartment, where he collapsed totally, while Maria Clemm told the good doctor that her son-in-law was deranged because Virginia could not live long.

Poe had been warned by another Southerner, the writer William Gilmore Simms, not to make any false steps at this crucial point in his literary career, when a single leading mistake might be fatal in its consequences. 'Remain in obscurity for a while,' Simms begged him. 'You have a young wife – I am told a suffering and an interesting one – let me entreat you to cherish her, and to cast away those pleasures which are not worthy of your mind, and to trample those temptations under foot, which degrade your person, and make it familiar to the mouth of vulgar jest . . . Do not suppose yourself abandoned by the worthy and honourable among your friends. They will be glad to give you welcome *if you will suffer them* . . .'

Yet Poe was driven to make three fatal errors, one after the other. Firstly, he went to Boston to deliver a lecture at the famous Lyceum. He usually spoke like the actor he was – by one account, his head was like a statue of Discrimination, his accent like a knife through water, his style pampering to the ear. Yet he decided to play a trick on the Bostonians and to read to his distinguished audience the boyish 'Al-Aaraaf' instead of a new poem – and then to declare that it was all the Frogpond of the North deserved! The prank naturally enraged the whole of that city.

He continued his folly by setting every tongue in New York against him because of his indiscretions and his petty vengeances. His pursuit of the flirtatious Mrs Osgood became more than an exchange of overwrought notes and poems – it became a rivalry for the affections of Mrs Ellet. Virginia knew about the gossip and read aloud to visitors the ladies' love-letters, sent privately to her husband. This provoked the descent of Anna Lynch and Margaret Fuller on the Poe household, the return of the love-letters, open scandal and threatened assault, intrigue and backbiting, until Poe seemed to be a worse philanderer than ever, even though his affairs of the heart reached no further than a look or a manuscript.

Worse still, Poe further alienated his chosen enemy, Rufus Griswold, who was also attracted to Mrs Osgood. Although Poe knew that Griswold had told abominable lies about him round New York, the two men officially patched up their quarrel out of mutual self-interest, and Griswold even contributed fifty dollars to the dying *Broadway Journal*, which finally folded in January, 1846. Yet Griswold was dissembling, waiting to destroy through forgery and lying the only genius he could call his friend.

Poe's search for distraction, his provocation of scandal, were a desperate flight from the demands of his wife with her terminal illness. He shook off the poison pens of New York and took Virginia and her mother to a refuge in Turtle Bay, then on to a cottage in Fordham of exquisite simplicity – the kitchen floor as white as wheat flour, the lack of furniture a virtue in the clean and charming rooms. There Poe plotted his final vengeance against his imagined enemies, for his sense of persecution was becoming a mania. He spoke to a librarian friend of a conspiracy among the other authors of America to belittle his genius and smother his work. In retaliation, he wrote for *Godey's Lady's Book* a scandalous series on the New York *literati*, savaging some of the men and overpraising the few women whom he admired.

This third sin was unpardonable. Only one of the injured writers lashed back, a certain Thomas Dunn English, who raked up every old scandal about Poe and also accused him of dishonesty and forgery. Poe sued him and the *Mirror* for libel, but his case dragged on – as did the foul publicity. Yet out in Fordham in that last year with his dying wife, whose disease was changing Poe's passion for her into an obsessive caring, all was at precarious peace in a waiting for the end. Virginia even sent her husband a Valentine, with the first letter of each line making up his name:

>   *Ever with thee I wish to roam –*
>   *Dearest my life is thine.*
>   *Give me a cottage for my home*
>   *And a rich old cypress vine,*
>   *Removed from the world with its sin and care*
>   *And the tattling of many tongues.*
>   *Love alone shall guide us when we are there –*
>   *Love shall heal my weakened lungs;*

And Oh, the tranquil hours we'll spend,
Never wishing that others may see!
Perfect ease we'll enjoy, without thinking to lend
Ourselves to the world and its glee –
Ever peaceful and blissful we'll be.

It was not poetry, but it was an enfolding love like Poe's lost love from Frances Valentine when he was a boy. Yet he could not keep Virginia alive through the long cold winter of 1846, although he and her mother held her hands and feet to keep them warm, as she lay on a straw mattress under the weight of his old West Point greatcoat and of Caterina, the tortoiseshell cat. 'He was noble, generous, affectionate, and most *amiable* (Dr Griswold's assertion notwithstanding),' Maria Clemm complained after the poet's death. 'Poor poor Eddie, it matters little to *him* now, but it almost breaks *my* heart to hear him spoken of so unkindly and *untrue*.'

In extremis, a brief and patronizing mercy came from the mob of New York scribblers, who put out an appeal for the Poes and collected sixty dollars for their use. The money provided some food and heat for the Fordham cottage, but too late to save Virginia, who died at the end of January. 'At death,' Poe had written to Lowell, 'the worm is the butterfly.' So the spirit of Virginia fluttered away at last – and Poe went into delirium.

The charitable lady, Mrs Shew, who nursed him through his brain fever, found a strangeness about his head. She thought that he must have a brain lesion, which produced a form of insanity from a drop of alcohol or opium. Other diagnosticians have suggested everything from a weak heart to diabetes. Mrs Shew noticed that, although his heart beat was irregular and his pulse intermittent, yet he had borne hunger and cold and extreme suffering of mind and body in order that he might supply food and medicine for Virginia. In Mrs Shew's opinion, there had to be some physical imbalance to explain his alternate saintliness and sprees – no nightmare of the soul – no desperate oscillation between agony and oblivion – just a warp under the skull or the ribs – as simple as that!

Pons visited the New York places where the Poes had stayed, and found – a cryptogram in Greek capitals, *Ypsilon Gamma*, over a black door in Amity Street, hinting at some mysterious fraternity or conspiracy of the *literati* against their chosen foe – the sagging banners round the United Nations Plaza, surrounded by glass towers and concrete walkways imprisoning the last few daffodils left in that desolate monument to the war of stale words – a Puerto Rican tarmac playground off Amsterdam Avenue, where lean brown youths raged behind wire netting at the opposite Louis B. Brandeis High School – and finally, Poe Park at Fordham – and his own brain fever.

What did he see on that hot day of nervous-bright cloud, but row on row of old Jews sitting on benches off the concrete paths that crossed the kidney-bean of brown grass in front of Poe's cottage, now removed to this ghetto of the ageing as if its white walls were the guiding ghost in Poe's vision of the awakening dead in 'The Premature Burial':

> I looked; and the unseen figure, which still grasped me by the wrist, had caused to be thrown open the graves of all mankind; and from each issued the faint phosphoric radiance of decay; so that I could see into the innermost recesses, and there view the shrouded bodies in their sad and solemn slumbers with the worm. But alas! the real sleepers were fewer, by many millions, than those who slumbered not at all; and there was a feeble struggling; and there was a general and sad unrest; and from out the depths of the countless pits there came a melancholy rustling from the garments of the buried. And of those who seemed tranquilly to repose, I saw that a vast number had changed, in a greater or less degree, the rigid and uneasy position in which they had originally been entombed. And the voice again said to me as I gazed:
>
> 'Is it not – oh! is it *not* a pitiful sight?' But, before I could find words to reply, the figure had ceased to grasp my wrist, the phosphoric lights expired, and the graves were closed with a sudden violence, while from out of them rose a tumult of despairing cries, saying again: 'Is it not – O, God! is it *not* a very pitiful sight?'

It was a very pitiful sight that Pons saw in Poe Park – the surviving old men in felt hats playing checkers, the remaining old ladies nodding and noddling at their chat – the hospital standing as their terminal on the square, to which they would soon be carted from their waiting-rooms in the high tenement apartments about – a deserted bandstand playing no heavenly music nor even a fiddle tune – and an undertaker's sign, declaring: THE FAMILY SHOULD GET TOGETHER TO DECIDE HOW YOU ARE BURIED.

Yet more pitiful to Pons was to know that these were the sleepers, fewer by many millions than those who were feebly struggling in general and sad unrest in the mass graves of the holocaust. From out the depths of the countless death-pits, a melancholy rustling seemed to sound in Pons's inner ear. It might have been a thousand plagues of locusts rubbing their dry wings and legs together. And the myriad scrapings seemed to make the sleepers on earth shift from the rigid and uneasy position of their indifference. If they would only listen, they would hear the tumult of the despairing cries of the murdered six million: 'Is it not – O, God! it is *not* a very pitiful sight?'

Pons had not seen it. He had escaped it. Now he was seeing some of those who had seen it and were marked by it until their dying days. He had not the heart to visit Poe's cottage, which was an irrelevance beside the thousands of old people expecting a decent human sort of death and trying to forget the obscene oblivion inflicted on the host of their kind.

Boing-boing, boing-boing, an ambulance passed wailing by, as it carried one of Pons's people to his terminal bed. It was like the dirge of 'The Raven', in which one of Poe's friends had found *the continuity of one unvaried emotion . . . liable to topple over into some delirium or an abyss of melancholy.* After visiting Poe Park, Pons knew that he would nevermore be able to forget the insane evil of the holocaust he had hardly avoided. Sadly, he said to himself, 'I am a Jew.'

Dupin did not scream as I had hoped. He started back at my rush into his room, then he set his face in a cold wrath, while I intoned:

'Is it not – oh! it is *not* a pitiful sight?'

'Take off that rubber mask, Ernest,' he ordered. 'Don't play the fool with me!'

'It's May Day,' I said, 'which is All Fools' Day to me.' I doffed my plague-mask – sold as Oscar the Unspeakable in the novelty store down the street. 'It's the day of the red jester!'

'Ordinarily I would encourage you to burlesque your fears – ' Dupin's anger at me, if he was not disturbed by something else, showed in a new gesture. He pulled at his finger-knuckles until each popped in turn like a firing-squad out of practice. 'But I have just been reading – before your recent intrusion – the first decent piece you have ever written or spoken about the fate of your people – and immediately, you throw it all away, and act like a buffoon – '

'Like Poe, you mean. I am exorcising his presence by playing out his cruder jokes – '

'Don't add insincerity to your vulgarity, Ernest! You're trying to *laugh off* what you declared had to be now your *one unvaried emotion* – the memory of the holocaust, of Rosa, of your dead family – '

'I can't *live* that way,' I declared. 'Even Poe ended "The Premature Burial" by making his hero give up his bugaboos.'

'But you were being human and sympathetic at last! Please don't give that up! Your account of Virginia's death was even romantic – her spirit fluttered away! I hate to say it, but for the first time I detected a note of compassion in you for poor Eddie Poe. When even his New York enemies showed mercy, so did you.'

Here Dupin strangely put his hands on my shoulders and almost pushed me back to sit on the couch.

'Ernest, develop that compassion! Try and understand and forgive Poe's deep flaws – his self-importance – his venom and his vagaries. *Because then you will understand and forgive your own!* Believe me.'

'I – I will try – ' I whispered. I felt my heart beat unsteadily, as if it were as irregular as Poe's. What was this curious metamorphosis?

'The secret of self is this – however wicked I AM – '

Was Dupin admitting his wickedness to me – or was he using the universal Ego?

'If I say, Ernest, I forgive you – then I say – I forgive myself also. Be gentle with others, then with yourself! Listen to me!'

Under the stare of Dupin's eyes, which his lenses had magnified into burning glasses, I had closed my own, as if he were putting me into a mesmeric trance. I lay back, letting his hands on my shoulders guide me into a position of rest.

'We all do wrong. We all do not understand. If we work on

understanding *one* other person – as a man tries to understand his wife in a long marriage and usually fails to – then we may begin to understand ourselves a little – the absurd, the partial, the trivial, the all-important person that is I! Your Poe did not destroy himself by his writing or even his critical attacks on others, but by his personal weaknesses – the wildness and the drinks and literary love affairs. Yet as he said, these were faults of the insanity which Virginia's illness caused in him – not the other way round. *There is usually a good reason for all our crimes and madnesses.* Believe that! Forgive that in others – then in yourself!'

As I lay back listening to this sermon with my eyes closed, I thought I could detect hysteria in Dupin's plea to me. Was he excusing himself? Was he, after all, in a conspiracy with my lawyer about my will, *which I had signed last week*, making Dupin the sole executor of my estate of half a million dollars and of my Poe collection? Did he not want me to *absolve* him, before he did away with me – to pardon him before he buried me prematurely and got his hands on my money – *what every Gentile wanted to do with every Jew*!!

While my mind was a maelstrom of such thoughts, my rational faculties kept my body rigid, as if in a trance. Then the imp of the perverse whispered to me, and – my hands flew to my throat – I choked and gasped, 'My heart – ' My throat rattled and my head fell to the side, while my eyes stared whitely – my lips hung slack and mute.

Dupin lifted his hands off my shoulders at last and stood upright, looking down at my still form. His back was to the window, leaving his face obscure, but – I swear I saw him smile – I swear I saw it! He walked quickly over to the telephone and dialled a number and spoke in French, a language I can understand – and not forgive!

'*Enfin,*' he said into the receiver, '*j'ai de la chance. Je peux toucher un gros boulot dans quelques mois, si nos amis puissent attendre un peu plus. Tu penses – ?*'

As he was listening for the answer, I rose unseen behind him, crept across the carpet, and put my hand over his mouth to stop his scream. He bit me, instead.

'Yah!' I cried with justification.

'You!' he shouted with anger, slamming down the telephone receiver. 'You dare!'

'Monster!' I shrieked, when I was not licking my infected hand. 'You know! You want to steal my fortune! You want to kill me!'

'Idiot – out! Get out of here! Get out of my life!'

He began beating at my chest, thrusting me toward the door, quite out of control in a French sort of a way. I had to embrace him in my long arms and hold him in a human straitjacket until he quite calmed down.

'You fool with your stupid tricks! To try to take *me* in, Charles Dupin! I thought – and you were playing your schoolboy jokes again!'

'More than that,' I said. 'I was showing up your plot. Whose *gros boulot*, may I ask? Whose fortune were you hoping to get soon to solve the financial problems of Comble, Dupin and Cie? Answer me that!'

He stepped away from me as if I had the plague. His voice was icy with disdain.

'My conversation on the telephone had nothing to do with you at all. I told you before that I had problems, which I would *not* ask you about. I now know how to solve them, *as you overheard*. When you rushed into my office with your silly mask on – surprise, surprise! – you stopped me from making the important call you have just spied upon.'

'Oh no, Dupin! You telephoned because you thought I was dead – because you knew the contents of my will, that I had made you my *sole executor* – '

'If you really think that,' Dupin said with contempt, 'change your will. Find somebody else you can trust – or is there nobody? Aren't you so damned unreasonable that I am the last person who will put up with you?'

I quite lost my breath at his audacity. How could he counter so fast, when I had exposed him for the villain he truly was? *Or was not!* I did not *know* he was talking of my fortune or of my will. He might have been talking of another stroke of luck. I had rushed into his room unannounced. His explanation was *reasonable* – and yet –

'Why did you not call the hospital *first* – or at least the undertakers?' It was a shrewd question. 'Were you not worried about me? I was mortally ill – dead, perhaps – '

Here Dupin began to laugh with an extraordinary snicker of superiority.

'I knew you were shamming,' he said. 'It might have been a self-induced fainting spell – but nothing to worry about. A slap on your cheek would have revived you. But I thought I'd take the opportunity to get on with some *serious* business. You have noticed, I suppose, that I am a bit nervous – I do have something on my mind, the problem with the wine company – '

Yes, Dupin was rational, too too rational. The conspiracy I had discovered by my ruse had made me seem irrational. I felt persecuted just like Poe did among the intellectuals of New York, when this man had always been trying to help me in his mercy.

'Oh, Dupin – ' I said, 'please forgive me. I have been disturbed too – more than I ever have been. To admit to the holocaust, to feel that I am a Jew too – Dupin, I am truly sorry.'

'That may well be,' Dupin said coldly. 'I could see his mercy was going to be strained without any of the gentle dew from heaven. 'But I am warning you, Ernest. Never play any of your tricks on me again. I know they're *your* childishness, not Poe's. And what is more – next time, *I shall retaliate in kind*! Or else I'll throw you out for good.' He pointed to the door. 'Now leave, and do Poe's death. And let me get on with my *important* business.'

9

Death is the Final Conspiracy

> My life has been *whim* – impulse – passion – a longing for solitude – a scorn of all things present, in an earnest desire for the future.
>
> EDGAR ALLAN POE

Poe's life ran to its end in three cycles of recovery, excitement, confusion and collapse. He knew his own weaknesses well enough. He had suffered so much hardship and denial that the attention of society easily went to his head. He spoke regretfully of the few men of genius who had not used up their energy, when they were young, in *living too fast* – thus were bound in middle age to make up for that deprivation. 'The earnest longing for artificial excitement, which, unhappily, has characterized too many eminent men, may thus be regarded as a psychal want, or necessity – an effort to regain the lost – '

When Mrs Shew and Maria Clemm were nursing him back to some sort of health in the Fordham cottage after Virginia's death, Poe had his only stroke of luck. He collected the largest sum of his life from his libel suit against the *Mirror* – $225 and costs. This money gave him the breathing and brooding space he needed to try to write the major works of his self-awareness and intellect. The first was his analysis of his relationship with love and death, the second was his solution to the riddle of the universe.

His poem 'Ulalume' is cast in the form of a dialogue between him and his Psyche as they wander the no-man's-land on the edge of his subconscious:

> *It was down by the dark tarn of Auber,*
> *In the ghoul-haunted woodland of Weir.*

His heart is volcanic, his talk serious, his memory palsied and treacherous, as he tries to come to terms with his need to love romantically a woman – *any* sympathetic woman – and yet remain constant to the beloved dead, particularly Virginia. He leads his gloomy Psyche towards the luminous stars of the Lion with their crystalline and Sibylline splendour; but he is stopped by the door of the tomb of his lost Ulalume. And he knows that the recurrence of passion which he craves is finally doomed by the intense memory of his past love. Virginia herself had been buried in a borrowed grave-plot under the cypresses below Poe's usual walk over the High Bridge near Fordham – and he could not forget her.

> *Then my heart it grew ashen and sober*
> *As the leaves that were crisped and sere –*
> *As the leaves that were withering and sere,*
> *And I cried: 'It was surely October*
> *On this very night of last year*
> *That I journeyed – I journeyed down here –*
> *That I brought a dread burden down here –*
> *On this night of all nights in the year,*
> *Ah, what demon has tempted me here?*
> *Well I know, now, this dim lake of Auber –*
> *This misty mid region of Weir –*
> *Well I know, now, this dark tarn of Auber,*
> *This ghoul-haunted woodland of Weir.*

Even the peevish sniping of such recent critics as Aldous Huxley at the vulgarity of 'Ulalume' with its lines that profess too much their musicality, cannot stop its mesmeric metres from sounding through the centuries to the hidden chords of our fears about love and death. If its meaning is obscure, it still speaks to us in the meaning we choose to give it. As Poe wrote himself, if it was worth explanation, it should explain itself. His originality as a poet was what he claimed it to be – ringing the changes on the slight varieties of metre and stanza to produce a musical beauty – something which he did most famously in his technical demonstration of his expertise, 'The Bells'.

The theme of that trivial and overrational declamation piece was suggested to him by Mrs Shew, who had begun to attract him through his gratitude. It was dangerous for a woman to do a favour for Edgar Poe. It often brought out his undying love, because he could transfer his ideal of Woman from one person to another, just as Ligeia had changed bodies, while remaining the same in spirit.

His solution to the problem of the universe was read to the uncomprehending Maria Clemm, who cared for his feverish enthusiasm while he was writing his philosophical prose-poem 'Eureka', and listened patiently to his brilliant and erratic theories. Like many Southerners, Poe believed in intellect rather than education, intuition rather than research, and the inspired amateur rather than the painstaking professional. So he induced and deduced his own solution to the absolute, because he found it intolerable that anything should be incomprehensible to his mind.

'My whole nature,' he declared, 'revolts at the idea that there is any Being in the Universe superior to *myself.*' So his Ego dethroned God and decided that his works came out of chaos and finally returned to chaos – this was their unity. 'Because Nothing was, therefore All Things are.' Since his own mind was limited, the Universe must also be limited. And because he had discovered the truth of the cosmos, 'Eureka' would revolutionize the mind of science. 'I say this calmly,' he stated in his confidence as a new Renaissance master of all knowledge, ' – but I say it.'

It was published without much success – and heard at Poe's occasional lectures in lyceums and taverns. The small audiences were universally mystified at its magnificent nonsense. If anything redeemed this long metaphysical treatise, it was Poe's dedication of it, not only to Alexander von Humbolt, but also:

> To the few who love me and whom I love – to those who feel rather than to those who think – to the dreamers and those who put their faith in dreams as in the only realities – I offer this Book of Truths, not in its character of Truth-Teller, but for the Beauty that abounds in its Truth; constituting it true . . .

In human love, in human intellect, beauty and truth lay apart from logic and fact. As Mrs Shew wisely began to remove herself from Poe's growing dependence on her, his devotion centred itself on Maria Clemm. He wore a gold ring, made up from her and Virginia's wedding rings entwined. And he wrote to her one of the more generous poems in the English language – its sincerity removing all mockery of its impossible subject, 'To My Mother'. The sonnet ended:

> My mother – my own mother, who died early,
>   Was but the mother of myself; but you
>   Are mother to the one I loved so dearly,
>   And thus are dearer than the mother I knew
>   By that infinity with which my wife
>   Was dearer to my soul than its soul-life.

Maria Clemm continued to mother him, while he worked on his metaphysics and tried to revive his project for his own *Stylus* magazine. The ambitious literary ladies such as the fat Mrs Lewis, who came out to Fordham seeking Poe's public praise of their poetry, were made by Mrs Clemm to pay in advance for his puffs, which she undertook to pull from his unwilling pen.

Yet this occasional flattery did not persuade him out of his venom against his enemies, real and imagined. After his friend Lowell had fairly called him three-fifths genius and two-fifths sheer fudge, Poe lashed at Lowell as a ranting abolitionist who deserved a good beating – and put an attack on him in the *Southern Literary Messenger*. His delusions of grandeur and wafer-thin skin against criticism had made him full of nervous aggression. He tried to defend these defects in his nature as part of his stock in trade, saying, *The man who is not irritable is no poet*. But the truth was that he was trying to justify his lack of control and excuse his excesses.

Mrs Shew fended him off by first making him her interior decorator, so that he might observe her happy and wealthy home – and then treating him as the necessary sacrifice for a new-found sense of religious duty. She would not allow him to visit her any more, despite his appeals and comparison of her to the lost 'Helen' of his youth, Mrs Stanard.

'My *heart* has never *wronged you*. I place you in *my esteem* in all *solemnity* beside the friend of my boyhood, the mother of my school fellow . . . as the truest, tenderest, of this world's most womanly souls, and an angel to my forlorn and darkened nature, I will not say "lost soul" again, for your sake. I will try to overcome my grief for the sake of your unselfish care of me in the past, and in life or death, I am ever yours gratefully and devotedly . . .'

Poe's vision of 'Helen', the ideal mature woman of his youth, had a third transmigration of souls. This last time, the woman was actually called Helen – a widow, six years older than Poe, but with the same birth date – Mrs Sarah Helen Power Whitman. She was the leading literary figure in Providence, Rhode Island, a poetess and priestess of the new vogue of spiritualism, who wore floating scarves and a miniature coffin round her neck, and who lived with her formidable mother and sister in a house of many drapes and few violet lights. She quietened her nerves and induced her dreamings by the use of a handkerchief soaked in ether. She actually began the affair by writing Poe a public Valentine, which asked the grim and ghastly Raven to visit and take her to some lofty eyrie. Poe decided to do that, when he had the time and money to spare.

His income now came chiefly from lecturing on 'Eureka' or declaiming 'The Raven'. After one successful lecture in Lowell, Massachusetts, he met the romantic love of his last years, Mrs Nancy Locke Heywood Richmond, the 'Annie' of his poem. In 'Landor's Cottage', he wrote of the effect she had on him at their first meeting – of her perfection of natural grace, of her enthusiasm and unworldliness and spiritual grey eyes. She was happily married, but she responded to Poe's need for sympathy and asexual love, procuring letters of adoration from him which still survive. She was his fair wild star, the one which made Agathos weep: 'Its brilliant flowers *are* the dearest of all unfulfilled dreams, and its raging volcanoes *are* the passions of the most turbulent and unhallowed of hearts.'

To 'Annie's' younger sister, Poe seemed the ultimate poet, 'so perfectly proportioned, and crowned with such a noble head, so regally carried, that, to my girlish apprehension, he gave the impression of commanding stature. Those clear sad eyes seemed to look from an eminence, rather than from the ordinary level of humanity, while his conversational tone was so low and deep, that one could easily fancy it borne to the ear from some distant height.'

In his overwrought moods, Poe liked the vision of himself as the damned soul in torment upon earth. When he travelled to Richmond to gather a Virginian subscription list for the *Stylus*, he went on a three weeks' social round of welcoming homes and taverns. The editor of the *Southern Literary Messenger*, perhaps in envy of his predecessor's fame, claimed that Poe was horribly drunk, expounding 'Eureka' every night to the audiences in the bar rooms, and telling them that he was an *âme perdue*, the victim of pre-ordained damnation. Other witnesses spoke of his gentleness, courtesy and genius. Somewhere between these extremes of behaviour lay the truth of Poe's return to Richmond.

At last, he now had the time and money to meet his predestined love in Providence – the third Helen. Wishing to be convinced, he persuaded himself that it was love at first sight. According to his letters to her, his love was more in his prose and his mind's eye than in his heart and his look:

> As you entered the room, pale, timid, hesitating, and evidently oppressed at heart; as your eyes rested appealingly, for one brief moment, upon mine, I felt, for the first time in my life, and tremblingly acknowledged, the existence of spiritual influences altogether out of the reach of the reason. I saw that you were *Helen – my* Helen – the Helen of a thousand dreams – she whose visionary lips had so often lingered upon my own in the divine trance of passion – she whom the great Giver of all Good had preordained to be mine – mine only – if not now, alas! then at least hereafter and *forever*, in the Heavens. – You spoke falteringly and seemed scarcely conscious of what you said. I heard no words – only the soft voice, more familiar to me than my own, and more melodious than the songs of the angels. Your hand rested within mine, and my whole soul shook with a tremulous ecstasy . . .

What Poe was describing was the intensity of his passion for his ideal unearthly woman, not a creature of flesh and blood called Helen Whitman. Poe was not only in love with love – he was in love with self-love, his conceit of himself as the turbulent poet, tortured by sentiment, and able to express all on a page. He proposed to his Helen of a thousand dreams immediately in a cemetery. She hesitated, but did not refuse him. She believed in her capacity for romantic passion just as much as she disapproved of the scandals which plagued his personal reputation. She made him swear to give up drink as well as other literary ladies. He agreed, persuading himself of the lie that he had met the first true love of his life.

When Poe had left Helen Whitman, he remembered Mrs 'Annie' Richmond, whom he loved as a woman rather than as an ethereal vision of a lost Helen. He began writing love letters to both women simultaneously and plunged into the heady drama of a torn heart and an impossible choice. After a long, hideous night of despair in Boston, he bought two ounces of laudanum and took one, determined to kill himself, childishly wanting his 'Annie' to come to him on his bed of death. Instead, he became delirious and his stomach rejected the fatal dose.

After this suicide attempt, he went back to Providence, where he behaved so wildly that Helen Whitman refused his proposal among the classic columns of the Atheneum. He drank himself into delirium and collapsed. A local Good Samaritan looked after him, had his daguerrotype taken, and packed him home to Fordham to recuperate. From there, he begged 'Annie' to visit him:

> Ah beloved Annie, IS IT NOT POSSIBLE? I am so *ill* – so terribly, hopelessly ill in body and mind, that I feel I CANNOT live, unless I can feel your sweet, gentle, loving hand pressed upon my forehead – oh my *pure, virtuous, generous, beautiful, beautiful sister* Annie! – is it not POSSIBLE for you to come – if only for one little week? – until I subdue this fearful agitation, which if continued, will either destroy my life or, drive me hopelessly mad – Farewell – here and hereafter –
>
> *forever your own*
> Eddy –

It is a letter of anguish and self-pity and desperation, yet there is no sentimentality or hypocrisy in it, except perhaps Poe's appeal to 'Annie' as a *sister*. When he had recovered and had realized that Annie would not leave her home and husband for him, Poe once again returned to Providence to marry Helen Whitman and to secure her eight thousand dollars to back his *Stylus* and his ambition. He dangled literary power in front of her as well as his person and his genius. Although he knew that his poverty and his excesses might damn him in her eyes, he gilded his prospects and his hopes:

> Would it *not* be 'glorious', *darling*, to establish, in America, the sole unquestionable aristocracy – that of intellect – to secure its supremacy – to lead and to control it? All this I *can* do, Helen, and will – if you bid me – and aid me.

Helen Whitman's formidable mother put the possibility of her aid for the *Stylus* beyond Poe's reach. He was made to sign a document, which transferred with his consent all his prospective wife's money to her mother's control before he was allowed to sign for the banns to be read. Even these were delayed while family pressure mounted on Helen against the marriage. Reports of Poe's renewed drinking and his love affair with 'Annie' and others reached Providence. Despite Poe giving a successful lecture there to an audience of eighteen hundred people, Helen Whitman's mother managed to break off the marriage and reduced her daughter to silence, nostalgia and ether.

Poe's humiliation led to his revulsion from the gossip and slander of the *literati*. 'From this day forth,' he wrote, 'I shun the pestilential society of *literary women*. They are a heartless, unnatural, venomous, dishonourable *set*, with no guiding principle but inordinate self-esteem . . .' His paranoia, fantasy, melancholy and solitariness grew, while he wrote his last tales of revenge and fortune. 'Hop-Frog' dealt with a dwarf jester avenging an insult on his true love in a back-biting Court by persuading the King and five nobles to dress themselves up as orang-outangs, then hitching the chain that joined them to a chandelier and burning them alive in their grotesque hairy suits. 'Von Kempelen and His Discovery' showed a scientist achieving the old alchemist's dream of turning lead into gold – this would have made the rush to the Californian mines unnecessary, something which Poe also stated in his poem 'Eldorado'. He set that golden place in the dreamland of the soul, not beyond the Rockies.

> Over the Mountains
> Of the Moon,
> Down the Valley of the Shadow,
> Ride, boldly ride,
> The shade replied,
> If you seek for Eldorado!

Poe himself knew where his treasure lay. Referring to the Gold Rush and its temptation for poor authors, he said that what was valuable to a poet could not be bought.

Love, fame, the dominion of intellect, the consciousness of power, the thrilling sense of beauty, the free air of Heaven, exercise of body and mind, with the physical and moral health which result – these and such as these are really all that a poet cares for: – then answer me this – *why* should he go to California?

Why indeed? Poe was better off at Fordham with the one woman devoted to him, Maria Clemm, as he wrote his final major poems, 'For Annie' and the famous 'Annabel Lee'. The first of them dealt with his slow recovery from his suicide attempt in Boston, the city of his birth and attempted death.

> *Thank Heaven! the crisis –*
> *The danger is past,*
> *And the lingering illness*
> *Is over at last –*
> *And the fever called 'Living'*
> *Is conquered at last.*

In this torpor of recuperation, probably aided by occasional small doses of opium, he reverted to his obsession over his dead loves that no longer seemed able to transfer their spirits to women other than Mrs Richmond. He made his Annabel Lee a child – and the hero a child – in their kingdom by the sea. They loved with a love that was more than love, until a chill wind blew and death – *a kinsman of hers* – took her to her sepulchre. But their souls remained together and communed through the night, the stars and the moon in her tomb by the sounding sea.

Poe's last period of creative obscurity was threatened by the failure of most of the periodicals for which he wrote. No money was being sent to Fordham – and he again began collapsing from nervous debilitation. Even Maria Clemm sometimes despaired of nursing him through his depressive illnesses, writing on one occasion to 'Annie' Richmond: 'I thought he would die several times. God knows I wish we were both in our graves. It would, I am sure, be far better.'

Yet Poe resembled his heroines, always returning from the grave of his disappointed hopes and weak body. A potential young backer for *Stylus* appeared and sent Poe fifty dollars to raise a subscription list in the South. Poe proposed to set off for Richmond again – *and made the fatal error of his life and death!*

(*I have underlined this, Dupin, and I have intruded, so that you should know I am aware of making the same mistake – and am doing it out of the perverse power of self-destruction that first attracted me to Poe – and, indeed, may have unconsciously induced the Jews to settle so heavily in Germany, the country of their fate.*)

Poe's choice of his final destruction was from a presentiment or a perversity – he seems even to have asked the envious Rufus Griswold to become his literary executor and edit his collected works. He then made his way towards the South, drinking in Philadelphia and falling into paranoia there. He said there was a conspiracy against him; he had overheard two men on the train plotting to kill him. He apparently spent a night in prison for drunkenness, then went with a friend, the editor Sartain, to the Schuylkill River, beside which he had lived with Virginia.

Once there, he seemed ready to commit suicide by throwing himself off a height, until Sartain managed to lead him away. Poe spoke of the white figure which had appeared to him on the prison walls, before turning into the evil black bird of cholera. Then he calmed down and admitted that the whole thing was a delusion of his excited imagination, and Sartain sent him on to Richmond. He wrote of the disaster to Maria Clemm:

My *dear, dear* Mother, –
 I have been *so* ill – have had the cholera, or spasms quite as bad, and can now hardly hold the pen . . . It is no use to reason

with me *now*, I must die . . . I was never *really* insane, except on occasions where my heart was touched. I have been taken to prison once since I came here for getting drunk; but *then* I was not. It was about Virginia.

By this time, Maria Clemm also believed in the conspiracy that surrounded her nephew. She loved him too much to distinguish between fantasy and fact – *or she knew of a plot!* 'I fear everything,' she wrote to 'Annie' Richmond. 'Do you wonder that he has so little confidence in any one? Have we not suffered from the blackest treachery?'

(*Have we not, Dupin? Conspiracies do actually exist, you know! They are not all paranoia. Before psychiatry was invented to explain them away, they were called plots, betrayal or the blackest treachery.*)

Poe went on to Richmond, where he recovered his health and balance of mind. He wrote back to Maria Clemm that he had been totally deranged for ten days, imagining the most horrible calamities. 'All was hallucination, arising from an attack which I had never before experienced – an attack of *mania-à-potu*. May Heaven grant that it prove a warning to me for the rest of my days. If so, I shall not regret even the horrible unspeakable torments I have endured.'

(*So Poe agreed that all was hallucination, which I do not yet – and you know why, Dupin! – And you will know better why, when you finish this Chapter of my analysis, which I will complete despite your plots – and mail to you from Paris.*)

To return to the regenerate Poe in Richmond. He found himself among friends, a true celebrity in his home city, a literary lion and an attractive lecturer. He began to court his first love again, Mrs Sarah Elmira Royster Shelton, now a wealthy and religious widow with fifty thousand dollars, who lived in the shadow of St John's Church and his mother's grave. She listened to his suit and, after one of his sprees, induced him to join the Sons of Temperance. He was so ill, indeed, after this one drinking bout that the doctors told him that he would probably not survive another.

This summary shock – and the possibility of a rich marriage which might finance the *Stylus* – sobered him wonderfully. Although Elmira was as shrewd as Helen Whitman and placed her money beyond his control, she did intend to marry her long-lost suitor and wrote to Maria Clemm to advise her of this, stating that she felt her lover's aunt was someone whom to know was to love.

Poe was now triumphant in his boyhood city, which had begun to enjoy his fame. His courtesy and air of distinction, his pallor and beautiful diction, impressed Southern society, although many were afraid of his scornful mouth and nervous temperament. On his last evening there, he was elated about his great error. He showed a young admirer a letter from his friend Rufus Griswold, accepting the post of his literary executor and flattering him.

(*Dupin, would you refuse to be my executor when it is a question of an estate worth half-a-million dollars?*)

He seemed to be falling sick again of nerves and fever, as he took the night boat to Baltimore at the end of September. He was only forty years old, but already broken in mind and body. At the prospect of returning north through Baltimore and Philadelphia – the cities of his early poverty and humiliation – he relapsed into paranoia. In his last letter to Maria Clemm, he told her to write to him under the pseudonym of E. S. T. Grey. He then disappeared for several days, until he was found in Ryan's Fourth Ward polls in Baltimore, dressed in the clothes of a derelict, drunk and dying.

He lingered on at the Washington College Hospital for some days of delirium, then died on the Sunday morning of 7 October, 1849. During his last attack of mania, he had shouted 'Reynolds! Reynolds!', the name of the polar explorer whose adventures had inspired his tales of the maelstrom and of the shrouded figure of perfect snow whiteness, which had met Pym at his final going down – and now would meet Poe.

There is no certainty about the events of his last days. The Doctor Snodgrass who rescued him believed he had been 'cooped' – made drunk and dragged from polling place to polling place to vote repeatedly for the machine candidate in the election then being held in the city. Later, the doctor made a *tour de force* of his one claim to fame. He declared that he and the poet had been kidnapped *by the two mysterious men Poe had feared*, and then dragged from poll to poll until Snodgrass had recovered from his drugged state and Poe was moribund. Then the kidnappers, according to Snodgrass, had decided it was futile to try to make a dead man vote and had packed Poe's body off in a hired hack to the hospital.

(*Most biographers dismiss this theory of conspiracy by the chief witness – but why should I, Dupin, after my Baltimore experience? Tell me that!*)

Poe's body was put in a cheap coffin and buried at the old Westminster Church, where his grandfather was buried along with many of the other heroes of the American Revolution. It was then a gothic and stately church in a prosperous part of Baltimore. It is now a crumbling ruin in a black slum, while the old houses bear names on their doors weirder than Poe's Al-Aaraaf or his Israfel or his Mummy Allamistakeo – *La-Ilaha Illallahu* and *Muhammadar-Rasul-Ullah* and *As-Salamu-Alaikem*. The church now offers guided tours of its haunted tombs and catacombs – (*and do not tell me, Dupin, that conspirators did not strike me down there – and drug me – and kidnap me to your secret psychiatric clinic!*)

Ernest Albert Pons was ending his analysis of Edgar Allan Poe's life and death by visiting the Westminster churchyard. Only six or seven people had appeared at Poe's burial, and the whole ceremony had been gabbled through in three minutes before he was interred. The burial of his personal reputation had been achieved almost as quickly by Rufus Griswold, *his chosen literary executor and executioner!* Writing in the New York *Tribune*, the trusted Griswold had assassinated the genius who could no longer reply to his lies. Although seeming to praise Poe, Griswold had declared that few would be grieved by his death, that he was almost friendless, and that he was arrogant and envious, cynical and treacherous, morbid and ambitious. It was not an obituary, it was the murder of a corpse.

And what happened to Pons, standing by Poe's grave, at the hands of *his* Griswold – *his* trusted executor – *his* DUPIN and his minions?? Pons walked from Poe's official monument by the churchyard entrance to look for the real tomb at the back. He refused to enter the church, which advertised a *mass common grave* of a hundred regular soldiers from the revolutionary war! Nor did he elect to view the Poe-like mystery of the bell-tower, where four had hanged themselves upon its ropes – the Egyptian and the Roman tombs, where derelicts still huddled and froze to death – the recess where the ghost of the teen-age girl was seen to pray – or the withered flowers that never bloomed on the poet's mortal remains! He was standing by the small stone marker over the original grave, where Virginia and Maria Clemm were also laid to rest in the end – when he was knocked and shocked – jumped and thumped – mugged, slugged, thugged, and drugged by *unknown and unseen assailants* – *In the pay of whom? Do you not know, Dupin? Who else knew Pons had to be in that graveyard about that time? Only you, Dupin – His executor!!!*

When Pons woke to the light of some future day – dull and heavy in the head – whom did he see by his bed but Dupin, wearing his concern like a surgical mask over his treachery. Why should their conversation be described except for one thing – *others* will know of it! That they will!

'My poor Ernest,' Dupin said, 'what bad luck! To be mugged in Baltimore! But if you will wander through these bad parts of town without taking precautions – '

'Dupin,' Pons muttered, 'why are you here?' He felt the bandage on his head that made him look like the sanguinary sultan out of the Thousand and Second Night of Scheherazade, and he wished he had a bowstring for Dupin's lying throat. 'Must you personally – be in at the death?'

'What are you talking about, Ernest?' Dupin still kept on his soothing voice. 'I do hope that the blow on the back of your head hasn't done any brain damage – at least, not more than was there *before* – '

Dupin was reverting to his usual waspish self, which was slightly reassuring. Pons could not bear his false face of caring.

'Because your agents failed to kill me – you've come down here to finish off the dirty work – '

'Ernest, if you talk as wildly as that – as your psychiatrist – I am going to have to recommend quite extreme treatment for you – '

Pons saw the trap. The first stage was only to kidnap, the second to kill!

'Have you committed me, Dupin? Without my consent? Am I a prisoner?'

Pons looked round his white room with its vases of petunias and pretty floral curtains – which did not hide the bars across the windows.

'Of course not,' Dupin said. 'You're in a nursing home. When the police found you unconscious and robbed by Poe's grave, they also found an envelope addressed to me in your pocket – for your analysis, I suppose. So they contacted me, and I came straight down to see you. Then I arranged for you to come here to recover. It's more of a rest home than a hospital.'

'I *rest in peace* here, do I?' Pons asked sarcastically. 'Quiet as the tomb?'

'What has happened to your head?' Dupin asked. 'You really are acting very strangely.'

Pons looked at the treacherous little man, smiling at him behind his rimless glasses, the epitome of the ordinary which is the true bland face of evil.

'You tried to have me killed, Dupin – to get your hands on my money!'

'Oh, come now, Ernest – '

'You were the only one who *knew* I had to go to Poe's grave. You had your killers waiting – '

'Ernest, please. Calm yourself, or I'm really going to have to tell the doctors to knock you out for a few more days with some jungle juice. Now listen to me – and be *reasonable!*'

'Reasonable? When I'm talking to my *murderer?*'

'Ernest!' Dupin's voice had the familiar shrill tone of authority. 'Do you know the statistics of mugging in a major American city? One in six citizens gets mugged or robbed every year. You have never been, to my knowledge. It was your turn, that's all. Your number came up, particularly as you were dreaming in a terrible crime area – '

Pons refused to listen to Dupin's reasoning. If he did, he would again fall into its snare of logic. In a charming room full of flowers with white sheets smelling of lavender, how could he possibly credit the conspiracies *which he knew to be true?*

'You *are* plotting to kill me, Dupin. It's in your interests – '

'I would be angry with you, Ernest, if you were not sick and shocked. It's not only the blow you got on your head. You had obviously filled yourself up with tranquillizers and amphetamines to get through your research on Poe's death, in case you linked it with your own. Now you've entered into his conspiracy theories at the end of his life. Doubtless, this last chapter will make me out to be a sort of Manhattan Machiavelli, not to mention a resurrected Rasputin. There are *no* conspiracies, Ernest – only in Poe's sick mind and your own.'

Pons looked at that serene rational countenance for any signs of guilt or remorse – and could only see the face of the good psychiatrist – and even worse, the Good Samaritan! If Dupin was so duplicitous, Pons knew that he would have to disguise his own intentions in order to survive.

'You're right as always,' Pons declared. 'Like Mussolini, Dupin is always right. I must have been thinking about the conspiracy theory of Poe's death – and how his trusted executor Griswold assassinated his reputation – when I was hit on the back of the head. Perhaps the blow lodged my fear in my skull, so that I woke up with it – and applied it to myself! Ha, ha – a simple delusion! Nothing more to it – forget it!'

Pons heard himself talking too excitedly, his voice squeaking with strain. Dupin was watching him with narrowed eyes, his mouth pursed. The psychiatrist then came to a decision and softened his face into a deliberate leer, which was meant to be a compassionate smile.

'Yes, Ernest, that must have been it – the knock on the head made you share Poe's paranoia. Look, let me go and talk to the experts here, and we'll have you right as rain in no time at all. Just let me fix everything – ' He began walking towards the door. 'Just relax for ten minutes. Empty your mind. Think of nothing. And I'll cope with everything. There, I'll leave the door open, so you'll know I'm not far away – '

Then he was gone to instruct his minions to finish off the murder. Oh, he would use the modern techniques – doping until there was a needle too much, injecting air into a vein, inducing a false heart attack – some sort of death without trace with a tame doctor to sign the certificate of natural causes.

Pons was dressed in minutes, his black suit looking ridiculous under the white turban of bandages on his head. Then he was out of the open door and hurrying down the corridor, smiling at the only nurse who passed him – and did not stop him, but merely smiled and said, 'Isn't it a nice day!' They are *clever*, these modern assassins! They give everything a façade of utter normality. But they did not deceive Ernest Albert Pons!

There was an open window leading to the garden – although a thorn-bush of roses had been carefully planted beneath it to deter all but the most determined escaper! Scratched but undaunted, Pons avoided the guards at the entrances and made his escape to France by a secret and unlikely route – Air Iceland!

(*Clever as you are, Dupin, you did not know I keep my passport in the bank with a few thousand dollars in a safe-deposit box in case I ever have to get away quickly from my enemies. And your secret agents will not find me in Paris! I shall go to ground, but you will hear from me soon. My analysis will be completed! And my analysis will not only reveal myself and Poe – but also show you up! You will notice that I have already begun to describe myself in the third person as Pons even in my meetings with you. And why? Because I have your number too, Dupin – and I will detach myself from you utterly!*)

10

Night and Fog

What the world calls 'genius' is the state of mental disease arising from the undue predominance of some one of the faculties. The works of such genius are never sound in themselves and, in especial, always betray the general mental insanity.

EDGAR ALLAN POE

Pons walked to the Charles Baudelaire monument between the cemetery wall and the burial vaults of the *grands bourgeois*. On the oblong graves lay broken enamel garlands of china flowers and stone laurel wreaths, their green paint washed off by rain. In the tombs with their iron doors forced wide, horsehair bulged from rotting hassocks – sprays of dusty lilies dropped their heads with little ping-pings to the touch – marble bibles opened at a blank page or on a sepia photograph of the dear departed in a high collar – empty display vases were smeared with soot – railings and chains were green with verdigris – and a fallen dwarf Christ lay with broken arms in a scatter of filthy wax roses. Forgetfulness fell from the air in this disenchanted garden of remembrance, where the French honoured their dead.

When Pons reached the poet's monument, he found Baudelaire showing a double face, as if he were another Dorian Gray. The young poet's head and chest brooded over the corpses of a dog and of the old poet, lying beneath in his winding sheet with his two feet bound together in one great flipper and his hands webbed into two fins. Corrosion already pitted the surface of the stone. Only the moss in the corners seemed always to have been there, along with the honeysuckle and the ivy climbing the wall, perennial and evergreen.

Crossing the Montparnasse cemetery to the actual tomb of Baudelaire, Pons fell behind a real funeral. The black hearse led the way with wreaths of floral tributes hanging in coloured lifebelts on its sides. At its back, the members of the family walked two by two, their mourning clothes shading their grief from dark black to violent blue. Behind them, four Citroëns idled along – and a pink Alfasud – choking the air with their exhausts.

By the time the procession had neared the grave, Pons could see that modern times had come to the cemetery with a vengeance. A red mechanical scoop had been the instant grave-digger. Four coffin-bearers, dressed in blue dungarees and peaked caps and workers' boots, unhooked the wreaths and carried them off, before returning for the corpse. Only a *flic* in shirt-sleeves seemed dressed for the occasion. Even the priest was late, speeding past the line of mourners to get to the grave on time.

The way to Baudelaire's bones lay past a monument that was a tale of mystery and the imagination – a gigantic garlanded phallus in honour of Rear-Admiral Dumont d'Urville, who had sailed round the world three times and had signalled the Venus de Milo in the Levant – how exactly was unsaid. After another hundred paces, three short steps led down to Pons's goal – a simple white vault with a plaque to Jacques Aupick, General and Senator and Ancient Ambassador to Constantinople and Madrid – to his stepson Charles Baudelaire – and to his wife, Caroline Archenbaut Defayes. *Pray for them*, it asked! But there was only a madman stooping over the tomb and arranging the five pots of geraniums left by the faithful in memory of the past. He soon hurried away, sucking at his empty cigarette-holder.

'He comes here daily,' the cemetery guard said to Pons without being asked. 'He likes everything in its place.' At least he was better than the madman in Baltimore who still leaves a bottle of whiskey for Poe's ghost on his birthday and on his grave.

On a black marble tomb nearby, a black cat was crouching. Its green eyes were burning as it waited to keep the rats from their chance at the dead. Pons went outside to the Saturday boulevard, where a market was being held under the plane trees. Men were taking up the road as they were always doing in cities – that was urban life – permanent earthquakes and instant crevasses.

On a corner of Edgar Quinet, a street performer was swallowing live frogs out of a goldfish bowl. He would gulp them down whole and hold them in his belly. Then he would belch and bring them up again – Hop-Frog, Hop-Frog – into the light of day. They looked no worse for wear than if they had plunged into a pond. And he would place them back carefully into their glass bowl – a man had to look after his investments, Pons supposed, just like he did.

Somewhere in Paris
June 1979

Dupin,
    I have been to Baudelaire's grave in the Montparnasse Cemetery, and I am still unsure whether Edgar Poe is not a creation of the French poet's imagination. I know I am not. I could not feel more Anglo-Saxon and alien in these harsh and smiling streets, which seem to include everyone except the American stranger. I am visiting the places where Baudelaire lived while he was translating his five volumes of Poe's stories. I am reading the countless essays which French critics have lavished on Poe since Baudelaire discovered him. And I am haunted by all those false correspondences in time and place that the rational process enjoys and tries to decipher, (I HAVE MY GRISWOLD – YOU – BUT WHO WILL BE MY BAUDELAIRE AND DEDICATE HIS GREATNESS TO PRESERVE MINE?)
    For instance, a man has been swallowing frogs for money not far from Baudelaire's grave. Then he has been bringing them up again. Am I supposed to think of the descent into the maelstrom? Or the premature burial? Is his success – and he did collect a few hundred francs from the crowd – due to the French obsession with frogs? Or to our universal love for the horrible and the grotesque, which Poe knew so well? So – is the frogman the symbol of the French passion for their Edgar Poe – a man employing a rational and brilliant method to exhibit in public a disgusting display of abnormal psychology?
    That same evening I read a long piece by Gaston Bachelard claiming that Poe was essentially influenced by the element of water – and stagnant water at that! He was a creature of the tarn, the cesspool, the dead sea – the shadow-sucking water that drinks your spirit before you drink it! But Hoffmann, who wrote those gothic tales always compared with Poe's, was said to be under the element of fire!

Discarding these theories as rubbish, I went after dinner to visit 60 Rue Pigalle, where Baudelaire once worked at translating Poe's *Histoires Extraordinaires*. I saw a glazed leathery man with a skin like a bronze lizard straight out of a Hoffmann story. He was swallowing turpentine and spitting out fire until he made a tongue of flame fifty foot long across Pigalle, driving the tarts and pimps right off their beat. A coincidence? A correspondence? Utter nonsense? Or the silly summer season for obsessed men looking for connections in a city of chaos? (PERHAPS THE FIRE-EATER WAS EVEN ONE OF YOUR SPIES!)

I have been wandering further in my search for the French vision of Poe, which Baudelaire created. I walked over to the Ile de France to see the Hotel Lauzun, where Baudelaire had stayed as a young dandy when he returned from his voyage to the East. I could not enter the locked green gates. The building was reserved for rich people now – no poets or inquirers admitted. Painters had just been working on the waterpipes that fall down from the young Baudelaire's mansard window on the third floor overlooking the Seine. Gold now pricked out the plunging pattern of waves and dolphins on the pipes. The drains looked like the way down to the City under the Sea! Do you remember Baudelaire's last two lines in 'The Voyage', which I will try to translate?

Plunge to the deep of the gulf – Heaven or Hell, who cares?
To the deep of the Unknown, to find the new, the *new*!

On his actual voyage, the young Baudelaire saw the whipping of a pretty negress on the island of Bourbon. He thrilled to it, recognizing the sadism in his desire. On his return to Paris, he found a black mistress, Jeanne Duval. So I walked down the Ile to where he had housed her nearby at 6 Rue de la Femme-sans-Tête. Yes, she was a stupid and drugged and greedy woman, who ruined his life, but she was not a headless woman – ANY MORE THAN I AM A HEADLESS MAN WHO CANNOT WORK OUT YOUR MACHINATIONS!

I don't think Baudelaire really reckoned with Poe's Southern fears of the abyss between black and white. He may have translated 'The Narrative of Arthur Gordon Pym' and have made it the most important of all Poe's books for the French – as it should be for everybody! Yet the black savages of Tsalal, whom Poe turned into the nightmare *figures of a slave revolt, are alien to Baudelaire, who found a perverse sensuality and an opium dream in the dark flesh of his mistress. He might have written, 'Do you know why I translated Poe so patiently? Because he resembled me.' He might have seen his own obsessions and hallucinations and half-conceived sentences already set down by the American poet, who claimed to be like Coleridge – startling himself into wakefulness from the dominion of sleep – and able to transfer its pictures into the realm of memory – to survey them later with the eye of analysis. But Baudelaire could never feel the extreme terror of black against white in the soul of a fearful man brought up to be a Virginian gentleman.*

I am not totally deluded, Dupin! As I read and consider Baudelaire's feeling that Poe was 'his likeness – his brother', I can see that other great men have shared my confusion of my identity with Poe's – unless he possesses herds of us like the Gaderene swine! Perhaps Baudelaire never thought he was Poe's double, his doppelgänger, his William Wilson – but he did believe in a curious correspondence and recognition – something which I will always do, even if this analysis is successful! WITH ONLY MYSELF TO LIVE THROUGH, I COULD NOT EXIST AT ALL.

Most American critics have never understood why the leading French poet of the nineteenth century should have spent sixteen years translating a mediocre and eccentric American writer, who thus became the chief influence on French literature from our shores. For where Baudelaire led, Mallarmé and Valéry followed in worship. Our critics – whom Poe despised so much himself! – think that Baudelaire's self-sacrifice must have transformed Poe's prose into something far superior to the original. The translator was the genius that the author was not – the copy is the work of art that the original failed to be! Heady stuff for me! What will their judgement be on 'The Facts in the Case of E. A. Poe'?

So I set out to compare the French translation line for line against the English. Naturally I used 'The Narrative of Arthur Gordon Pym'. How often have I said to you, Dupin – The great opening words for me are not – 'In the beginning was the word and the word was God' – but – 'My name is Arthur Gordon Pym'? And do you know how Baudelaire translated it? Not colloquially as any Frenchman would – 'Je m'appelle Arthur Gordon Pym (I am called Arthur Gordon

Pym).' Not even dramatically – 'Qui suis-je? Arthur Gordon Pym (Who am I? Arthur Gordon Pym).'

No, he put down the exact and simple phrase – 'Mon nom est Arthur Gordon Pym.' It was a literal translation, no tricks at all. I tell you, Poe speaks directly through Baudelaire's French version. Although my own French is far from perfect, I suspect the impact of Poe here is the same as in the English language. He startles and sends us back to our dreams – but they value him for it.

So the problem remains. If Baudelaire adds so little, why do the French think Poe a genius, and our critics usually think him a confidence trickster? I think it is because the French admire his mental fight to organise his fearful passions. Poe worked so hard to find a form and style to use as a harness on his nightmares – his poems, indeed, lose much of their visionary terror in the overwound clockwork of their effects and repetitions. Yet the French have always tried to govern their natural anarchy and love of liberty with the worship of Reason or Napoleon. Poe could well be a god here – no man ever tried harder to exert a rational control on an unbalanced self.

Also I suspect that the things we find horrible in Poe – the teeth pulled from Berenice's living corpse – the sudden decomposition of M. Valdemar – the severed mother's head in the Rue Morgue – the French enjoy with their relish for physical facts, not to mention the guillotine! Poe tended to place both his most horrible and most rational ideas in France – LOOK AT THE CHARACTER OF DUPIN AND THE CRIMES HE HAD TO SOLVE, WHICH WERE TRANSLATED FROM AMERICA! Everything is, after all, oral in our medicine – nice and clean and sterilized. It is rectal here – thermometers and drugs, they go up your ass. So perhaps Poe is only truly appreciated by those who think shit is rather more important than toothpaste!

Seriously, to know how Poe is honoured in France has helped me. After all, it is no joke to be told in America that I have spent the last twenty years pretending to be a charlatan! Like Baudelaire, I would hate to imitate anyone short of genius.

I have been lucky enough to find and buy the two little etchings of Baudelaire by Manet. The first shows a young dandy in outline and profile, cocking up his nose even higher than the brim of his top hat. The second shows a pale ascetic with a dome of a forehead brooding above a severe black suit. If it isn't the older Baudelaire during the time he was translating Poe, then it is a portrait of Poe himself! Or of Roderick Usher or William Wilson! Or the spirit of Poe possessing Baudelaire while he was posing for Manet!

Do you know, Baudelaire even claimed a Poe-like false ancestry – forefathers who were idiots or maniacs – the victims of terrible passions in stately mansions? And he said that he was the only child of a marriage that was unbalanced, pathological and senile! He really had to declare that he was more of a Poe than Poe himself – as I used to do – and now DO NOT!

I TELL YOU, JUST LIKE DOGS GET TO LOOK LIKE THEIR MASTERS, SO DO WE BECOME THOSE WE LOVE AND RESEMBLE. IF WE LIVE OUR LIVES BY THEM, THEY LIVE AGAIN IN US!

I slip back – that is how terrible this cure of yours is. As I understand more, I understand less. I revert to those happy days when I knew I was E. A. Poe. The discovery of his history and reputation is not only the discovery of myself – it is also the loss of myself more completely in him as I find more and more correspondences.

I am tired and I shall end my letter, Dupin. You still have the power of making me try to be rational and to explain myself – as the other Dupin did to his creator. Tomorrow night, I am determined to try a shock therapy – to cure my worst perversity! Poe – Baudelaire – and I, Ernest Albert Pons? One – or three?

Walking from Montparnasse the next day on his pilgrimage to see the two busts of Baudelaire that he knew were in Paris, Pons became tired. He had passed the lobsters hiding behind the artificial rocks in their killing tank inside the Closerie des Lilas – and the incredible fountain between the Observatory and the Luxembourg park with its eight angry turtles spouting jets of water over the heads of dolphins and sea-horses with plunging front hooves and shark's tails, rearing away from a pillar on which four naked olive nymphs were dancing in a circle and carrying the world in a metal cage above their heads. Once he had passed this fantasy of Arnheim along the avenue of dripping chestnut trees towards the bust of Baudelaire, he could not imagine that he had not dreamed it. So he turned back – and there it was. He walked on again.

The poet's monument had been tucked away in the English garden of the park. It was facing the locked gates leading to the

Rue Auguste Comte. Baudelaire looked as if he were in a mild mood, gently smiling to find himself facing the road named after the positivist thinker – and equally amused at the efforts of the School of Horticulture to train trees and shrubs into triangles and pyramids and horizontal bars. Evidently, the authorities had not wanted him in the public park at all, so they had placed him out of the way, hoping that nobody would notice him. Yet there he was, as unlikely as the fountain had been.

It was a long walk down the Boulevard Saint Michel across the Seine. Yet Pons feared to arrive at the new Pompidou Museum at Beaubourg, where the other bust was said to be. So he took a detour through the little park at the back of Notre Dame to see his favourite view of all in Paris – the cathedral as fantastic as Pym's ship sailing on its imaginary voyage with its black spire rising like a mast to its cross-trees – its grey roofs blown sideways like mainsails – and the prow of the chapel breaking in waves of flying buttresses that fell back in a foam of stone on to the green leaves beneath.

The Beaubourg museum was more horrible than he had expected – the nightmare of progress so feared by Poe – a vast bulbous hangar enclosed in bursting tubes and struts, in which a clanking mechanical dragon spat out kiddie-cars at him, while a revolting cube of oozing plastic guts sent him hurrying to a transparent intestine that transported the mob on elevators up to the gallery floors. Once there, he found himself wandering willy-nilly past the impressionist and cubist masters of France, unable to look at the pictures because of the green and silver tubes and ducts twisting above his head.

He felt he was caught in the digestion of the building. Soon its exposed tripes would engulf and excrete him down to the square below. He did discover a bronze head of Baudelaire by Duchamp-Villon, but it was as bald and shiny as a polished kidney. So Pons fled for his life and reason into the old part of the city outside. He collapsed in the nearest café to see if two *marcs* could restore his energy for the evening of his sexual and other experiments.

The first part was easy. The streets were alive with black girls touting for a living in the most expensive city in the western world.

Pons let himself be taken by a siren from Martinique down some narrow stairs into a private club, which he hoped was called *Luxe, Calme et Volupté*. Beyond the red door, there was a little bar, a few chairs and tables, some reproductions of Josephine Baker and Mistinguett, and a three-piece Caribbean band playing steel drums. The confined noise hammered nails into his ears, but soon he was deaf enough to endure it. He did not want to speak because he had nothing to say. In that way, the hellish music was a good excuse, until it stopped for an interval.

– Her name was Monique – she said. Monique from Martinique – like a *chanson*, Monique from Martinique – Yes, she would have champagne – Yes, she would have more champagne – Yes, *monsieur* was very kind – and not so very old – quite young in fact – he must not think of himself as old – and yes, when they had had one more bottle of champagne, she could ask the proprietor to go with him – yes, yes, yes – he did have the air of a generous man –

The hundred franc notes disappeared from his wallet faster than the dead leaves of the fall. Even when he left the club with Monique, the cab back to his hotel was another hundred francs, as was the night porter who forgot to see Monique going upstairs with him. 'You'll save the supplement for a double room,' she whispered to him in consolation. And it was only two hundred francs more for Monique to strip herself half-naked – and three hundred francs to be all naked for all the night.

– Was *monsieur* still generous?

Monsieur was.

Pons had drunk too much to make love to his black beauty, though he tried. She was pleased to earn her money so easily, so she did not try too hard. Pons thought he understood Baudelaire better now – the sexual indifference or impotence, the slow stroking of the velvet flesh, the mercenary and careless woman doling out her rationed caresses. He tried to feel Poe's horror for the dark and the forbidden, but the champagne had dulled him into an acquiescence in this curious new wickedness in his life. This was maturity – with an *older* woman – the European corruption – none of the child whores and arrested development of America!

When he brought out the two prepared clay pipes stuffed with opium, he expected Monique to refuse. But she accepted one and lit both of them and inhaled from hers, smiling at the smoke in her lungs. She was sitting cross-legged on the bed, the brass rails at its head backing her nakedness – and with the smoke making veils of incense about her ebony skin – she became the Eidolon named NIGHT – or the Sleeper Irene with her Destinies! So Pons heard himself declaiming:

> 'At midnight, in the month of June,
> I stand beneath the mystic moon.
> An opiate vapour, dewy, dim,
> Exhales from out her golden rim,
> And, softly dripping, drop by drop,
> Upon the quiet mountain top,
> Steals drowsily and musically
> Into the universal valley.
> The rosemary nods upon the grave;
> The lily lolls upon the wave;
> Wrapping the fog about its breast,
> The ruin moulders into rest;
> Looking like Lethe, see! the lake
> A conscious slumber seems to take,
> And would not, for the world, awake.
> All Beauty sleeps! – and lo! where lies
> (Her casement open to the skies)
> Irene, with her Destinies!
> Oh, lady bright! – '

There was a rapping on the far side of the room wall, and a voice shouting threats.

'He's right,' Monique said. 'Shut up.'

She fell asleep soon, her pipe half-smoked, and breathed heavily, while his thoughts meandered in a mazy motion –

He did not plunge into maelstroms – scrabble at coffin lids closed above him – bury pale figures with bloody mouths – hear hearts beat louder than grandfather clocks – meet the Red Death face to face! If anywhere, he strayed to the Domain of Arnheim and the Island of the Fay. His opium dreams were of flowering gardens and mysterious waters and wraiths as beautiful as his nostalgia for the girls of his summer holidays, always gone for ever with the train back to Brooklyn.

He had meant to try to see whether he could write under the influence of opium. But of course, he did not. What had Cocteau written? *One must not be cured of opium, but of intelligence.*

He slept until late next morning. He woke to find that Monique was still sleeping. She seemed alien, almost intolerable. He wanted to be alone. His mouth was dry, his head was full of sand. He went to the bathroom and drank a pint of tap water and felt no better. He walked over to the window and looked out at the plane trees. The pen and paper on the little writing-table were untouched. Nobody wrote directly under the influence of opium – not Baudelaire – not Poe! It was the work, not the dream, that finally mattered. Or everybody would write because everybody could dream.

He looked over to the bed where Monique was stirring and asking for her breakfast.

'Please go at once,' Pons said.

He could hear the meanness in his voice. He could identify the sour taste in his mouth as disgust. Finally, he was an American, not a Frenchman. He knew how Poe must have felt after a debauch – guilty, angry, exhausted, estranged.

When she had gone, and when he had written down this episode, he would leave the city of Baudelaire. It was only a French vision of Edgar Poe, after all. Not the man himself.

Before Pons had finished his writing, he was responsible for two discoveries and one act of bravery. The French newspapers were full of the new Bordeaux scandal, concerning Comble, Dupin & Cie! Now he understood why Dupin was so self-assured and authoritarian – he was one of the *Chartronnais*, those Protestant masters of the wine business, who had imposed their control on the vineyards by the ruthless use of their capital and control of the market.

(*Did you, Dupin, as a boy drive down the only street in France where your kind of merchant prince insisted that the traffic use the left hand side of the road? Is that why you have driven ahead on your own wrong way ever since?*)

Comble, Dupin & Cie was being accused of adulterating its French wines with inferior Algerian imports in order to make up a loss estimated at *half a million dollars!* (*A convenient sum, Dupin – just right, I would say!*) Nobody would buy the old firm, because its distinguished name now stank on the palates of the wine-tasters. It was a scandal that would have even made Edgar Poe ashamed. And as for Ernest Pons, he understood why he had been mugged and left for dead in Baltimore!

His second discovery incidentally concerned Dupin. The method of reasoning which Poe gave to his great detective was not original. It was the method of Voltaire's *Zadig* – or *Destiny*. Zadig was nearly put to death twice for reasoning out the whole of an affair from one glance at an animal passing by. That was why Poe had made his Dupin a Frenchman, in homage to the inductive logic of the great *philosophe* – and the ingenuity of his thought. That was why he had discounted his own cleverness in unravelling a web, which he had spun for the express purpose of unravelling.

(*You do not fool me, Dupin – for I know you have allowed me to spin my own web to trap myself – but I shall break out!*)

To find that final liberty – to prove his bravery on his own – Pons went to the cinema to see *Night and Fog* – Alain Resnais's documentary about the concentration camps. What could he say but – he saw what he had never allowed himself to see before – what he could hardly bear to see now. The sights were so horrible that he often shut his eyes – then sights more horrible would bleed behind his eye-lids – death-pits – and the victims of the plague. There was no escape left for Pons from his own.

With *Night and Fog*, another film by Resnais was playing – *Hiroshima Mon Amour*. Again Pons could hardly bear to look at the screen – the pitted and warped and charred victims of the terminal bomb – the lovers' bodies dissolving into atomic dust – the shocking shaven head of the girl, maltreated for loving an enemy soldier – and the straight cutting from past to present *so that recent horror was the here and now!* Was there no end to the foul murders of this age – no way for Pons to flee once more into the terrors of time past or of the soul – terrors so alien, so distant, so wrapped in the pleasant thrill of melancholy that he could *forget* the obscene insanity of modern massacres.

No, there was no refuge, because there is no coincidence – only the chance of one's destiny, from which the Zadig or the Dupin in each of us may induce what must be done to reach a solution. Pons had not intended to pick up the *Herald-Tribune*, which described the Festival of Horror! The Poe films of Roger Corman were all to be shown – and exhibitions of comic books – all the child's paraphernalia of the burlesque, with which we laugh away our fears in case we may believe them.

Even so, Pons might have avoided the Festival; but he could not yet return to America and the plots of his Dupin! He was still on the run – and he would try to analyze Poe's influence on mass taste and the modern psyche, especially as – the Festival was being held in BERLIN! The city of his infancy – of his Rosa – of his guilt! He had to go.

(*Dupin, you see how I am free of you! Without you, I am going to Berlin. I am a Jew. I was a Berliner. I will return. Braver than MacArthur, I will return! What are you to me now, Dupin – and what is Edgar Poe?*)

11

The Return of the Raven

> The theatrical profession embraces all that can elevate and ennoble, and absolutely nothing to degrade. If some – if many – or if nearly all of its members are dissolute, this is an evil arising not from the profession itself, but from the unhappy circumstances which surround it . . . The writer is himself the son of an actress – has invariably made it his boast – and no earl was ever prouder of his earldom . . .
>
> EDGAR ALLAN POE

Pons went to mock the eight Poe films made by Roger Corman – and emerged a convert from the cinema. The director had chosen two actors to play the double nature of Poe. Vincent Price played the world-weary gentleman, somewhat surprised as an American aristocrat to find himself associated with a horror tale at all. Peter Lorre played the European Imp of the Perverse, goggle-eyed at the grotesque and burlesque situations of the scripts, which wisely preferred buffoonery to fidelity, laughter to the loathsome. As a journalist, Poe himself had loved hoaxing the masses – and in Corman and Price and Lorre, he had found his modern pranksters.

The Raven was the most absurd of the films, with Boris Karloff joining in the romp to make up a trio of incompetent sorcerers. Karloff had actually managed to change Lorre into the famous black bird of prey on the bust of Pallas – though when Lorre was released from his tar and feathers, he still looked like a plucked carrion fowl. As in Poe's more ridiculous fantasies, such as 'The Man that Was Used Up' or 'A Predicament', Lorre was as gleeful with his sorceries as a schoolboy with his tricks. At the comic climax of insane cannons and snakes as neckties, Pons found himself laughing like a child at a practical joke.

Tales of Terror had the same knockabout element, mixing the ribald with the horrid as Poe had often done himself. If 'Morelia' had lost all the romantic gloom of the original story, Price decomposed very glutinously into brown gravy in the case of M. Valdemar, while Lorre had a fine time as a mocking mason, walling up his wife and Price and his black cat Pluto in 'The Cask of Amontillado'. *The Tomb of Ligeia* also lost Poe's romantic sense of love beyond the grave, but added a black pantomime finale with Ligeia coming back from the vault again and again and again – with Price unable to kill her serial spirit. If Price seemed to walk in his sleep through *The Fall of the House of Usher* and *The Pit and the Pendulum*, he was superb as Prince Prospero in *The Masque of the Red Death*, into which Hop-Frog's revenge was inserted. His sardonic sadism flourished in a world where horror was perpetrated – not just to view the blood and pain – but to see whether it had a value of its own above good and evil.

And the ending of the film! And the poster! These reminded Pons of why he had come to Berlin, and why he could not laugh away his fears. When the Red Death held illimitable dominion over all, Death's messengers reported to their master that only the dwarf jester and five other people remained alive in all the world. While in the poster – Price's face was made up of tortured and dying people – as in an Archimboldo painting – or in a death-pit!

The best of the other horror films, dedicated to the perennial haunting imagination of Edgar Poe, was *Spirits of the Dead*, three tales filmed by Vadim, Malle, and Fellini. Vadim made a nonsense of 'Metzengerstein', playing the young Jane Fonda as a wicked countess in love with her brother, whom she burned to death, but who returned as a black stallion to rape her into a corpse. Malle made a far better job of 'William Wilson' with the satanically smooth Delon breaking down into a convincing paranoia and double identity – even though Bardot was compelled to bare her back for a whipping sequence. Yet Fellini was supreme, transcending his material in 'Toby Dammit', and making of Terence Stamp a fallen angel – a fading, self-pitying matinée idol, doomed to a last death-ride in his red Maserati – and ending with a small child picking up his severed head, which he had bet to the Devil.

Yet the films became coarser and further from the spirit of Poe.

They seemed to hang the magic of his name onto any shoddy material of their fancy. The most recent version of *The Murders in the Rue Morgue* had Herbert Lom returning disfigured from the grave to menace half-dressed beauties, their legs spread open before his hairy claws. *City under the Sea* dredged up no fantasy of drowned palaces, but a silly Egyptian underwater hall off Cornwall, where carnivorous gillmen ate scuba divers. And as for Corman's last Poe picture, *The Haunted Palace*, it had no demonic insane mind with vast forms dancing behind the red-lit sockets of its skull, but Vincent Price as a warlock, burned alive and risen again for some purpose Pons was too bored to discover.

Yet even if Poe's ideas were now treated in a vulgar or trivial way, they had lasted. He had proved himself capable of haunting the mind of mankind in the age of mass entertainment. He had known in his own time how to exaggerate the horrible in order to appeal to popular magazine taste. He did not know, however, that his exploitation of his nightmares would prove evergreen, ever-seen, evermore – that his presence, recognized or invisible, acknowledged or ignored, would live through the cinema in the mass imagination – or that his spirit would be as undead as Ligeia's, because of the vigour of his will. Like her, he did not yield himself to the angels – *nor unto death utterly* –

So Pons tried to concentrate on Poe – and failed. The dead poet no longer stalked with his quick, erect gait through the halls of Pons's imagination, which were now hung with images from *Night and Fog*. What was the bedchamber of the Lady of Tremaine to the gas-chamber at Belsen? What was Ligeia's raven hair to the countless tresses shorn off Jewish women and piled as high as the pyramids for stuffing pillows? What were Berenice's small, white and ivory-looking teeth to the tens of millions pulled from the jaws of the camp victims for the gold in their fillings? What was one man's sensitivity and suffering to the holocaust or to genocide?

Resnais was the Baudelaire of modern times – and Adolf Hitler was its Edgar Allan Poe – and Joseph Stalin its Red Death – and the atom bomb its King Pest. Horror now lay in the deliberate killing of the millions, not in the ticking of time or the creeping of decay or the scratching of obsession or the stealth of corruption in each one of us. Concentration camps were the maelstroms of our creation – nuclear dust our version of the plague. The gloomy fancies of Poe, like those of Hoffmann and Grimm, should only frighten children now – not the creatures capable of a Final Solution to the whole human race.

So Pons went on to the exhibition of comic books at the Festival of Horror – and found Poe occupying a whole special issue of *Creepy* magazine. As he leafed through the pages of comic strips he saw – a girl in a nightdress shrieking 'Mother! NOOOO-O-O-O!' as the barbarous ape graphically slashed off the mother's head before 'ultimately *choking* the lass and stuffing her lithe frame up the *narrow* chimney' – the Man of the Crowd translated into a Psychic Vampire living off the Souls of Others! – and ghoulish drawings of skeletons and victims of the plague – while at the end of the magazine, Pons found that he could buy twelve recordings of Poe's tales, so well done that 'the horrible word pictures of Poe's diseased psyche seem to materialize before your eyes: rotting castles, scurrying rat-things, the walking-dead in their pale shrouds seem to vibrate in the air as the words of the world's greatest macabre storyteller ripple the ether!'

At one time, such demeaning of genius would have rippled Pons's ether into a lightning storm. Now he smiled and shook his head and understood. Poe, above all, had wanted to be *read* – and romantic poets, in a way, were always children, loving the chant and wonder of the language more than its brute meaning. Immaturity was their passion – look at Virginia! – and a necessity in their nature and their rhymes. It was better to transpose Poe into the comic strips and moving pictures of the illiterate fantasies of adolescents than to leave him mouldering on the back shelves of libraries. Old tales into book dust do go – unless they are made visual for modern taste! What child in love with mock monsters could resist:

> A Man Fearing His Wife's Teeth!
> A Demon Unfolding A World of Unspoken Dread!
> And Deathly Masonry!

When Pons was weary of the halls and cinemas of the Festival of Horror, he walked the streets of Berlin in the new anonymous fawn mackintosh that he had bought in Paris. The city itself had been obliterated – and had risen again in blocks of houses that avoided the memory. Revenge from the sky had burned Hitler's capital as certainly as Sodom, while he was suffering his premature burial in his bunker. Yet so tenacious was humankind to what it had known, that Berlin had been built again to await its next destruction. The site was apt enough for a Festival of Horror, for terror now had no name or face or place, but lurked in the universal city of concrete and initials and identical rooms.

Even the Berlin Wall failed to impress – gimcrack and ugly – a silly barrier in the battle for the divided mind of man. Yet as Pons walked the streets of his childhood, unseen and unseeing, he felt foreboding grow on him like a hump. There was a sense that *some one – something* would appear – and throw him back into time past. There were still linden trees in Berlin – and little girls in white dresses playing under them – Rosa, Rosa – And there were the inexplicable men, waiting and watching in the quartered city – agents of the O.G.P.U. or the C.I.A. or DUPIN – of one of the major conspiracies that manipulate our minds!

Instead, he met Toby Dammit in the flesh – Terence Stamp or his double – sitting at the next table in a café – an angel fallen from the screen into the seat nearby. Pons complimented him on his performance and said Poe himself would have been proud of him. And the angel nodded as if such hymns of praise were his due – and left soon afterwards to escape just another fan.

Yet the star in the flesh had turned the image into truth. Now Toby Dammit would always rise from the printed page in the wicked beauty of the actor – and Pons would forever see Poe's character with Fellini's eye. The picture of the screen and the memory were substantial. The spirit did pass into the body. The dead lived – and their performance for good or ill – and could not be ignored.

Pons knew he could not linger in a place which had no meaning now that he was there. Only a stupid fear had kept him from Berlin for so long. He had been deterred by an evil which he had invented. There was nothing to confront in this labyrinth of the obvious. His Minotaur lay elsewhere. Yet he still had one errand to perform.

He had seen the glassblower in a side street – an Italian, who had brought his art from Murano, moulding his fantasies into whirls and weaves and warps of red and purple and green threads, tangling in set snakes like a dead Medusa's hair. When he had heard what Pons wanted, he had laughed and refused – yet when Pons had insisted, he had accepted the money and the message.

So Pons watched while the man blew the large black bottle from his blow-pipe, shaping it with the fiery tongs, then cutting the porthole in its side. He pierced with a hot needle two pricks above the hole – he never used *wire!* – then he shaped a flap with two small glass hooks – and lo and behold! it fitted the gap in the black bottle, so that Pons could open its side and put his hand within and feel that there was enough room – *quite* enough room – for his manuscript – when, oh God! he would be going down –

He could not delay the real purpose of his journey to Germany any longer. He took the train to Auschwitz – as his people had been forced to do. Of his own free will, he visited the camp, now preserved as a memorial. When he saw it, he knew that he had always seen it – and that he would always see it, even when he was not there.

'Born again,' the President of the United States claims to be and uses the White House as his nursery school in government. 'Born again,' Monos says to Una in Poe's 'Mellonta Tauta', explaining how the process of dying has changed his consciousness of *being* into an abiding sense of *place*, so that his grave has become his home. 'Born again,' Pons also claims, because he too is taking his first steps in learning to be a responsible Jew in modern America, and because the process of mass murder has changed his consciousness of being Poe into the abiding sense that the graves at Auschwitz should always have been his home.

Flying back to his Poe shrine in Brooklyn as he writes these lines, Pons knows that he has to set down his final analysis of the poet to free himself from the shadow of the Raven and prove himself a man in his own skin. Like Hitler, he has tried to make his apartment into a bunker and exclude the truth of a suffering world. Now he will barricade himself within for his own final days, postponing the invasion of Dupin's red hordes or secret agents – WHO MUST COME SOON! – in fire and black ruin – *to terminate his case!*

12

MS. Put in a Bottle

> If any ambitious man have a fancy to revolutionize, at one effort, the universal world of human thought, human opinion, and human sentiment, the opportunity is his own – All that he has to do is to write and publish a very little book. Its title should be simple – a few plain words – *My Heart Laid Bare*. But – this little book must be *true to its title* . . .
> No man dare write it. No man ever will dare write it. No man *could* write it, even if he dared. The paper would shrivel and blaze at every touch of the fiery pen.
>
> EDGAR ALLAN POE

As in the case of M. Valdemar, I have been collecting the facts about E. A. Poe for nearly seven months, holding the dead man in a trance without attempting to examine his nature. My work has been something of a biography and an autobiography, an inquiry and a quest, but not an analysis or an obituary. If I now succeed in suggesting the essence of the man – and if he is not like myself – then he should pass utterly from my person – shrink – crumble – absolutely rot away beneath my hands. I will risk that final interrogation and judgement – to be free of his corpse that will not die – because – he has mesmerized *me* for quarter of a century, while I have only begun to exert the force of my mind over his will for the past half a year.

The facts of Poe's childhood gave him reason to evade responsibility all his life. If the Freudians are correct, and nobody can ever right the consequences of the years of infancy, then Poe was always doomed – *as he wished to believe he was*. How could the child of a lovely consumptive actress – born in the Romantic Age largely invented by Lord Byron – reared in the self-dramatic Southern tradition – not explain his moods of depression as a constitutional melancholy – or his morbid fantasies as a *family* taint? Such inherited characteristics excused him from the need to combat them.

Poe justified the heroes of his *Tales of Mystery and Horror* as he justified himself. Because the hero of 'Berenice' was born in the chamber where his mother had died, he is always haunted by her shadow – vague, variable, indefinite, unsteady, but inescapable even in the sunlight of his reason – so he is driven to obsession and monomania. The hero of 'Eleonora' comes from an ardent, fanciful and passionate race – and so calls himself mad, because he lives between a disease of thought and the shadow of doubt – the heights and the depths of perception. And Roderick Usher, Poe's other self, is dogged by the family evil – a morbid acuteness of the senses and an anomalous sense of terror.

Poe could explain and disclaim his actions because of his young dead mother and vagabond fickle father – and make the same excuses because of his treatment by his foster family. Frances Valentine Allan loved him and protected him, then died on him in his early manhood. John Allan educated him to expect to become a Virginia gentleman, then tried to destroy him as an intellectual upstart and a sexual rival.

Again the fault of Poe's disappointments seemed not to lie in him, but in his rearing. He claimed he had been taught to expect an allowance and an eventual fortune from his foster father – and a gentleman's education and position without much effort of his own. In fact, he took none of the care of a charity child to win the difficult favours of John Allan, who was also a merchant in his affections. He had all the gracious impudence and wild arrogance of the young Virginian aristocrat without any of the necessary financial or social standing. His defects actually increased his assertions. His vulnerability exaggerated his boasts of quality. He felt forced into the role of playing the young Byron to impress his friends – then found himself trapped by his own words into the pride of the poet.

His disgrace over his gambling debts could have sobered his character, just as his Army experience could have disciplined his behaviour. Yet his constancy to his image of himself as a romantic poet was magnificent. And by the age of twenty-two, he did manage to have published three small books of poems, which exceeded promise and hinted at more than talent. His foster mother's death, his brief reconciliation with her husband and strange postscript at West Point summed up his excuses for failure and ended his illusions that he might be a rich heir or a soldier of fortune and fate.

The truth of such an upbringing was more blessed than damned. There was no period in childhood or adolescence when Poe was not loved. Except for his infancy, he was raised in plenty and well-educated for the time. To the rest of the poor Poe family, he was the prince of every chance. He could not complain of being a poet *damné* because his good luck failed to continue, or because his foster father forced him to make his own way in the world. He chose to isolate himself from the routes of commerce; he was not excluded by John Allan. His view of himself as persecuted and isolated was that of many a spoiled child who thinks himself more clever than his society.

The contemporary picture of the Byronic troubadour informed Poe's opinion of himself and inflamed his actions. Because he wanted to act out the tragedy of a lost soul, he had to exaggerate his trials and his solitude – when, in point of fact, he could bear loneliness so little that he demanded a mother figure all his life. He may have been deprived of his own mother and his foster mother, when he was old enough to be a Sergeant-Major – yet such was his sense of loss that he could not be happy until he had found his aunt Maria Clemm to play their role. Poets *damnés* should hardly be so dependent.

As an actor's son and a Southern student, Poe's sense of drama did often damn his reputation. His heredity and his Richmond boyhood played their part in making him overplay his own. If the role of a *chevalier* from the *Chansons de Roland* or from Walter Scott was Poe's saving grace in polite society, it was also his inferno in case of debt or slight. He treated his creditors as if dishonour lay in their trying to collect what he owed, and he insulted his critics as if words were bullets in a duel to the death. Such exaggerated notions of chivalry and pride made him less the Byronic knight than the bar-room actor, not quite sure of his ground as a Virginian aristocrat, but sure that his companions would applaud him as superior to their sort.

His vanities and vagaries in the publishing cities of the East Coast made and enhanced an ambiguous fame. He learned too quickly how to provoke and excite an audience, how to draw blood with his pen or comment with a hoax. Yet as he publicized his poetry through his exploits, so he declared that it should be treated as the expression of pure beauty and truth, and that his criticism was the creation of a genuine philosophy of American letters, not a servile imitation of the English. Like a classic Greek hero, everything was too much in his responses and his gifts, so that he was hounded for his insolence by men and the gods.

His presentation of himself as a mysterious and doomed person – lucid, but also in search of the ultimate sensation – sparked speculation and suspicion equally. His tales of horror and ratiocination gave him a popular audience, fascinated by his command of nightmare and induction, while they deterred finer intellects, whom he wooed by his essays on cosmic theory and poetic principle. He wanted to dredge the deeps of the unconsciousness – yet also to stimulate his mind to the utmost height of reason.

He reached out for more than he could achieve – and so surpassed his education and his talents. If such a stretching of the intellect and of obsession is a kind of genius, then he had that – when his body and his spirit were not failing him. His tricks of style and repetition could obscure his qualities, just as his wearing of his originality on his black silk stock could repel as well as appeal to the romantic sensibility of his time. Yet if he played out the expectations of his age, he found in them the inspiration to write what he had in him.

His victory and self-sacrifice lay in his insistence on living a writer's life, when it imposed on him poverty and denial. He despised the literary market, yet he had to exploit it. He always bit the hand that fed him in case it began to patronize him. He boldly attacked the dominant men of letters for their self-serving, then served himself and his friends as a gentleman should. He was a manipulator and a mesmerizer of his audiences, who then declared that he was a lover of solitude and the simple life. He admired the inventive ferment of the period from spiritualism to electrical experiments, yet decried progress, praised slavery and longed for a luxurious feudal life in some time past.

In such a quandary of contradictions, violently at war within himself and with all cliques that were not his own, Poe took to drugs to find a truce which could never last. Alone, his drug was opium; in company, alcohol. Other writers who used opium such as Baudelaire and Cocteau recognized that some of Poe's stories were almost clinical descriptions of the various stages of dreaming under the influence of drugs. Poe did not so much *need* opium and its derivatives to stimulate his imagination – and to dull his quivering sensibility – in order to write; but it was the fashionable drug for romantic writers – mysterious and soothing and haunting – and it was easily available in his brother's and his wife's medicines.

Poe was using no more than the normal barbiturates of his age – opium was actually an ingredient in most 'female remedies'. Yet its use did enable him to describe many of the common dreams and fears of mankind – at least, those of a gothic age in which opium was aspirin. As D. H. Lawrence wrote of him so well:

> Poe knew only love, love, love, intense vibrations and heightened consciousness. Drugs, women, self-destruction, but anyhow the prismatic ecstasy of heightened consciousness and sense of love, of flow. The human soul in him was beside itself. But it was not lost. He told plainly how it was, so that we should know.
>
> He was an adventurer into vaults and cellars and horrible underground passages of the human soul. He sounded the horror and the warning of his own doom.
>
> Doomed he was. He died wanting more love, and love killed him. A ghastly disease, love. Poe telling us of his disease: trying even to make his disease fair and attractive. Even succeeding.
>
> Which is the inevitable falseness, duplicity of art, American art in particular.

We are doomed, if we act as if we were. Poe was doomed to want too much – of drugs, love, fame, genius – and occasionally alcohol. His bouts of drunkenness and his public courtship of literary ladies gave his enemies their excuse to destroy a man greater than themselves. He knew that his generous and loving behaviour to his aunt and dying wife – his dedication to his craft as a poet and critic – were his salvation, just as he knew that playing the role of the editor and lecturer in the bearpit of the city was his destruction. Yet he craved both the simple and the social life until he was as used up as the body of his military hero tortured by the Bugaboos.

The abnormal psychology of many of Poe's characters made him even more vulnerable to his destroyers, led by Rufus Griswold. Poe did put much of himself into Roderick Usher and William Wilson and the narrators of his tales who describe themselves as 'I'. Yet he was not writing autobiography, but an exaggerated version of certain hidden traits in many men of intelligence. He employed the literary conventions of his time to explore the unknown recesses of human nature. The device of a narrator was common to most adventure stories; what was original was the use of the form to hide a voyage into the unconsciousness or in quest of metaphysical truth.

Even his excessive tales of horror were in the contemporary gothic mode. As he wrote to Thomas White in defence of the plot of 'Berenice', such tales on the verge of bad taste were exactly the sort that made leading magazines like *Blackwood's* popular. As the first men in English letters had written such stories as 'MS. Found in a Mad-house' and 'Confessions of an Opium-Eater', Poe also asserted the value of his gothic style. In point of fact, he was writing better than he knew, by converting the merely eerie and weird into the obsessive and the psychological.

Like many other writers, he discounted his tales written for the market. He despised his novel about Pym because of its critical and commercial failure, and he thought little of his horror stories, hardly aware that he was researching into the secret and universal terrors of mankind. He thought that he was only appealing to a popular taste for the grotesque and the macabre, not to all who crave for an understanding of their unspoken fears.

He considered that his genius lay in his poetry, in his principles of composition, and in 'Eureka'. He was wrong, because he overwrought their shape at the expense of his inspiration. At the best, they were incantations; at the worst, mere jingles tinkling with 'The Bells'. His despised popular stories of ratiocination were his original intellectual contribution to the pleasure and mental processes of man. Even in his own time, his achievement was recognized by Martin Farquhar Tupper in the London *Literary Gazette*:

> Induction, and a microscopic power of analysis, seem to be the pervading characteristics of the mind of Edgar Poe. Put him on any trail, and he traces it as keenly as a Blackfoot or Ojibway; give him any clue, and he unravels the whole web of mystery: never was bloodhound more sagacious in scenting out a murderer; nor Oedipus himself more shrewd in solving an enigma. He would make a famous Transatlantic Vidocq, and is capable of more address and exploit than a Fouché; he has all his wits about him ready for use, and would calmly investigate the bursting of a bombshell; he is a hound never at fault, a moral tightrope dancer never thrown from his equilibrium; a close keen reasoner, whom no sophistry distracts – nothing foreign or extraneous diverts him from his inquiry.

If his Dupin stories invented detective fiction, his literary hoaxes did much to invent science fiction. Jules Verne acknowledged his debt – and even finished *Arthur Gordon Pym* in a simple way, making the white shrouded figure at the Pole a magnetic rock, which drew Pym irresistibly into its embrace through the iron barrel of his musket. Once more, Poe transcended his intentions, infusing his hoaxes with a sense of fantasy and marvel and cosmic awe. Others had written forgeries of the past like Ossian, but Poe dreamed of the false traveller's tale of the future – and of a new genre that would dominate the imagination of the space age.

His unearthly sense of the struggle between good and evil, light and darkness, gave Poe his most disturbing characteristic – his need for a split life of restraint and wildness, simplicity and spree – and his legacy of the double and warring identity that lies suppressed in every man. William Wilson is its clearest expression – but even Prince Prospero kills himself as he tries to stab the Red Death which lies within himself – and in 'The Purloined Letter', Dupin *is the reverse image of the blackmailer D*——, '*a desperate man, and a man of nerve*'!

So Poe played out his personal conflict between his private and his public life. Possibly Southern and Victorian conventions put too intolerable a strain on the imaginative people of the period. Possibly social hypocrisy was so pervasive that the reaction from it led to self-destruction. Poe certainly thought so. 'When *shall* the artist assume his proper situation in society – ' he demanded, 'in a society of thinking beings?' And answer came there none.

Yet he had also been brought up as a fundamentalist, who believed in the struggle of the soul of man between heaven and hell. He might mock at the existence of the Christian God, but as he tried to stride the stars, he was always terrified at the pendulum and the pit below. In a violent time of religious frenzy, inventive fervour and coming civil war, Poe expressed these excesses *in extremis*.

He was less his own victim, perhaps, than the victim of a community which let its writers starve. After he left his foster home, he always lived on the margins of existence, even if he put on a good face in the salons. Poverty drove him to the worst of his work – and some of the best. If he had been able to indulge himself as a gentleman, he might have been less of a scribbler in pursuit of fame and genius – a good defence against lack of means. He even seemed to make his strange death part of the cult which he created about his life.

In the final judgement, he was successful in what he aimed to do – to create an impression about his power and his originality – and a legend about his life and work. What is personality, Muriel Spark has asked, but the effect one has on others? Living is all the achievement of an effect – and that Poe did achieve. He broods over our time as he did over his own. He calculated and contrived – and won on his own curious terms.

This obituary has not turned out to be a psychoanalysis. There is good reason for it. Poe's works have an intrinsic meaning in themselves – they are more than a dossier for a modern Dupin to read by laying out the poet on his couch – *or his imitators!* So has each man's life an intrinsic meaning, which he must discover hardly through his follies and his defects. If he is weak enough to put on the *persona* and ape the *psyche* of a mesmerist like Poe, it may also be his condition of survival and the first step in his self-awareness.

We do not know ourselves until we may know another. We cannot value ourselves until we can judge another. Now that I have judged Edgar Poe – tried to appraise and blame him, whom I know so well – I find – *I am not as he!* – I never was anything but his presentation of his public show – I acted badly what he acted well, but untruly – My name is and always was Ernest Albert Ponz – I say again, MY NAME IS AND ALWAYS WAS ERNEST ALBERT PONZ –

There is a voice at my door – it is the voice of Dupin himself! – I shall not open it! The seven locks will keep him out! The bars will hold him on the far side! Yet *what* are his awful shrieking words?
 'Rosa! Rosa! Come and meet your Rosa, Pons! Come on out! Meet your Rosa from Berlin!'
 As I write these words, my pen sticks to the paper – I SHALL NOT MOVE – I shall not go to the door! God help my poor soul!
 'Rosa!' A girl's voice is now shrilling in my ears – 'I am Rosa! Come back to you, my love!'
 I may not resist my fate. I must go! My will is powerless. The mind of Dupin *conquers all* – even the WORM! Look! I will put my MS. in my bottle – close the glass lid – and rise – and, oh God! – going down –

New York Daily News, 13 September 1979.

A TALE OF THE GROTESQUE AND ARABESQUE

The body of Ernest Albert Pons (45) was found in Brooklyn Heights, after police had broken into his apartment. He was in an advanced state of decomposition, owing to the recent hot weather. An autopsy will be carried out in spite of the bad state of the cadaver.
 Mr Pons was a recluse and collector of Edgar Allan Poe. His only recent contact, his psychiatrist and literary executor, Dr Charles Dupin, told our reporter that Mr Pons had been suffering from an acute persecution complex since the previous spring. His physical condition was poor, and the balance of his mind was disturbed. Once he even dressed up in the mask of a victim of the bubonic plague on a visit to Dr Dupin.
 After a trip to Europe, Mr Pons had returned to complete a

manuscript now in the possession of Dr Dupin. Some weeks previous to his patient's death, the doctor had visited the Brooklyn apartment in an effort to communicate with Mr Pons. Determined to try shock therapy in a last effort to gain entry past the barricaded door – and to make his patient more rational – Dr Dupin took with him a past friend of the deceased, Ms Tilly Zimmerman, whom he had dressed in a child's white dress and Shirley Temple wig.

Announcing that he was accompanied by 'Rosa', the first love of Mr Pons, Dr Dupin persuaded his patient to open the door partially on its chain. But when Mr Pons saw the figure in white and curls, he shouted 'Reynolds!' and slammed the door shut in the doctor's face. After repeated efforts to contact Mr Pons over the succeeding weeks, Dr Dupin sent for the police department, who found the decomposed body of his patient lying by the door.

It appeared that he had suffered a heart attack when he saw the figure in white, and fell against the door, closing it with the weight of his body. The door was unfortunately made of steel and soundproofed, so that Dr Dupin could not have heard his patient dying on the other side of it. Dr Dupin defends his use of such shock therapy. He had warned his patient that he would enter into Mr Pons's own fantasy world and bring him back to reality by proving to him that his fears and practical jokes were all grotesque illusions.

'Of course, if I had known the effect of using his methods to try and cure his disease,' Dr Dupin says, 'I would not have played back on him the joke he had played on me. But it seemed a simple and safe technique at the time. I would say with the original Dupin – perhaps the mystery was a little *too* plain.'

Ms Zimmerman would not talk to our reporter, but a spokesperson said on her behalf: 'Ernest Pons was a great human being and a warm caring individual. Tilly was just trying to get him to relate more.'

Editorial Notes

At the request of Dr Charles Dupin, the literary executor of Ernest Albert Pons and the President of the Pons-Poe Foundation, which has been formed to encourage research on the life of Edgar Allan Poe, I have been appointed literary editor of Mr Pons's manuscript, which will be the first publication of the new foundation.

Dr Dupin wishes to make the following points about *The Facts in the Case of E. A. Poe*:

It is a case history of an identity crisis and of a persecution complex – and should only be read in that light.

It grossly misrepresents Dr Dupin's own character and methods of analysis. Only because of his past relationship with Mr Pons, and because of his feeling that the work may be of minor value in the annals of psychiatry, does he permit its publication in its original form.

Although it was an irrevocable clause of Mr Pons's will that Dr Dupin could not serve as the President of the Pons-Poe Foundation without publishing the manuscript unaltered and unabridged, Dr Dupin wishes to make it absolutely clear that personal and professional considerations have reluctantly persuaded him to respect Mr Pons's last wishes, particularly as Mr Pons was deluded that he might suffer, like Edgar Poe in his letters, from the forgeries of his literary executor.

Dr Dupin is himself working on a companion volume to *The Facts in the Case of E. A. Poe* in order to set the record straight. He will comment on the various inaccuracies in the text, particularly in relation to Mr Pons's fantasies about the nature of psychiatric treatment and about Dr Dupin's own business dealings, which have always been of the highest integrity.

From my own point of view as an independent literary editor of the manuscript, I also wish to make the following points:

I have accepted the task of editing Mr Pons's book as an author of some standing in the profession. My opinions are *not* those of Mr Pons and are not influenced by the fee paid to me by the Pons-Poe Foundation.

I consider the work to be of interest outside its narrow application as a case study in psychiatry.

Firstly, Mr Pons had a considerable knowledge of Edgar Allan Poe. When he does not intrude personally into his text, he has written an intriguing biography and analysis of his subject. If I were not bound by the clauses of his will to edit the text as it stands, I would be tempted to remove all the personal references and publish a conventional biography of Edgar Allan Poe, written by Ernest Albert Pons and completed by myself.

Secondly, Mr Pons's methods of comparing Poe's past life to his own recent quest after his subject do much to bridge an unfortunate fault in the writing of biography – the difficulty of relating the subject's old influence and times to his present appeal. For instance, Mr Pons can evaluate Poe's effect on the horror cinema in a manner which a more formal study might exclude. He can also use Poe's life and prose to show up the follies and errors of modern days. Like a new Candide as well as a born-again Edgar Poe, Mr Pons's commentaries serve as a judgement on what we have become as well as on the poet we have lost.

Thirdly, even with its flaws and lack of revision, the manuscript seems to deal freshly with some basic problems for biographers – the connection between the writer and the material, the limited understanding possible between the living and the dead, and the impossibility of being both objective and entering into an understanding of the subject. By identifying himself wholly with Poe at the beginning of the work, then by divorcing himself from the poet's character, Mr Pons has provided a new solution to the *process* undergone by biographers during their long period of study – the initial attraction to, the following revulsion from, and the final synthetic verdict on another person, who may often impose his style and thought on the effort to describe him.

There are those who may be irritated by the interweaving of Mr Pons's story with Poe's. Those who are strongly interested in Poe may not want to read about automobile journeys and long psychiatric sessions with Dr Dupin. And yet Mr Pons does serve as a catalyst between a modern sensibility and one of more than a century ago. He accepts psychiatry in a way that Poe could not. His perceptions – and the pressures on him – are different from Poe's, and in that difference we can see the contrast of their experiences in America.

There is also the question of the methods used to discover *The Facts in the Case of E. A. Poe*. They all derive from the poet himself. The long conversations between 'I' and Dupin, the opposition between the emotional and the rational, the process of ratiocination and deduction, the elimination of partial hypotheses, the elaborate voyage that is also a journey of the mind, even the element of hoax and crude jokes – all these techniques once used by Poe relate him through Mr Pons's words to our time most faithfully. There is much to be said for letting the subject of a biography set the terms of the inquest upon him. Why, even the fact that I am only the editor of this book seems to suggest Poe's own role in *The Narrative of Arthur Gordon Pym!*

Set a Pons to catch a Poe, Dr Dupin said to his patient. Biography is autobiography, Dr Dupin also said. I believe that through his obsession that he was Poe, Ernest Albert Pons stumbled on an original way of translating the psyche of one age to a very different one, and of recreating a dead man's personality through his increasing awareness of his own.

I shall end my editorial notes by stating that my brief in preparing this manuscript is limited. I am not a literary critic and do not wish to comment on the quality of the work. In respect to Mr Pons's wishes, I have tried to produce it in the form which he appeared to suggest from his working papers before his unfortunate death. He left a note that he would wish it distributed hand-written on parchment and put inside a bottle. This has, unfortunately, proved too expensive. Still, in the words of his mentor and subject: 'To be appreciated you must be *read*, and these things are invariably sought after with avidity.'

ANDREW SINCLAIR, Ph.D., F.R.S.L., *Editor*.

A Short Bibliography

(Although Mr Pons's library contained every known work by or about Poe in the original edition or in facsimile, the following books and articles were found beside his manuscript and his desk.)

The Complete Works of Edgar Allan Poe (J. A. Harrison, ed., 17 vols, New York, 1902).

The Letters of Edgar Allan Poe (J. W. Ostrom, rev. ed., 2 vols, New York, 1966).

The Works of the Late Edgar Allan Poe, with a Memoir by Rufus Wilmot Griswold (4 vols, New York, 1850-1856).

Allen, Hervey, *Israfel: The Life and Times of Edgar Allan Poe* (rev. ed., New York, 1934).

Bachelard, Gaston, *L'Eau et les rêves* (Paris, 1942).

Barine, Arvède, *Névrosés: Hoffmann, Quincey, Edgar Poe, G. de Nerval* (Paris, 1898).

Baudelaire, Charles, *Oeuvres* (J. Crépet, ed., 19 vols, Paris, 1923-1953).

Bonaparte, Marie, *Edgar Poe* (2 vols, Paris, 1933).

Broussard, Louis, *The Measure of Poe* (University of Oklahoma Press, 1969).

Campbell, Killis, *The Mind of Poe and Other Studies* (Cambridge, Mass., 1932).

Carlson, Eric W., ed., *The Recognition of Edgar Allan Poe* (Ann Arbor, Mich., 1966).

Eliot, T. S., 'Edgar Poe et la France', *La Table Ronde*, December, 1948.

Fagin, N. B., *The Histrionic Mr Poe* (Baltimore, 1949).

Gill, W. F., *The Life of Edgar Allan Poe* (Boston, 1877).

Harrison, James A., *Life and Letters of Edgar Allan Poe* (2 vols, New York, 1903).

Hoffman, Daniel, *Poe Poe Poe Poe Poe Poe Poe* (New York, 1972).

Howarth, William L., *Twentieth Century Interpretations of Poe's Tales* (New York, 1971).

Ingram, John H., *Edgar Allan Poe, His Life, Letters, and Opinions* (2 vols, London, 1880).
Jackson, David K., *Poe and the Southern Literary Messenger* (Richmond, 1934).
Jacobs, Robert D., *Poe: Journalist and Critic* (Baton Rouge, 1969).
Joyce, J. A., *E. A. Poe* (London, 1901).
Krutch, Joseph Wood, *Edgar Allan Poe, A Study in Genius* (New York, 1926).
Lauvrière, Emile, *Le Génie Morbide d'Edgar Poe* (Paris, 1935).
Lawrence, D. H., *Studies in Classic American Literature* (London, 1924).
Lefubure, M., *Samuel Taylor Coleridge: A Bondage of Opium* (New York, 1974).
Lemmonier, Léon, *Edgar Poe et les Poètes Français* (Paris, 1932).
Lowell, James Russell, 'Our Contributors, Edgar Allan Poe', *Graham's Magazine*, February, 1845.
Mabbott, Thomas O., ed., *Merlin, Baltimore, 1827, Together with Recollections of Edgar A. Poe by Lambert A. Wilmer* (New York, 1940).
Mallarmé, Stéphane, *Oeuvres Complètes* (Henri Mondor and G. Jean-Aubry, eds., Paris, 1945).
Mauclair, Camille, *Le Génie d'Edgar Poe* (Paris, 1925).
Messac, Régis, *Le 'Detective Novel' et l'Influence de la Pensée Scientifique* (Paris, 1929).
Miller, Perry, *The Raven and the Whale* (Boston, 1956).
Moss, Sidney P., *Poe's Literary Battles* (Durham, 1963).
Pope-Hennessy, Una, *Edgar Allan Poe: A Critical Biography* (London, 1934).
Quinn, Arthur Hobson, *Edgar Allan Poe: A Critical Biography* (New York, 1941).
Quinn, Patrick F., *The French Face of Edgar Poe* (Carbondale, Ill., 1957).
Ransome, Arthur, *E. A. Poe: A Critical Study* (New York, 1910).
Riding, Laura, 'The Facts in the Case of Monsieur Poe', *Contemporaries and Snobs* (New York, 1928).
Robertson, John W., *Edgar A. Poe: A Psychopathic Study* (New York, 1923).
Rousselot, Jean, *Edgar Poe* (Paris, 1953).
Sinclair, David, *Edgar Allan Poe* (London, 1977).
Stanard, Mary N. intro., *Edgar Allan Poe Letters Till Now Unpub-*

lished in the *Valentine Museum, Richmond, Virginia* (New York, 1925).
Stedman, E. C., *Edgar Allan Poe* (Boston, 1881).
Stovall, Floyd, 'Poe's Debt to Coleridge', *University of Texas Studies in English*, 1930.
Symons, Julian, *Edgar Allan Poe* (New York, 1978).
Tate, Allen, *The Forlorn Demon* (Chicago, 1953).
Valéry, Paul, 'A Propos d'Eureka', *Variété* I, Paris, 1926. 'Situation de Baudelaire', *Variété* II, Paris, 1930.
Wagenknecht, Edward, *Edgar Allan Poe: The Man Behind the Legend* (Oxford, 1963).
Walsh, John, *Poe the Detective* (New Brunswick, N.J., 1968).
Weiss, Susan T., *The Home Life of Poe* (New York, 1907).
Whitman, Sarah Helen, *Edgar Poe and his Critics* (New York, 1860).
Wilbur, Richard, 'The Poe Mystery Case', *New York Review of Books*, 13 July 1967.
Willis, Nathaniel P., 'Death of Edgar A. Poe', *Home Journal*, 20 October 1849.
Wilson, Edmund, 'Poe at Home and Abroad', *The Shores of Light* (New York, 1952).
Winwar, Frances, *The Haunted Palace: A Life of Edgar Allan Poe* (New York, 1959).
Woodberry, George E., *Edgar Allan Poe* (Boston, 1885). *The Life of Edgar Allan Poe, Personal and Literary, with his Chief Correspondence with Men of Letters* (2 vols, Boston, 1909).

ALSO AVAILABLE FROM VALANCOURT BOOKS

Michael Arlen	Hell! said the Duchess
R. C. Ashby (Ruby Ferguson)	He Arrived at Dusk
Frank Baker	The Birds
Charles Beaumont	The Hunger and Other Stories
David Benedictus	The Fourth of June
Charles Birkin	The Smell of Evil
John Blackburn	A Scent of New-Mown Hay
	Broken Boy
	Blue Octavo
	The Flame and the Wind
	Nothing but the Night
	Bury Him Darkly
	Our Lady of Pain
	The Face of the Lion
Thomas Blackburn	The Feast of the Wolf
John Braine	Room at the Top
	The Vodi
R. Chetwynd-Hayes	The Monster Club
Basil Copper	The Great White Space
	Necropolis
Hunter Davies	Body Charge
Jennifer Dawson	The Ha-Ha
Barry England	Figures in a Landscape
Ronald Fraser	Flower Phantoms
Gillian Freeman	The Liberty Man
	The Leather Boys
	The Leader
Stephen Gilbert	The Landslide
	The Burnaby Experiments
Martyn Goff	The Plaster Fabric
	The Youngest Director
Stephen Gregory	The Cormorant
Thomas Hinde	Mr. Nicholas
	The Day the Call Came
Claude Houghton	I Am Jonathan Scrivener
	This Was Ivor Trent
Gerald Kersh	Nightshade and Damnations
	Fowlers End
	Night and the City

Francis King	Never Again
	An Air That Kills
	The Dividing Stream
	The Dark Glasses
C.H.B. Kitchin	Ten Pollitt Place
	The Book of Life
Hilda Lewis	The Witch and the Priest
John Lodwick	Brother Death
Kenneth Martin	Aubade
Michael Nelson	Knock or Ring
	A Room in Chelsea Square
Beverley Nichols	Crazy Pavements
Oliver Onions	The Hand of Kornelius Voyt
J.B. Priestley	Benighted
	The Doomsday Men
	The Other Place
	The Magicians
	The Shapes of Sleep
	Saturn over the Water
Peter Prince	Play Things
Piers Paul Read	Monk Dawson
Forrest Reid	Following Darkness
	The Spring Song
	Brian Westby
	The Tom Barber Trilogy
	Denis Bracknel
Andrew Sinclair	The Raker
Colin Spencer	Panic
David Storey	Radcliffe
	Pasmore
	Saville
Russell Thorndike	The Slype
	The Master of the Macabre
John Trevena	Sleeping Waters
John Wain	Hurry on Down
	The Smaller Sky
Keith Waterhouse	There is a Happy Land
	Billy Liar
Colin Wilson	Ritual in the Dark
	Man Without a Shadow
	The Philosopher's Stone
	The God of the Labyrinth